I0534887

Second to Surrender

Moonlight Rogues, Volume 2

Alexa Whitewolf

Published by Alexa Whitewolf, 2018.

This is a work of fiction. Similarities to real people, places, or events are entirely coincidental.

SECOND TO SURRENDER

First edition. November 21, 2018.

ISBN: 978-1-9994499-2-6

Written by Alexa Whitewolf.

"Don't you think I'd stop if I could? It's not the past. It's not the future. It's my every day, and it's not going away. Those monsters in the night you fear as a kid? Well, they're every-fucking-where for me."

-Tristan Cayne, *Second to Surrender* -

Author's Note & Acknowledgements

Since the beginning of this series with *First to Fall*, I knew it would be different. Dom and Tristan are two very unique characters. But added to that, Tristan has some baggage that's not as easily understood as Dom's.

Post-traumatic stress disorder (PTSD) has been somewhat of a fascination for me. Members of my family participated in various wars around Romania when I wasn't even born. Add to that the Communism era, and the remaining half are still recovering (or ignoring) the effects of those historical events on their personality, and their lives, overall. More so than that, my interest in PTSD comes also from the admiration I have for the soldiers who are putting their lives at risk only so we can have another tomorrow. They deserve compassion and accolades, not misunderstanding and shunning.

And while this is all fiction, I tried to the best of my ability to be real with Tristan's PTSD symptoms and anxiety attacks. Please note, it's still a fictional book. If you or someone you know suffers from PTSD, please speak to a qualified professional who can help. And if this topic could have the potential to trigger, you may want to skip this read and head on to Book 3, *Third to Tumble*.

Overall, I hope you enjoy the storyline. Yes, it can get heavy at times, but it's got the badassness of werewolves, some of the characters from Book 1 and a few more, and a love story for the hopeless romantic ☺. Do consider leaving a review at the end, even a few words make a difference!

As usual, a huge thanks to my family and furbabies for helping me through this! And the team behind this book who helped edit, design the cover, encourage me—I can't thank you enough!! An extra hug to Y. Nikolova with **Ammonia Book Covers,**[1] who brought my vision of the cover to life with her awesome talent!!!

And last but not least, thanks to my readers!

Happy readings,

Alexa

---

1. https://mobile.twitter.com/AmmoniaCovers

∞ ∞ ∞

CHAPTER ONE

∞ Visitante ∞

"We are all <u>visitors</u> to this time, this place. We are just passing through. Our purpose here is to observe, to learn, to grow, to love... And then return home."

-Australian Aboriginal Proverb-

Tristan

Nothing's ever smooth in this pack. After the fight with the Reapers and Dom winning over his vrykolakas, we have to make sure humans don't find dead carcasses of things they can't explain.

So we spend the major part of the day cleaning. By the time we're done, the bonfire draws my attention. It's turning to ashes the last evidence of what transpired here, and I'm not sure if that's a good thing.

Out of the corner of my eyes, I see Luz dozing off against Dom's shoulder, and the lucky bastard has the most content look on his face. He should. He has no idea how feeble such happiness can be – or maybe he does.

Unable to look at them without feeling envy for what they have, I turn to the flames once more. They soar against the night sky, burning through the scent of death. It's not enough to completely clear the air, and the smell wafts to my nose. It's choking me, blurring my vision. Only it's tears in my eyes, not the smoke.

My mind pulls me somewhere else, as it's prone to do since I came back. It's not the clearing I see, nor my friends. I'm surrounded once more by the rage and bloodshed of war.

Ghosts of the past take shape in the smoke, and I lose sight of reality.

"Down, Tristan, down!"

I turn to the guy who's yelling, but he's blown off in a pile of dust. Horror fills me as his remains shatter everywhere around me. Then I turn to the tank, and the horde of creatures coming our way.

We were sent in to evacuate, but they hadn't told us the danger would still be around.

I watch helpless as another comrade gets torn to shreds by bloody canines. Then I lift my weapon, aiming.

My hand still shakes as Lucas' voice that pulls me back to the present. "I think we're all on the same wavelength here, but just to make sure. If any of you see vrykolakas running free in town, going forward, you report it to Dom or me. They're Dom's pack, so it will be his decision how he deals with them. But we will have no vigilante murders, you hear me?"

The alpha gets what he wants, and I nod. I've had my experiences with the vrykolakas, but if Dom can keep them in check, that earns him a measure of respect. And a certain length of rope. I just hope he doesn't hang himself with it.

Finn and Dom nod as well, and my gaze is drawn once more to my friend. He shifts his stance, as if sensing Luz's uneasiness in her sleep, and she snuggles deeper into his chest.

It takes a moment for his next words to penetrate my mind. "We hear you. What about Jared? Finn, what was your take on it?"

My gaze shifts to our Irish buddy, the fourth member of the pack. He's been uncannily quiet, but his ability with emotions has come in handy more than once. He takes his time, eventually saying, "There's a lot of resentment from Jared, more so than his usual racist shite. But I doubt we'll be getting trouble from him. He may be a wanker, but he's not a nutty one."

Lucas nods, rubbing the back of his neck. "Grazie, Finn. I thought as much. But his pack is a different story."

Dom straightens up at that, his jaw tense. "What, you think they'll try something?"

Lucas meets his gaze, shaking his head. "Not towards you or Luz. But there's a strong chance the Reapers will rebel against their leader. They saw him get his ass kicked by a human woman, and there's all the other stuff." Another frown. "Which reminds me. What was it you told Jared about a deal with a *zmeu*?"

Dom has the grace to look sheepish. After a few beats, he says, "When I was fighting Radu, he said Aiden wanted to undermine Jared because of his weakness towards us—letting us settle in—and the recent deal he made with a zmeu. In Romanian mythology, they're, umm…"

"Dragons." All eyes turn to Finn, but he keeps his gaze locked onto the flames. "I read about them in New York, when I was researching your past with Luz."

I say nothing, but my jaw clenches. We had hoped to avoid this, but it seems to be as inevitable as an incoming hurricane. If the Reapers start unraveling, there will be more violence, which means the humans of Rockland Creek will be at risk.

It's bad enough we're the only non-murderous wolves around here. We're also the only protection standing between humans and lunatic Reapers, whose bite can turn any of them into a monster by the next full moon. And now, we have to deal with a *dragon*?

My head drops in my hands. A familiar wave tightens my chest, making it harder to breath. How the hell are we supposed to face this, when already... *Merda*.

Arms wrapped around my knees, I dig my nails through the clothes, hard enough to draw blood. The pain centers me, enough so that I manage to avoid losing my shit in front of all my friends. *That's the last thing I need right now.*

My wolf tries to nudge to the surface, but I'm afraid to let him. As a lobisomem – Brazilian werewolf – I can choose to suppress him or work with him. He's the most primal part of me, ruled by raw emotions, and if I can't control myself, there's little reason to hope he would. It's one thing to shift, another to let him fully drive. So I push him back down, and take a deep breath instead.

When I look back up, the tension is palpable among us. Lucas does his best to diffuse it. "Radu may have lied about it."

His pitiful attempt at reassurance doesn't fool anyone, so Lucas picks up the thread of the conversation. "Whether there is a dragon or not, we can only wait and see. But as for the Reapers and their potential unfurling... If they *do* fall apart, the reality is we may have a bunch of rogue wolves on our hands."

A deafening silence descends on our group, with only the crackling of the flames breaking it. It's a reality I tried to prepare myself for since setting foot in Rockland Creek. I knew then the four of us might not last, stubborn as we all are. Yet against all odds, we did.

The Reapers are another story. Ruthless, hateful, they're only held together by fear of their alpha. Now that their respect for him is gone, they're a ticking bomb ready to explode. And there's the issue of the dragon. How the hell are we even supposed to fight something like that, if it comes to it?

"If it comes to it..." Lucas meets our gazes above the fire, oddly echoing my thoughts. "We may have to step in, fix things up."

Dom glances at Luz, ensuring she's asleep, before meeting his gaze. I read the worry in there for his mate, but his response is nonetheless sure when it comes. "Whatever happens, I'm in."

Finn nods. "And I."

They all turn to me, the only one who hasn't answered. I'd been avoiding all their gazes, but I force myself to meet them in turn now. In response to Lucas' dark glare, I nod. "Sim, claro, me too. You know it."

"Bene, it is settled then." Lucas nods, and his eyes drift to Luz. "You made a bold decision tonight, and you have my respect forever. But I swear to all that's holy, Dom, if you hurt her, I will have your hide."

Their banter tunes to the background, and I find I'm unable to stay still. Something's going to happen, I know it will. The *instinto* hasn't steered me wrong yet, and my gut's clenching like it feels it coming.

As if the universe hears me, the ring of a cellphone interrupts our little get together. Everyone turns to me and it takes me a second to realize it's coming from my back pocket. I pull the phone out, staring at the unfamiliar number.

"Yeah?"

There's a pause at the other end, followed by a whisper that roots me to the ground. "Tristan?"

I jump to my feet, almost stumbling over and into the flames. My mouth opens in wordless stupefaction. *Could it be...?*

"I'm in trouble. Por favor, Tristan. *Please*. Can you help a girl in need?"

Everything fades around me as images from a different past, almost a different life, assail me. Then the inflection registers, and I know it's not *her*. Which leaves only one other person who could sound exactly alike. "Dani? Where are you?"

Another pause, another whisper. "On my way to town... Your town."

My hand clenches around the phone. *Is Izzy with you?* It's what I want to ask, the words almost burning my tongue. But I can't. I won't. "Não se mova. I'll be there in a few."

I hang up, running a hand through my hair. Then I become aware of the dead silence surrounding me, and look around. My gaze stops on Dom and Luz. "I've got to go."

Before any of them can say a word, I take off. *What the hell is going on?*

Daniela

The dark of the night gives way to headlights and lamp posts. We're nearing the town, or at least that's my best guess. It's getting harder and harder to ignore the butterflies swimming in my stomach.

Tristan's stupefaction had been more than evident when we spoke. And it's not like I'd wanted to call on him, for obvious reasons. He's demanding, a leader, a soldier, and did I mention demanding? Plus, we have a history—and no, not in *that* way.

It's a simple story, really. Boy meets girl. Boy falls for girl. Girl breaks boy's heart. Boy goes into the army. But girl is determined to see him suffer...enough to make sure he can never return home upon his return.

Okay, so maybe the story's not that simple. The girl here was my twin sister Izabella. Not that it matters, since she's gone now. But I know it'll matter to Tristan... It's not like they ever had their closure. And now, there's no way they ever will.

A throb to the side of my head draws my attention. I shouldn't be getting upset. It's not Tristan's fault he left – and left me behind. He needed to escape, and had I known what was good for me, I would have, too.

My throat closes up and tears well in my eyes. No freaking way I'm crying on the bus. A deep breath later, and I try to pull myself together. The pull is heavy in my bones, the cry of the wild. My right hand, squished between the window of the bus and my thigh, curls inwards. I bite my lip hard enough to draw blood.

It doesn't hurt. None of it does, not anymore. My family made sure of that. But how far can I run, and for how long? They'll find me, sooner rather than later. Lobisomens are great trackers. And then what?

I just hope Tristan can help me out. Because there's no way I'm going back home to face off my crazy relatives. Hell-to-the-fucking-no.

The bus stops in the middle of a deserted parking lot. I see a long, winding street to the right, full of small mom and pop shops. Opposite, on the left, there's nothing – only a forest calling out to me.

My breath catches in my throat and I grab my bag, stepping off the bus. With quick, efficient movements, I pull my hair in a ponytail and fix my backpack on my shoulder. I left Bow's Arrow in a hurry and didn't bring much with me. Hopefully, Tristan won't mind.

Here's to hoping the hours it took me to arrive served to ease up on his surprise.

Tristan

I couldn't believe it when I got the call. *Dani...*

Merda! Images of dirty blonde hair, smiling amber eyes, a mouth begging to be kissed run across my mind as I'm driving over the speed limit. Replaying the conversation in my head does nothing to calm my fast-beating heart.

Tristan, I'm in trouble. Her words go on a loop around my head. Even as I'm driving, other images hit me—of Izabella, with her hazel eyes and tempting mouth, an exact copy of Dani except for the eyes. They'd been twins, once upon a time when we were all young.

I push back the rest of the memories, the pain, the betrayal and heartache. It has no place in my head if I'm to help Dani. But as I pull into the parking lot of the bus station, I can't help my wayward thoughts.

What could have happened that drove her all the way here...away from her pack, from her sister? *I guess I'll find out soon enough.*

Turning off the ignition, I get out of the car, lock it behind me, and wait. And wait some more. Dani had said she was on her way, but the bus is nowhere close.

The ring of my phone jostles me. "Yeah?"

"Where did you run off to, mate? It's been hours and we haven't heard a word."

I don't appreciate Finn's keen sense of everything on a regular day. So for him to be calling me now, it does nothing to calm my nerves. "Nowhere you need to know."

Finn is silent, and the next time he talks, I can hear the smile in his voice. "Who's Dani, then?"

"Shut your mouth." Then I notice the bus pull in. A glance at my watch and the sky confirms the sun's already rising. The door opens then, to let the passengers out.

"I have to go. *Adeus.*" I'm sure he doesn't appreciate my quick goodbye, but I've got more pressing matters on my hands. And I've waited long enough.

Travelers get off, and I know their type. Was one of them, not so long ago. Empty faces, lost souls, looking for escape – a way out. But then a figure at the back of the line draws my attention, and I have to cross my arms over my chest to avoid running towards it. A scene plays in my head, fleeting like a bird...

"What are you thinking about?" Izabella's under me, arching her body towards mine. Our bodies are slick with sweat from what we just shared, but the temptation in her hazel eyes says she's ready for more.

"You," I whisper, rubbing my nose against hers. "You're beautiful."

She smiles, her arms wrap around me, and I'm done for.

The figure getting off the bus doesn't have hazel eyes, though. They're dark amber, almond-shaped like a cat's, and arresting enough to root me to the ground. As if I could move. As if I could breathe.

It's not her. It's not Izabella. That's done, man.

No matter what I tell myself, seeing Dani – it's a shock to my system. And then the surprise morphs into anger. I had my shit under control. It was handled, as much as it can be. And now, I'm not even talking to her yet, but emotions from the past rise within me.

I've done everything possible to forget Izabella. Still, with Dani in town it won't be long before those ghosts come back to haunt me. And I can't have that, not with the Reapers ready to snap to pieces, a dragon running rampant and an innocent walking in the midst of it all.

The last thing I want is to turn into another sappy version of Dom. Falling in love again is not a possibility. I'm way too damn damaged for that. And even if I wasn't, it sure as hell can't happen with Izabella's twin sister.

I need to talk some sense into this girl and send her packing, before she becomes a complication.

Daniela

Already antsy at being so in the open, with the sun up, I tap my foot and scan the surroundings. My eyes linger on a guy leaning against a black SUV, arms crossed over his chest, baseball cap pulled low over his brow.

I can't see much of his face, but his body—holy shit. I avert my gaze before my wayward hormones get the best of me. Life as a wolf is difficult—being an unmated one is even more so, making the females prone to bouts of insanity.

At least in my pack. And for a very good reason. My jaw clenches and I force the unwanted thought away.

"Where the hell is he?" I keep looking around, but Tristan is nowhere I can see.

Then I hear my name called out and search for the voice. It's coming from the SUV guy. And now he's walking towards me, his stride long and purposeful. When he's close by, he shifts the hat on his head and I get a full view of his face.

"Tristan?"

My surprise is snuffed out by the anger radiating off him. "What the hell are you doing here?"

I gape at him, uncomprehending. He hadn't sounded annoyed over the phone, but I guess the hours it took me to arrive didn't help. Still, from there to be so rude... "Nice way to greet an old friend, *velho* amigo," I retort with sarcasm, stressing the *old* mention. "If that's how you treat your buddies, I shudder to think what you make your enemies go through."

The words give him pause – at least enough that I can catch my breath. I hadn't expected the circles under his eyes or the haunted look, like his soul is displaced and can't find peace. I also hadn't counted on the muscles. No wonder I didn't recognize him. Holy shit, the *muscles*. He'd been fit before, but the army must have seriously kept him in shape.

"Desculpe," his gruff apology is enough to make my gaping mouth shut. I hope I haven't drooled. To my annoyance, Tristan gives no indication he's just as easily affected. Instead, he pulls off the baseball cap, revealing a cropped head of hair, which he rubs in obvious agitation.

I have to give something back. At the very least, despite his obvious discomfort, he's making an effort. "It's okay," I say, and try to reach out and hug him.

He jerks out of the way. A flash of pain appears on his expression, too quick for me to be sure. Then he's shaking his head. "Knee-jerk reaction. It's been a long...few days."

Something about his tone tells me I've picked the wrong time to come to town. Then I smell something woodsy off him. My nose turns up in the air, and I grimace at another scent. "Were you at some kind of...bonfire?"

He nods, then shifts on his feet. This guy standing in front of me, it's not Tristan. He didn't use to be this wary, this edgy, this... I shake my head, trying to remove the cobwebs of the past. What good will it do us? *I'm not the same, either.*

As if to remind me of the fact, the burn on my left shoulder intensifies. I try to roll it back, and the movement draws Tristan's attention. "Your bag's heavy." It's a statement, followed by the most innocuous gesture – he reaches for it.

I shake my head, taking a step back. The air between us clears, and I can breathe in again. Which I do – deeply. If he moves any closer, I may spontaneously combust. *Stupid hormones.*

"Your bag's hurting your shoulder," Tristan repeats, hand still outstretched. "Let me take it."

My eyes move from his impressive shoulders to his face once more. "You don't seem that happy to see me. If this is a bad time, I can leave."

Tristan doesn't offer empty reassurances. At least that much hasn't changed. Instead, he sighs and runs a hand over his head again. "It'd probably be better if you did, I'm not going to lie. But you've travelled all this way, so the least I can do is buy you a drink."

Wow.

As I stand gaping at him like a fool, he shifts again. With each passing moment of my silence, he grows more and more restless. His eyes dart around, and my sense of paranoia resurfaces.

It's nothing compared to the energy rolling off him. "We should go."

Before I can say anything, Tristan reaches over for my backpack, pulling it out of my grip. I hesitate, and the pause is enough to drive his gaze back to mine – *into* mine. Because if there's one thing I'm sure of, is that Tristan's melty chocolate eyes see way too much of me.

"What is it?" The roughness of his voice causes shivers to run down my back.

I should've listened to Izzy. I should've... Shaking my head, I try to avoid Tristan's staring. "Nothing, I'm fine." It comes out rude, but then again, what does he expect after his jarring welcome?

Something gives though, because in the next moment he's shouldering the backpack and jerking his head towards the SUV. "Come with me."

I weigh my options, glancing at the now empty bus. To go right back is impossible. Anywhere else is a liability. Staying here, at least, has the merit of a potential protection.

A cry in the sky draws my gaze, and I could've sworn it's a raven. But the black bird, whatever it is, circles again once and disappears. The sky is too damn clear today.

"Dani!"

Tristan's shout demands my attention. He's standing by the SUV, holding the passenger door open for me. And this time, I let my feet carry me towards him.

∞ ∞ ∞

CHAPTER TWO

∞ Dúvida ∞

"Doubt is not a pleasant condition, but certainty is absurd."

-Voltaire-

Tristan

I shouldn't have picked up the damn phone. Better still, I should've thrown it away when I left that cursed town. Why didn't I change my number? Out of some misplaced nostalgia that's now biting me in the ass?

Merda! My hands tighten on the steering wheel and I do everything I can to avoid looking at Dani.

It wasn't meant to be easy, our reunion. Not when she's the exact copy of Izabella. And the last time I'd seen my ex, it had been with her legs up in the air and the pack's beta between them.

"I can feel your anger, you know," Dani whispers.

She's staring out the window, head tilted to the side as if hiding her face from me. And my stomach churns. She doesn't deserve this – paying for her sister's mistake. It was Izabella who drove me out of town, her I have an issue with.

Dani... She's only ever been good to me.

A heavy sigh escapes my lips and I pull the car over to the side of the road. I'm still clenching the steering wheel, taking deep breaths to rein myself in. A tantrum will only spark my wolf into morphing, and that's a pain I don't need right now.

Headlights in the distance come closer, and at first I only notice them out of the corner of my eye. Some stupid car with their lights still on during the day. Then I take a closer look, and the glare sparks another memory.

The headlights. The desert. Middle of the night. So much blood....

"Tristan?"

Dani's voice gets through the fog and I snap to. She's reaching out for me again and I jerk away, slamming into the driver's window. She looks shocked – and I can't really blame her. It's the second time I've done this, without much explanation. But I'm seeing those curls again, the eyes, the mouth, and my mind is somewhere else.

"I'm not her, you know." It's another whisper, this one bitterer.

"I know."

Dani looks away. A beat of silence stretches between us before she finally speaks. "This was a bad idea, but I didn't have a choice. I know you have your new pack, and I was hoping for protection."

The soldier in me stands to attention. "From what?"

A shudder runs through her, and the fear emanating from Dani is tangible, enough to taste. This is the same girl who used to believe in fairies and unicorns when she was young, and promised to forever be by her family's side.

What could have scared her so much, enough to leave Bow's Arrow? The mystery nags at me, and I have a feeling I won't like it when I solve it.

Not that Dani's making it any easier for me. She's silent for so long I don't think she'll answer me. When she does, it's not what I expect.

"You've made it clear I'm an inconvenience, so I won't bother you further. Just bring me to the alpha of this town and I'll plead my case to him directly."

I straighten from my hunched up position by the window. "Dani, I–"

"No." Her eyes flash my way, the amber darker – wary. "I didn't come here to hatch up old history. And judging by your scent, you can't give me what I want anyway. So let's cut the bull, and bring me to your alpha."

Being dismissed like this doesn't come easily, especially not from her. This isn't the young woman I left behind, she's cutthroat and...

"What happened to you?" The question pushes unbidden past my lips, but it's too late to take it back.

Dani's expression shutters and she turns away from me. "I grew up."

Her entire body language is meant to block me. And for a moment, I want nothing more than to shake some sense into her. What no one has done with me, when this gripping dread takes hold of me. But I also know it's the dread that keeps me going, like a comfort blanket.

So I keep further questions to myself and put the car back in gear without a word.

Daniela

I should've known this wouldn't be easy. Heaving back a sigh, I try to tune Tristan out.

It's hard. I haven't been around a werewolf like him for a while, and my senses are tingling. He should be forbidden fruit, but it's not like Izabella's around to care.

And for a moment there, he looked at me – really *looked* at me. Like he saw me, not some ghost of his ex-lover. Maybe things would be settled if he knew the truth once and for all... But I doubt it.

Plus, if Tristan knew everything that happened since he left Bow's Arrow, he wouldn't help me. He'd be too focused on seeking revenge, and probably die in the process. And that's a chance I can't take.

After long moments of silent driving, he pulls in front of what looks like a bar. A neon light spells out The Cave and the building looks old, some colonial antique style. Tristan gets out of the car, and I follow him inside.

"What is this place?" I ask him, expecting he won't answer. "Why are we here, Tristan?"

He throws me a look. "To meet some people." Then he heads in, and I've no choice but to follow.

The place is less crowded than I'd thought. Dismissing the bar, Tristan heads straight for a corner booth where two other guys are seated, along with a female, eating some kind of brunch. Their wolf scents hit me from a distance – except for her. *She's human.*

Tristan stops dead in his tracks and whirls to me. "Yeah, she is. And under the protection of our pack, so lay off it, Dani."

He turns away without giving me a chance to explain and I gape after him. Then I shake myself out of the daze. *This can't be normal, him hearing my thoughts. Can it?*

Something nags at the back of my mind. Our pack was tight-knit, but a connection like this would come only from something deeper. And Tristan left long ago, so there's no way any of that remains between him and any wolf in Bow's Arrow... *If it does, I'm double screwed.*

Instead of focusing on things I can't control, my gaze falls on Tristan's new pack. The redhead is leaning against one of the guys – blonde and blue-eyed, he's a straight Apollo. He notices us first, and surprise flickers in his eyes before a smirk tugs at his lips. Tristan's by their table now, and I reluctantly trail behind him.

"So that's where you disappeared to, mate?" The question's from the second male. With his dark hair and green eyes, I would've pegged him for a Celt even without the Irish lilt in his voice. It makes me uneasy, being around a wolf with his capacities. *If he figures out what I can do...*

"Bite me, Finn," Tristan near-growls. He reaches behind him without looking and grasps my hand, pulling me forward. I nearly stumble into the table, but catch myself in time. It's uncanny how he knew exactly where to reach for me.

Oblivious to my stupefaction, Tristan introduces me. "This is Daniela Da Silva, an old friend. She needs to speak to Lucas. Where is he?"

Three pairs of interested eyes turn on me, but it's the redhead who speaks first. She stands and smiles broadly, holding out her hand. I hesitantly shake it. "I'm Lucrezia – but everyone calls me Luz. This is Dominic – Dom – Konstantin, my boyfriend, and Finn McConnell." She introduces first the blonde-haired guy by her side, then the Celt.

I nod at each of them, then bite my lip. How much does she know, and what can I say in front of her? This is why I avoid packs. Especially packs with mated females. The bond between her and Dom is strong enough even I, a stranger, can feel it.

The Celt speaks next, probably sensing my discomfort. "Luz knows about us, so feel free to speak your mind around her."

A relieved sigh escapes me. "I've travelled a way from my old town, and I'm afraid only your alpha can help. Is he around?"

I notice the glance between Dom and Tristan, before his light blue eyes settle on me. "Lucas is unavailable for the day, perhaps a bit longer. Other business has him occupied. I'm his beta, perhaps I can help?"

While I appreciate the thought, I'm shaking my head before he's done. "I'm here to ask for protection, but the details are too sensitive to share around." I bite my lip again. "The less you know, the better off you'll be."

Rather than dissuade them, my words only spark curiosity in all of them. *Shit.*

Tristan snorts by my side and mutters something akin to, "Welcome to my world." Then he addresses Dom. "I'll get Dani a drink."

"She could join us," Luz offers.

They may not see the tension in Tristan, but I do. And the last bit of hope I had about him being okay with my presence here crumbles to dust. "It's okay," I smile feebly, then turn to the bar before they can see my tears.

"Two whiskeys," Tristan orders by my side, then takes a seat next to me. I guess people in Rockland Creek make it a habit of drinking during the day, because the bartender doesn't even blink.

"I don't need you to babysit me," I whisper into my drink.

"Doubt that."

His mutter aggravates me more than I can say. I throw back the drink, then stand. Even with me upright, we're barely eye level. Damn him and his height – and those *malditos* broad shoulders that draw my attention every two seconds like clockwork.

"You know what, Tristan? Call me when your alpha's around. I don't want to *impose* in the meantime."

His eyes narrow on me, glinting molten chocolate in this light. "What the hell are you going on about, carinho?"

I shove his chest – hard. Not that it has any effect on him. "Don't freaking call me darling. I'm not Izabella."

He stands at that, his eyes flashing. "You think I don't know that? I'm not delusional, Daniela."

"Really? 'Cause from where I'm standing, you're definitely not in your right mind." I take a step back, scanning him up and down. "Matter of fact, you sure you're fit to be rescuing anyone?"

Tristan growls, and I distinctly hear his teeth snap together. "You have no idea what you're talking about."

"Really?"

He shakes his head, then downs the rest of his drink. "I came when you called, didn't I? Should earn me a measure of trust, if nothing else."

I shake my head. "It was a mistake. You shouldn't have. You and I – we have nothing." Having delivered my scathing reply and gotten the satisfaction of seeing the startled look in his eyes, I walk away.

Tristan

I'm still standing like a dumb idiot when someone taps my shoulder, drawing my gaze away. Luz's red curls and green eyes greet me. There's a twinkling in their depths that spells trouble for me.

"So, friend, huh?"

My jaw clenches at her words and I look back to the other side of the bar, where Dani's resolutely ignoring me. *How in hell...* I can't. I look at her, but it's another I see. And I. Can't. Disassociate.

Fuck me.

Another poke, this time more insistent, focuses me back on the fiery redhead by my side. I glance around the bar, looking for Dom. He needs to come and gather his mate, but he's too busy looking smug and leaning against a wall.

He doesn't have to speak for me to get his meaning. *You're on your own.*

Screw you too, buddy.

Dom shrugs, and Luz pokes me again.

"What?" I unclench my teeth long enough to spit it out.

She grins as if I've just awarded her the best gift. "Nothing..." Her eyes flicker to Dani, and the grin widens. "She's pretty."

So is her twin, who broke my heart.

The words are on the tip of my tongue, but I bite them back and grunt instead. Luz rolls her eyes, more than used to our caveman ways by now – or so I'd hope, considering the wolf she's shacking up with.

As if on cue, Dom finally moves off the wall and joins us. His arm wraps around Luz, pulling her back against his chest. She melts into him, and I look away. Needing to escape their love, their connection that stirs my wolf. He demands one of his own – and my eyes land on Dani, again.

Merda.

"She's got you twisted already? Now that's a record if I ever saw one."

I scowl back at Dom. "You've no idea what you're talking about, meu amigo."

"Hmm." Dom arches an eyebrow. "I may not be Finn, but that's a helluva spitfire you have there. Plus, she's from your old pack, meaning she gets your crazy shit. You can't ignore a girl like that." His gaze falls on Luz. "Trust me, I know."

A snort escapes me, and my expression eases. "I've no intention of chasing her."

"And why not?" Something about Luz's question gives me pause. Her eyes are inquisitive, as if she understands there's something holding me back.

Not that I can talk about it. "We've got history, her and I. And not in the way you're thinking, Lucrezia. It's...complicated."

Her green eyes are a little too eager, and I refuse to explain myself. *Screw it.* I signal the bartender for another shot, and practically rip it from his hand. I'm not like Dom and the others – alcohol *does* get to me. It doesn't make me drunk, but it numbs everything – my senses, my nightmares, my wolf.

And right now, I need it. So I gesture for another. Luz whispers something to Dom, who rests his hand on my shoulder. I shrug it off.

There's a guy getting closer to Dani, talking to her and offering to buy a drink from the way he's gesturing. A growl escapes me, and Luz's chuckle half-registers.

"He's a goner."

"Would you two get a life?" It's thrown over a shoulder, because I'm already moving towards trouble.

Daniela

I feel him standing behind me, but don't turn around. Instead, I increase the charm up a notch and focus all my attention on the guy. He was nice enough to buy me a tequila shot – which I downed like there's no tomorrow. A second followed. And a third.

Numbness is the name of the game right now. It's all I'll have tonight, and I need it more than anything. Probably not the best way to deal with problems, but try being me for a second. With a family as fucked up as mine is, I'm better off forgetting.

Plus, why should I give Tristan the time of day? I mean, I hadn't expected him to actually be nice to me, considering what Izabella put him through, but some acknowledgement of a friendship we'd shared a while back would have been better than this.

The hurt makes my insides clench, but I keep on a neutral expression for my companion. He's a nameless face right now, designed to keep my mind off the one wolf it shouldn't linger on.

My mark throbs again, and I move my hand to rub it. Time is running out, or it did as soon as I left Bow's Arrow. And they'll come looking for me. My eyes close against the wave of despair threatening to overwhelm.

There's a thought, a darker one, that goes on a loop in my head. *What the hell am I going to do if Tristan doesn't listen, if I can't get protection here?*

As if sensing my doubt, another wave rises within me. Only, it's not despair. It's something very, very tangible. It rumbles within me, eager to come out. Panic freezes me, before I jump into action, motioning for the bartender to serve me another drink.

It's a temporary solution, but I don't intend to show my hand in this bar full of wolves. It'd be suicide, for one. For another, I definitely wouldn't be getting any protection out of it.

So yeah, the tequila helps by keeping everything at bay. At least, until Tristan speaks.

"Can I talk to you?"

I don't bother turning around. "Nope, I think we're done for the night. Call me if your alpha resurfaces."

Silence only answers, then the growl at my back pulls me out of any wayward thoughts. Before I can tell him to piss off, Tristan grabs my arm and jerks me off the barstool. Then he drags me behind him and through the doors heading at the back.

In the distance, I see Luz leaning against Dom. They're both watching us and smiling like they know a secret I don't. And hell if I don't wonder what it is.

Then we're outside, and it's pouring rain. Cold rain, in the middle of winter. It's darker outside, way too dark for only mid-afternoon now. I glance upwards at the sky, noticing the thundering clouds. A shiver runs through me, but it has nothing to do with the weather. My werewolf blood keeps me warm enough.

No, what really scares me, is what I see perched atop a building – a raven. Its moonshine eyes are fixed on us, head tilted to the side like it's listening. Panic seizes me again, and I try to run back inside. But Tristan is faster.

"Stay," he growls. "We need to talk, away from prying eyes."

My gaze lifts again to the raven. Its beady eyes are still on us. I shake my head, trying to rip myself from his grip. "Let me go, Tristan!"

He frowns, his eyes scanning me up and down. We're both soaked through our jeans and jackets now, and my hair is plastered to my face. But still he looks, until I'm forced to meet his gaze. And the burning fire in it scorches me.

"Tristan, I—"

Something snaps in him, and I swear I hear it. Before I can draw another breath, he pushes me against the wall. I yelp when my back hits it, but his mouth falls on mine. And trust me when I say, I don't pull back from it.

∞ ∞ ∞

CHAPTER THREE

∞ Irresistível ∞

"Love is an <u>irresistible</u> desire to be irresistibly desired."

-Robert Frost-

Tristan

I don't know what possessed me, but it's not an action I'm fully aware of. One minute I'm angry, the next I just want a taste of her lips. And boy, do I get one.

Dani clings to me like she's drowning, and not even the hard wall at her back is enough to distract us. Her mouth moves against mine, taking charge of the kiss, even as her arms wrap around my neck.

My hands go of their own accord to her hips – I'm lost in the daze. Past, present, future – Izabella, Dani. It's a mess in my head, but this kiss feels nothing, *nothing* like what I've had before.

My wolf, who never pokes his head out, growls in appreciation and settles back.

"Am I interrupting?"

I stop, panting against Dani's lips. Her eyes are dazed, looking at me like she doesn't recognize me. Then I glance over my shoulder to see who spoke.

Now my wolf is wide awake. The presence of another male, interrupting us and drawing Dani's attention, is enough to make me lose my tight rein on him. The haze of rage dawning on me is unfamiliar, and I take a step back from Dani, hoping it'll help clear my head.

Only, it doesn't. She's looking all kinds of flushed and confused, those amber eyes staring at me as if seeing me for the first time. And when they drop to my lips, I clench my jaw and turn away, towards the last person I want to see.

The newcomer smirks, all white gleaming teeth and cold onyx eyes. The moon shines on his ebony skin – all of it on display. He's wearing only an open jeans jacket, with a pair of jeans. And he's barefoot. A ring around his bottom lip, another around his right eyebrow, and two more on each ear. Shaven head, cocky demeanor...

"Reaper," I spit. His face is familiar, from an encounter months ago. "Cade, is it?"

He smirks wider, his eyes settling on Dani behind me. "If you ever want what he can't give, just come see me, sweetheart."

Dani says nothing, and my fist clenches, ready to pummel into him. I take a step forward, but she snaps out of her daze and touches my shoulder. "Don't."

Cade taunts me, hands in his pockets. He's not afraid, not even a little thrown off, and that pisses me off more. "Was there a point to your interruption?"

He laughs as if I said the funniest joke, then shakes his head. "Just sniffed a new wolf in town." His gaze goes on Dani again, and he licks his lips. "I was curious. Can't really blame me, right, buddy?"

I step forward at that, towering over him. He's a head shorter than me, not that it seems to stop him from acting stupid. "Do I look like your buddy, *idiota*?"

Cade narrows his eyes. "Careful, pal. We should all be on our best behavior around such a wonderful...specimen."

Again, he looks at Dani. This time I can't help myself. I shove him backwards, and he moves with the flow, but doesn't seem surprised. Or annoyed.

Dominate! Claim your turf. My wolf's restrained shouts don't help. But he's right about one thing. That cocky smirk? I need to wipe it off.

Before I can, Dani speaks, sounding exasperated. "Seriously, Tristan?"

I turn to her, scowling. "Yeah, fucking seriously. Go back inside and wait for me."

Her eyes flash with annoyance, and for a moment I fear she won't listen. Then she nods, once, and stalks off. When I look back to finish what I started, Cade is gone.

Fuck.

Daniela

I'm shaking by the time I enter the bar again, and not with the chills. That kiss... It's all I can think of. And what would have happened if that Cade guy hadn't interrupted.

Did Tristan kiss me because I look like Izabella? Or was it something more?

It can't have been, my rational mind points out. All it is, is chemistry – for all the wrong reasons. But my hormones tell me different. And not even two shots of straight-up whiskey can convince them otherwise.

"You okay?"

The Irish lilt drags my darkened gaze away from another drink. The Celt – Finn – joined me by the bar, and those emerald eyes seem filled with concern. For a stranger. *This guy wouldn't last a minute in my pack.*

I shake the thought off, then nod to him. "Sure. Peachy."

His gaze lingers on me a moment longer, then he smiles. It's sad, like he knows what I've been through. Before I can say anything, he gestures to the bartender for two more drinks.

I down the one in front of me, and Finn pushes another towards me. "Your story isn't easy to understand," he says after a beat. "I'm especially intrigued why one such as you, with a future as bright, would leave that behind... Would leave your pack behind. Lobisomem, is it?"

"Lobiso*mens* for the plural," I correct half-heartedly. It's the name given to us by history, the wonderful trackers of the Brazilian forests, led by the Amazon women. *What a joke.*

My glare is still focused on the dirty counter, and the drink calling out to me. Finn's not done talking, though. "One would guess something bad happened, grave enough to chase you away."

I meet his gaze then, waiting for the rest. Waiting for him to out me, to tell his friends I'm a fraud. Instead, his expression softens. "Like I said, not easy to understand at all."

Relief courses through me, headier than any alcohol. "Damn straight." I try to take a sip, but his hand reaches out to stop me.

"And it won't get easier with alcohol."

I glare at him, but he doesn't seem impressed. A more genuine smile plays on his lips now, like he's amused. "You've got spunk, lassie. But be careful your stubbornness doesn't get you into trouble."

His eyes flicker to something over my shoulder, and mischievousness sparks in their depths. Then he leans closer to me, whispering in my ear. "I know you sense my abilities.

And I feel yours. You should come clean while you can. Tristan isn't one to forgive easily."

Before I can say anything, he's shoved back from me, and Tristan gets in his face. "Are you done yet, meu amigo?"

Finn glances between us, chuckling. "I wasn't aware Daniela was spoken for."

"I'm not!"

My shout is muffled by Tristan's growl. "She's not available."

Finn throws me a look full of meaning, then heads back to the table. Dom and Luz's curious gazes are on us, and I realize they must have seen everything. *Wonderful. I'm barely in town a few hours, and I'm already causing problems.*

"No, you're not." Tristan turns to me, frowning. "And you need to stop berating yourself over this. Will you tell me what brings you here?"

I gape at him. This is the second time he reads my mind, and he seems to not even be aware of it. Then the alcohol in my blood sparks my fury, and I stand. "Are you *kidding me* right now, Tristan? First you're rude as hell, then you kiss me, and now you're acting like a barbarian. And you think I'm going to trust *you*?"

His expression shutters, and the emotion in his eyes vanishes. "You called me, remember?"

I'm panting, halfway between a need to gouge his eyes out or fuck him senseless. Problem is, I can't quite decide which is more appealing.

Locks of red catch my eye, and Luz bounces up next to us. "Dani, since you're new in town, why don't you stay with us? Dom has a spacious bungalow."

"She can stay with me," Tristan growls, not taking his intense chocolate eyes off me.

Dom joins his girlfriend then, and taps his friend's shoulder. "No offense, but it looks like you need some time apart to cool off."

Tristan opens his mouth to speak for me again, but I beat him to it. "That would be really nice, thank you."

I leave with them before anything else can escalate. My mind needs a breather, as do my hormones... And hopefully this pack's alpha will be back in town before I lose control of both.

No sooner do we get to Dom's house, that Luz pulls me aside and pours me a glass of wine. Dom takes one look at us, then steps to Luz and nuzzles her neck.

"You got this, iubirea mea?"

"Mhm," she nods, throwing me an amused look. Then her full focus turns to him, and her hand lifts to his cheek. "Get some sleep. You need it."

He closes his eyes for a second as if relishing her touch, then waves at me and leaves to the bedroom. Once the door is closed, Luz pushes the untouched glass of wine towards me.

"Okay, I promised myself I wouldn't pry. But you and Tristan... You've been practically sizzling since you walked in together. Is there something there?"

I take a sip of the alcohol, pondering my words. She's so easy to like, and their offer to stay here practically saved my butt tonight. Would it be so bad to actually talk, rather than resort to silence?

It's been a long time since we've had someone to trust... My wolf nudges, seeking that same sense of belonging, and a sigh escapes me. "Probably not. My pack... The way it works with females my age, in my pack, is you've got to be mated. If you're not, well, you kind of go crazy."

Luz's eyes widen. "Sex crazy?"

I snort into my glass, then take another gulp before answering. "Pretty much. The longer it goes, the worse it gets. And once our wolf sets her sight on someone... Well, time runs out pretty fast."

"And for you, the aim's on Tristan?"

I lower my lids at that to hide the tears. "Yeah. I didn't mean it to, but it's not like I can control this kind of thing."

Luz is silent this time, sipping her wine and staring at the countertop as if it holds all the answers. When she finally speaks, it's not what I expected. "But would it be so bad? Acting on it, I mean. If it's been so long, and you're not mated anyway, would it really be the end of the world if you sleep together?"

Her question has me pensive for a long time. In the end, I shake my head. "I don't know, Luz. There's so much history there, it would only lead to complications."

She makes a non-committal sound, then shifts the conversation to my old town. Without getting into details, I describe Bow's Arrow and my childhood – at least the better parts. The dark ones, well, she doesn't need to be burdened with those.

By the time I go to sleep, all I can think of is her question. *Would it really be so bad, to give in?*

Tristan

The wrench slips out my hand and clatters to the floor with a loud clang. Boots step into my vision, and I scowl at the newcomer. "What do you want, Dom?"

There's a pause, then, "How about you tell me what's going on, Tristan?"

I slide from under the car and glare at him. "None of your damn business." Then I dive back under.

Out of the corner of my eye, I can still see him there. "You're not getting the hint, *meu amigo*."

He snorts and taps my work boots with his. "Oh, I do. Believe me. But Finn didn't leave me alone when I was working on Luz, so I don't intend to leave you alone, either."

I move back out, glaring at him this time. "You're meddling."

His blue eyes light up. "I know." He's enjoying this too damn much, like he's no longer alone.

And it sinks in then, his lighted demeanor. "It's not the same like you and Luz, man. My wolf didn't ask for Dani. It wanted Izabella, probably still does – and she broke my heart."

The smile slips off Dom's face and he frowns. "I should say I'm sorry to hear that, but I'd rather not lie to your face." He pauses again, struggling with words. "While I'm sorry you're hurting over something that happened so long ago, maybe it's time to let it go. To move on."

"Whatever, man," I growl and get back under the car. Eventually, Dom walks off. And no amount of work calms me down.

That night, I'm at The Cave, drowning my sorrows in some good whiskey. They've set up a dance floor in a corner and Luz and Dom are fooling about, with Finn looking on and grinning like an idiot. Then I see his gaze slide to a strawberry-blonde girl off in the corner, nursing a soda.

She's young for you, bud.

Finn throws me a look across the distance, arching an eyebrow. *Ah, it speaks. You're out of your misery, then?*

He shouldn't have heard me, not in human form. Once more, his gifts get on my nerves and I slouch over my drink. *Fuck off.* I signal the bartender and he refills my glass. I'm in the process of downing it, when I smell her.

Sure enough, when I look over my shoulder to the entrance, Dani walks in. My eyes roam over her. She's dressed in jeans and a casual black tank top, with a black leather jacket over. In winter, she should be freezing. Yet only her cheeks are flushed.

She looks around, and her gaze stops on me – then moves past. I shouldn't be feeling hurt or angry over her indifference. My blood pressure spikes up, and before I know it, I'm half-standing – then a hand on my forearm pulls my attention.

"Don't." I glare at Finn, knowing now what Dom went through. It's hard to listen to your better judgment when your wolf is telling you otherwise.

Finn's eyes glitter as if hearing me, and he smiles. "You can't start something in front of the humans. Neither you nor Daniela can control yourselves. If you want something, get it – but outside."

He leaves as abruptly as he showed up. When I glance around again, Dani's no longer in the entrance. Worse. She's on the dance floor, laughing at some guy – human, to boot.

Daniela

I feel him staring, and try to shake it off. Tristan is not why I came here – not to Rockland Creek, and not to this bar. And since his alpha has not yet made an appearance, I'm stuck. I wanted protection, and now I want fun. Neither have anything to do with him.

Or so I keep telling myself.

Then the guy I'm dancing with wraps his arm around my waist, pulling me flush against him. A growl meant for my ears only reverberates, and I shiver. "Give me a minute," I say, and step out of his arms. He looks disappointed, but he'll get over it and keep his jaw. 'Cause as sure as my next breath, there's one wolf in this joint ready to lose it.

Without looking at Tristan, I pull my jacket back on and head outside. His footsteps trail behind me, and I can feel him physically like a flame over my body.

The minute we're outside, he reaches for my hand and pulls me to him. "What are you doing?"

We're a hair's breadth apart. I can smell whiskey on his breath, but his eyes aren't clouded. And all I want to do is shout and make it clear he can't be bossing me around. Only the minute I fall into his chocolate burning stare, my mouth goes dry.

A hum starts in my body, and I know where this is heading – ready for it. It's as inevitable as the moon rising, and my own destiny. I couldn't stop myself if I tried, because I've been yearning for this for way too long.

So I don't.

My body leans forward, and then I'm on my tiptoes, mouth brushing his. "Shut up," I whisper against his lips, before pulling him into a kiss.

His hands tighten on my hips, as if ready to push me away. Then they dig in, pulling me closer – impossibly closer. The evidence of his desire is hard against my belly, and my wolf purrs in appreciation. *Yes...*

Tristan drinks my moans, then one hand digs into my ponytail, and he forces my head away. I'm panting, practically climbing on him. My hormones are out of control, but it's more than that. My wolf seeks his, like this was meant to be, like it's more than just a quick fuck.

It can't be.

Tristan's eyes narrow on my face, and I wish to hell I knew what he was thinking.

Tristan

My nostrils flare, taking in Dani's arousal. Even more alluring is the surrender in her eyes. She takes one look at me and I read no hesitation, no games. Just pure want – and it stokes the need inside me even more.

I drop my mouth to hers again, this time less gentle. She took me by surprise the first time. It won't happen again. My free hand moves under her ass, and with one movement I've got her legs wrapped around me, and her sweet moans in my ears.

Then we're moving, and the first I reach is the wall of the building. Dani's pressing against me, asking for more. My wolf scents hers, the lobisomem hormones in the air, while the rational part is dimly aware of our open surroundings.

Releasing her hair, my hand meets hers, grasping it and holding it above her head. I do the same with her other hand, until all that's holding us together are her legs wrapped around my waist, and my powerless surrender to the heat between them.

A door opens and closes in the distance, and I freeze. The sound is loud in the night, the boisterous voices even more so. It's a cold shower I didn't need – one I want to reject. Dani feels my annoyance, and pulls her mouth from mine.

"Your place. Shift."

It's three words, but it's all I need. I nod and move off her, and the second after I'm in wolf form. Lucas would be losing his shit if he knew I did that so close to humans, but no freaking way can I wait.

I glance behind to make sure Dani's shifted too, and notice her sandy-colored fur in the corner. She nods, and then we're sprinting across the distance, finding our way to my place.

We run up the fire escape, and I morph again. The darkness and lack of moon covers us, but just barely. If any human looks up, they'll see our naked asses.

Impatient, I snap the handle on my patio door and push inside. Dani tiptoes behind me, but the minute after I've closed it, I'm on her. Her skin is soft underneath my fingertips, her reactions spurring me on. She arches her back against the wall, then lifts one leg enticingly around my waist.

Next thing I know, she's pulling me flush against her moistness, and fuck if I don't lose it right there. I groan against her heat, and my hands move of their own accord to her breasts. The lamp light from the outside casts a faint shine inside, illuminating her creamy skin.

"Dani..."

Something akin to satisfaction flashes in her eyes at me using her name. Then she pushes more against my hands, and I drop my mouth to her skin. She tastes sweet, like vanilla and cinnamon all mixed together.

A groan leaves my lips, and then she shifts her hips, enough to make me slide inside her halfway. I freeze, glancing up. And those amber eyes staring at me, that sexy smile, it's my undoing. I drop my mouth to Dani's once more, and lose myself inside her.

∞ ∞ ∞

CHAPTER FOUR

∞ Desculpa ∞

"An <u>apology</u> is a lovely perfume; it can transform the clumsiest moment into a gracious gift."

-Margaret Lee Runbeck-

Daniela

Memories of last night flood me. Tristan kissing me, licking my skin, tasting me... Looking at me like I'm his one and only.

I blink against the sun – and the moment I do, the illusion is shattered. Tristan is awake, head in his hands by the side of the bed. And somewhere deep in my chest, my heart curls up and shrivels in pain.

As if feeling I'm awake, he lifts his head towards me. Those chocolate eyes are all kinds of confused at the moment, and I gulp. Attempting a blank face, I ask, "You okay?"

Tristan holds my gaze for a moment longer, then looks away. "Not really."

I wait, hoping he'll follow it with something else. But he doesn't. He gets up, and my mouth waters as I take in his naked body. He's ready for more – and I am, too. But instead of coming back to bed, he turns his back to me and pulls on a pair of boxers.

"I need a shower," he mutters, and walks away.

For a long, humiliating minute, all I can do is stare at the spot he last occupied. Tears well in my eyes and start dripping down my cheeks. I'm only aware of them when they land on my hand, and for a second, the tiniest of moments, I consider giving in and allowing the weakness to take over.

But I won't.

Gulping past my sorrow, I stand from the bed and start pulling on my clothes. I'm only thankful that in the darkness of the night, he never got to see the mark on my back. Even now, it throbs, warning me I'm running out of time. So no way I'm going to stand here and wait for him to return and kick me out, when it's obvious he can't even stand the scent of me on his skin.

And to think I believed there had been something special... *Fool!*

"Dani, I—" Tristan walks in then, and stops in his tracks. His eyes narrow when he sees me buttoning my jeans and hastily pulling on my t-shirt over my bra. "Going somewhere?"

I ignore the way his voice gets to me. It's gone low, and there's a flicker of something in his eyes – hurt? Too little, too late. I'm too far gone, my defensive walls too high up, to care.

"What's it look like? Away from here."

My treacherous eyes can't help roaming over him, and I notice his skin and hair are not wet. *He didn't shower, then?* I shake my head of the thought. It shouldn't matter. It doesn't mean he changed his mind.

"And why, carinho?"

All colors drains from my face then. "I told you never to call me that," I hiss. *That's what you called Izabella. I'm not her.* The words tear at my heart, but I bite them down. The anger only covers what I'm really feeling – the pain that I've been a replacement, and nothing more.

Tristan looks taken aback, then shakes his head and takes a step forward. "Dani, I'm sorry. Can we talk about this?"

"There's nothing to talk about," I mutter and try to move past him. But he steps in my way.

"I think there is."

My eyes meet his then, and I try with all my might to ignore the heat emanating from him. My wolf wants to cuddle, wants to rub noses, to get back in bed. What we shared last night... It can't have been only me.

Sensing more tears gathering, I scowl. "You were an itch I had to scratch! This doesn't mean anything, Tristan. It doesn't give you some claim over me."

"Claim?" He snorts, moving closer. My wolf reacts, wanting to get out, but at the same time my mouth waters at the way his muscles rip. All I want is – *no*.

"I don't want to claim you," Tristan says. "But I'd like to know why the hell you used me."

"I think we both know who used who last night." Then I pick up my jacket and walk out the door.

Tristan

The arena is deserted – it should be. This gym was shut down three months ago for illegal fighting, and it's been empty ever since. Graffiti line the wall, and cans of beer and sugary drinks are piled up on the floor.

But that's not why I'm here. That's not what I care about. What I want, more than anything, is to get this fucking pain out of my chest and stop feeling like I can't breathe. So I do the only thing that seems to calm me down these days.

I fight.

The old gym equipment may be used and out of shape, but it does the trick. My fists hit the worn leather without care, not even when my knuckles start bleeding. I know all it takes is a quick swipe of my tongue and they'll heal.

Hours later, I'm sweating and panting – but nowhere closer to getting the peace of mind I want. And Dani's to blame for this.

Her sweet skin, that pouty mouth and those eyes begging for more. Always more. Last night was – I don't even fucking know. But it was the first I've slept so soundly since coming back to the mainland.

And that's also Dani's fault.

"Merda!" My shout echoes in the darkness. There's no electricity in this place, but I welcome the dark. I always will – unless it's at night time, in my own place. That, I can't deal with.

I'm so focused on punishing myself, on trying to forget Dani's sweet sounds, that I don't hear the door open and close. Then a scent hits me, and I whirl around with my fist up.

Dom ducks me, and backs up a few steps. "Easy, camarade. What's gotten into you?"

A grunt is all he gets as an answer, and I go back to beating the punching bag. Dom's silence feels pensive, until he speaks again. "Tristan. Stop and talk to me, man."

When I don't listen, Dom reaches out and grasps my elbow. I try to yank it out of his grip – damn vârcolac strength. Chains would've been less secure than his mighty fist.

I scowl instead. "What do you want?"

"You didn't show up for work and Finn thought it best I come to check out this place." He pauses, frowning. "What's gotten into you?"

Dani.

Instead of admitting it, I shake my head. "Nothing. Needed a day off. Plus, Lucas isn't back yet, so it's acceptable, no?"

Dom tilts his head, those blue eyes flickering with something akin to amusement. "Mhm, acceptable. Sure." A pause. "So this has nothing to do with Dani?"

The punching bag looks way more appealing than answering that question. So I go back at it.

Daniela

Ducking under a tree, I make my way back to the civilization of Rockland Creek. For the past few hours since taking off on Tristan, I've been in the woods. Running as a wolf has its perks, one of which is that I don't have to feel emotions. What I focus on is nature, and the call of the wild.

Now that I'm walking back on human legs, the return to reality jolts me. Tristan's words – or lack thereof – hurt me, but what did I expect? He's in no shape to make proper decisions, not when he has so much to deal with in his own head.

Doesn't take a genius to see his demons swimming under the surface. Or maybe it takes one to know one.

The problem is, I can't wait. My hand lifts to my shoulder, rubbing the mark against the t-shirt. I grimace at the pain, but it ebbs away, at least for the moment. It will come back. It always does. And I need to find protection – soon.

I bend under another tree, and emerge past it, slamming into someone.

"Well, well."

Startled, I glance at the newcomer. It's the same man from the other night, who'd interrupted our kissing. My confused expression must tip him off, as he smirks.

"I'm Cade Nielsen. We've met before."

Crossing my hands over my chest, I let my gaze roam over him. He's dressed like before – only in a different pair of jeans. His ebony skin has no tinge of frostbite, and his wolfish intent this close to me is clear in those onyx eyes.

Only problem is, I'm not in the mood. "Yeah, we did," I say, and move around him.

Cade lets me take a few steps away, then jogs to keep up with me. "In a rush?"

"Yup."

"Running from someone?"

I throw him a look. "What's it to you?"

He shrugs. "I know the type, is all."

That makes me stop and tilt my head. "Type?"

"Wounded creatures, ye females," he says in a bad accent. It's terrible enough to make me snort, then I grace him with a chuckle. "What do you want, Cade?"

"Why, the pleasure of your company, of course."

I hesitate. Despite having been here only a short time, I'm distinctly aware of the rivalry between Tristan's pack and Cade's. It was evident in the way he spoke last night, calling him a Reaper.

"Aren't you and Tristan's pack enemies?" I frown, still keeping my distance.

Cade throws his head back and laughs, then shakes it and takes a step closer. "Ah, we are. But that's not *Tristan's* pack, darling. It's Lucas'."

The reminder seems incongruous, and only becomes clearer with his next words. "If it's an alpha you want, you're better off coming with me."

I look him up and down, doubtful. "You don't smell like an alpha to me."

A hint of steel enters his eyes, and the smirk becomes frostier. "Good scenting, darling. You really would do well with us." A pause, then, "True, I'm only a beta. However, things change all the time in my pack. I assure you, if it's protection you're in need of, you'd be better off with us."

"Tempting as that might be, I'm in no rush to make decisions." The lie burns its way past my lips, and I try to make it sound real. "But I'll keep the offer in mind."

I turn to leave, but he shadows my steps once more. Not even my annoyed glare is enough to throw him off. "Seriously?"

Cade shrugs. "The woods aren't always safe, darling. Best to walk around with company."

If that's a veiled threat, I choose to ignore it and huff instead. "Fine. Walk me back to town, then."

Something flickers in his eyes and he smirks. "With pleasure."

Tristan

Dom's gaze on me grows heavier by the minute. And what's even more annoying is the noise of the idiotic tennis ball he keeps throwing against the wall.

"Are you done yet?" I throw over a shoulder.

"Depends," Dom grins. "Are you?"

I glance at my cracked knuckles, finally taking in my exhausted muscles. My workout clothes feel – and smell – like I've been drenched in the sewers.

"Probably."

Throwing my shirt to the ground, I head to the changing rooms. The shower here still works – or, the cold water does, at least. After a scrub and putting on a fresh pair of clothes, I head back out. One lick of each hand, and the wounds start closing.

Dom's still there, leaning against a wall and waiting patiently. "Don't you have a girlfriend to see?"

"I do," he grins again. It's annoying how happy he is these days. "And the longer I stay with you, the worse the need to see her gets." He pauses, growing serious. "She's worried too, you know."

I sigh. "Tell Luz she has nothing to worry about. I'm fine."

"Bullshit."

I stare at him, he stares right back. Neither of us backs down, and I recall our last bonding moment – kicking Tommy's ass. Then defeating the pack of Reapers, and the vrykolakas. Finally, I sigh.

"Dani and I, we slept together. Last night. And I might've acted like a dick this morning."

Dom tilts his head to the side. "Because...?"

Running a hand over my face, I whisper, "Because I finally had a good night's sleep."

"Is that all?"

I shrug. "Sure. That, and the fact I dated her *twin* sister."

Dom's mouth drops. "Well, shit." He stares at me for a beat, then says, "That's a little piece of info you probably should've shared earlier, buddy. We might've laid off, understanding what you're going through."

A snort escapes me. "Sure you would've."

Dom rubs his chin and admits, "Mm, maybe not. Still, we would've all understood better." Another beat of silence. "So, what are you going to do about it?"

I run a hand over my face, trying to think past the haze of everything. "Talk to her. Try to explain."

He grins like I've handed him an early Christmas present. "That's a good start. Come on, I'll give you a ride."

∞◆∞

I get out of Dom's pickup and head into Claws Auto Shop. Or, I'm about to. Then I smell her – and someone else. My wolf growls, but already Dom has a restraining hand on me.

"Breathe. It's a Reaper."

Sure enough, within minutes Dani turns the corner accompanied by none other than Cade. It's not what I want to see, and the leash on my wolf snaps a little more. Regardless of what happened last night, she came here seeking protection and I'm determined to make her understand she has a safe haven with me.

Daniela

Tristan's staring at me with hurt in his eyes, and for a moment I almost feel guilty. Then I remember which of us reacted bad this morning, and remind myself I'm not doing anything wrong by strutting around with another wolf.

Keep telling yourself that. I ignore the annoying voice at the back of my head, and turn to Cade. "Well, you've walked me back to safety. Thanks, I guess."

His gaze flickers between me and Tristan. "My pleasure, darling." Then he drops his head, and his lips briefly linger on my cheek. "The offers stands."

Out of the corner of my eye, I see Tristan moving towards us, his stride agitated. Cade pulls back with a satisfied smirk and salutes him. "Later." Then he's gone, leaving me to face the incoming storm.

Rather than yell at me or acknowledge my departing companion, Tristan says, "Can we talk?"

I follow him into a corner, unsure of what to expect. "We said everything we had to this morning."

"No, we didn't." He grabs me by the shoulders, and there's real sincerity in his voice. "I'm sorry, Dani. Your coming here, I haven't exactly been a good sport about it. Yes, we have history, especially where Izabella's concerned."

My mouth opens on a retort, but Tristan lifts his index to my lips. "Wait, please. I really do apologize for giving you a hard time since you arrived. And..." His hand falls back down then, and the look in his eyes changes. "What happened last night, I don't know what it was. Não tive má intenção..."

I didn't mean to do that. In his emotional state, he's reverted back to our native language, and I gulp. These are not the words I need to hear.

Yet before I can interrupt him, Tristan goes on, "I'm not going to say it was a mistake, because I honestly don't know. But you do have a safe haven with me, Dani. Until you're ready to talk, to tell me more about what brought you here. And until Lucas is back. Please don't go making rash judgments...not when you have a pack ready to help you, right here."

Try as I might, I can't help gaping at him. "You mean it?"

His eyes soften. "Claro, beleza."

Those are the words I'd been waiting for, ever since stepping foot in here. And probably much longer. Telling him that, though, would be crossing that line again. So I hug him and pray he doesn't see my tears when I say, "Vai, esquece."

Forget about it. If only I could, too.

Despite Tristan's reassuring words, I still think it's too early to go back to his place. So that night, I'm bunking with Luz and Dom once more. The vârcolac leaves us girls to chat, and Luz slowly works up to the subject of Cade.

"Who was that guy you came in with this afternoon? That window to the reception area doesn't hide much."

I tear my gaze from the fireplace and meet her curious expression. "A Reaper, Cade."

Luz nearly chokes on her drink. "Jared's new beta?"

I wait until she catches her breath, then ask, "Yeah, you know him?"

She nods, biting her lip. "Just, be careful. I've had encounters with them, and they're not, umm, as friendly as you might think."

"I'm pretty sure Cade only offered me protection because he sniffs my lobisomem abilities."

"Protection?" Luz's eyes are wide, and I realize I shouldn't have shared that part, so I try to backtrack. "But he's not even the alpha, isn't that, I dunno, disloyal?"

A shrug escapes me. "Who knows? Things seem to run differently around here. And I didn't accept, don't worry. I mean, it's tempting because it would've solved all my problems and I wouldn't have to wait for Lucas to come back. But... I'd have to be pretty desperate to get into bed with the likes of them." The mark throbs on my shoulder, reminding me I *am* pretty desperate. I ignore it.

Luz nods at my words, then adds, "What abilities did you mean? And what did you call it? Lobo-something?"

"Lobisomem. It's what my type of werewolf is." I run her through the quick history, then shrug. "As for the abilities, well..."Another oops on my part. "My kind of wolves, we're great trackers. Aside from being able to shift our forms, enlarging our body mass, we can pinpoint a scent from miles away and even figure out its rank within a pack."

"So you'd know if it's an alpha, a beta, or the like? Neat!"

A chuckle escapes me, and I take another sip of wine. Before long, Luz retires to sleep, and I snuggle on the couch. Sleep is hard to come over me, and when it does, it's restless.

I thought I wasn't seeing right. But nope, there goes my lucky streak – right along with the freaking raven hovering outside in Dom's backyard. I glance at their bedroom, then tiptoe closer and exit the patio doors. The blasted bird doesn't run off, only watches me with moonshine eyes. A shiver runs up my spine. Could they have found me already? Could *he* have found me?

"What do you want?"

My whisper is barely audible, but the bird cocks its head. Then it croaks once, twice, enough to let me know it's not just a simple bird. The shivers intensify, and next thing I know, my teeth are chattering.

I look back at Dom's house, and a part of me wants to go and wake them up, tell them what's happening. Then I think back to what my family's capable of, and I know I can't put these nice people in danger. Especially not Luz, who's been so kind already, but whose mortality makes her so damn fragile.

Which means there's only one other person who can help me out now. Tiptoeing back, I pull on my jeans and jacket, grab my backpack and head out the door.

The night is silent, but the moon's glare is impossible to resist. I check around to make sure I'm alone, then duck in an alleyway. I look at my hand, and in front of my eyes it blurs – into claws, and a paw with fur. I gulp, fearing the change. Last time, I'd...

I shake it off, and slowly, my hand returns to human form. Then something flies in my face, and I wish I'd gone with the freaking change.

Tristan

"Where is she?" After a sleepless night fighting my own demons, I came in early to grab Dani and ask her to come back to my place as of tonight. Only problem is, her scent is nowhere around Claws Auto Shop, and something unsettles inside me.

Luz looks up from the reception desk with a pretty frown on her face. I see out of the corner of my eye Dom lift his head from the hood of the car.

Chill, I'm not looking for a fight, I tell him.

Then watch your tone with my girl.

I sigh, and amend my statement. "Have you seen Dani?"

Luz tilts her head to the side. "What makes you think I would have?"

"Lucrezia..." My teeth are gritted and I'm clenching the side of her desk with enough force to hear a crack.

She drops the report then and looks to the inside of the garage. Dom is out the second after, Finn following closely behind. The vârcolac speaks first. "She wasn't on the couch when we woke up this morning, and her backpack was gone."

I glance between them. "Why the hell didn't you call to tell me?"

Luz bites her lip. "We thought she came to you, Tristan."

One moment I'm staring at her, the next my fist is in the wall, cracking it open. Luz jumps, Dom moves in front of her, and Finn shifts his stance to block me just in case.

I scowl at them. "She's not with me, and I need to see her."

Dom frowns. "Maybe you should've thought of that before making such a mess of things."

My feet move towards him, but Finn steps between us, hands lifted in a sign of peace. "Enough, mate. Let's not waste time with this crap. Where would she have gone?"

I shake my head, running a hand down my face. "Don't fucking know." Out of the corner of my eye, I see Luz biting her lip. I know that look.

"What is it?"

"Um, Dani might've mentioned something last night..."

That draws my attention and she cringes under my glare. "Tell me."

"She only said there had been other options presented to her for protection..."

I take a step closer. "By whom, Luz?"

"Cade."

The words that escape my mouth then aren't growls, they're a mix of inhumane animal sounds and swear words. Then I'm out the door, in my pickup, with Finn's shouting echoing in my ear.

Hell if I'm going to let my girl end up with the Reapers.

I ignore the other question – why she'd even think about it, after our talk yesterday – because it's not one I want to ponder too closely.

CHAPTER FIVE

∞ Quebrada ∞

"A <u>promise</u> must never be broken."

-Alexander Hamilton-

Daniela

The woods blur before my eyes. How long have I been running? I glance behind – why didn't I shift yet? I've been so panicked I ran on human legs and I know they're not as reliable as a wolf's.

As if to prove me right, I trip over a large tree root and go sprawling down.

"Merda!"

My palms hit the ground in anger, and I'm tempted to curl onto myself and refuse to face reality. The raven – again. In Rockland Creek. I know it's a messenger, but who will they send? How much time do I have?

The answer is impossible to ignore any longer – none. As if on cue, my mark throbs again. I groan against the pain, waiting for the wave to pass. Then I shrug the jacket off my shoulder, followed by the top of my t-shirt. I crane my neck to see as much of it as I can, but it's useless. The biggest observation I can make is that it's red, inflamed and angry-looking.

Time's run out, and I've only myself to blame. Tristan blinded me with his wounded soul and my hormones didn't help. I shouldn't have listened, shouldn't have waited.

And now it's too late and they'll come for me.

A shudder runs through my body, despair clawing at my very soul. I can't do this alone. And while all I want is to go back in Tristan's arms, I know it's not possible, not when he's got his own demons to fight and he's still pining after Izabella. There's only one place I can go, and it's where I should've gone since the beginning.

On wobbly legs, I stand and dust myself off. Then I let the shudder morph into more, and my wolf takes over. Once I'm on four paws, I take off on a run.

The barn looks ancient against the green of the hills, but the scent doesn't lie. Cade's in there.

So I strut over to the entrance – then two men block my way. Pierced from head to toe, in black leather and bulky as hell, they're aiming for intimidating.

I keep walking, but with each step my wolf gives way to the human. Not once do I stop. By the time I'm a foot away, I'm back on human feet, tossing my hair back and pulling it up in a ponytail.

The men don't look as self-assured anymore. I think it's the first time they've seen a wolf girl turn and not end up naked.

I smirk. "Disappointed, boys?" Without giving them a chance to answer, I nod to the barn. "Where's Cade? I need to speak with him."

They share a look, then one goes inside, while the other watches me like I'm a freak. It's not the first time. *Won't be the last.*

Then Cade walks out, his eyes lighting up in anticipation when they land on me. "Well, this is a surprise. To what do I owe it?"

I met his gaze full on. "What does it take to join the Reapers? I'm pretty sure I have it."

Tristan

My phone's buzzing on the passenger seat, but I'm too wired to stop and check it. It would mean time lost, and I don't have that. What the hell possessed Dani to go to the Reapers?

You know what.

The treacherous voice at the back of my head is right. *I possessed her.* Drove her away acting like a callous fool. Taking what I wanted and unable to deal with it. And when I had the chance to explain myself, to make things better, I acted like a love struck fool and kept my mouth shut.

"Merda!" The light is red and I strike the wheel twice, three times with my hands.

My breath is coming in short pants now. I'm so damn aggravated at myself, at the world. At freaking Izzy who ruined me. And Dani, why...

Then I hear a *pop-pop-pop* and I'm gone. No longer there. At the back of my head, I know it can't be guns. *Must be kids playing with fireworks.* Not that it matters, because I can't rationalize it. Everything slows down, my vision narrows.... then speeds up. My breathing comes in fast, too fast. *I can't –*

I'm hitting the wheel again, but this time to ground myself. Clenching onto the leather, muscles straining against it, nothing helps.

The sound of guns. The smell of blood. Creatures of the night. Smoke. Fire. Shouts. So much blood. And then in the darkness, a creature comes out, more zombie than real. I shoot – but it's still walking. Still coming towards me.

I can't be having this now. Dani needs me to pull myself together. The realization takes a bit to come through, then I'm back in my car. Behind me, honks are going galore. The light is green.

My foot hits the gas by reflex and I drive off. I'm on automatic, my actions no longer controlled by logic. If they were, I would have known driving after that episode is not a good idea.

By the time I finally come to my senses, shake off my sweaty muscles and look around, I'm parked somewhere. There's a structure in the distance – a barn. And acres upon acres of land. I've gone past a metal gate, and pulled over into a shaded corner.

A glance up tells me the afternoon is coming to an end. *Where the hell am I?* And the better question is, how much time went by? Am I too late, or is Dani already...

My phone buzzes again. This time, I pick up. "Yeah?" It comes out scratchy, and I clear my throat.

"It's me," Dom says. "Where are you?"

"Hell if I know. Some compound out of town. With a barn."

"In your car?"

"Yeah, why?"

"Finn says he can track your GPS. Lucas won't like this, man. You took off without permission."

"You'd know all about that, meu amigo."

"Yeah, but don't go getting ideas." He pauses, and I hear Finn muttering in the background. Then Dom comes back on the line.

"Tristan, listen to me. You're in Reaper territory. Whatever you do, *don't* go in. We're coming, and we'll get Dani back together."

"Dani?" Everything else is a haze. I drop my phone and step out of the car, taking a deep breath.

There's manure, animals, the scent of the Reapers and then...

"*Dani.*"

My wolf, suppressed for long, isn't taking it any longer. He's at the surface, ready to strike, egging me on. Each step is taken by *us*, propelling *us* closer, until I stop thinking, stop resisting.

I run to the barn, shoving past the two wolves who try to stop me. With them on my heels, I barge through and stop dead in my tracks.

Dani's inside with Cade, facing him. He's holding her hands in his. Something about that gesture, the tilt of her head, stabs me with enough pain to have me gasping.

Still, I manage to speak past the agony in my chest. "What the hell are you doing?"

She barely spares me a glance. "This doesn't concern you, Tristan. Walk away."

"Like hell I will!"

The stubborn tilt of her head tells me she's not about to give in. And she's still avoiding my look, focused on Cade instead.

Dani may not get it, but Cade is bound. And I don't see any alpha around to sanction this. "You can't integrate her into your pack unless you get confirmation from Lucas she's not with us."

"What makes you think Lucas didn't agree?" She's still avoiding my look, but her biting words carry a sting that's not entirely Dani.

I glare at her, starting to seriously get annoyed over this. "Enough."

Dani looks up at my tone. Whatever she sees in my expression, it's enough to get her to stop. She goes back to pretending I don't exist.

"Leave us," I tell Cade.

He looks down at Dani, a smirk playing on his lips. "Remember what I said, darling. You've got a sure thing here – if you're brave enough to reach for it."

Before I can stop him, he drops his mouth to hers and kisses her. It's only a few seconds, but at the sight of him on her, something in me snaps and I stalk over. One-handed, I shove Cade off Dani and use my free hand to punch him. Considering my last few workouts at the gym, Cade stumbles backwards, and I'm pretty sure I hear a crack.

Cade wipes at his mouth, but dismisses me in favor of Dani. "Chat soon." Then he's out, waving to his two wolves to follow him.

Once he's gone, I stare at Dani, trying to quiet my breathing. Cade, the Reapers, it all fades to the background. Nothing else matters, at least not now, except for her and me.

I failed my buddies in the field, and I've sure as hell messed up multiple times since coming back. But this...Dani... It's something I can fix, something I owe her. She never deserved whatever it is that had her running here, and one way or another, I need to communicate that to her.

Quick on the heels of that realization comes another, tempering my wolf and the words on the tip of my tongue. *I've come here to get her back, not push her away.*

"Querida–"

Dani backs away, as if my using the endearment is too painful to hear. "Don't." Holding up her hands, she adds, "I don't get why you came here. Out of some misguided sense of responsibility because we shared one night?"

She glares at me, but I see the hurt under the surface. "Or is it because of Izzy? Whatever it is, *don't*."

Daniela

Tristan's quiet for a long time, and I curse the history that links us. It's that same history that had me thinking I could find solace here. The same damn thing that blinded me and had me falling into his arms.

I've got no one to blame but myself. And by making this choice, coming here, this was me trying to start fresh. The

Reapers may have been the worst pick, but they're no worse than my family.

Before I can walk away and finish what I started with Cade, Tristan speaks softly. "It has nothing to do with Izabella."

Christ, even the way he says her name sounds like he's still in love with her. The truth about my sister is on my lips, eager to tumble out, but I swallow it past my dry throat.

"Dani, look at me."

I blink away tears and meet his eyes. Tristan takes a step closer, his expression pained. "Why did you come here, to the Reapers? I thought... After we last spoke, you were meant to wait."

Unable to hold that gaze filled with so many emotions, I pace away, running a hand through my hair. "You wouldn't get it."

"Try me."

I shake my head, facing him again. Telling him about the raven is a no go. "I'm running out of time, Tristan."

He takes another step closer. "What makes you think that?"

My mark throbs, and I wince. He frowns, probably noticing the pain in my expression. *If only you knew...*

"Knew what, Dani?"

I shake my head, gesturing to him, taking this new distraction rather than focusing on the truth behind my decision. "Are you so far gone in your head, fighting your own demons, that you don't realize what's going on?"

My bringing up his demons is enough to get his walls back up. "What are you going on about?"

"You can hear my thoughts, Tristan. Like you did just now!"

He frowns, crossing his arms over his chest. "That's not true."

"Really? How did you find me here? Why did you sleep with me? And what makes you so intent to protect me?" With each question, I take a step closer, until I'm standing only a foot away from him, on the verge of tears again. "Don't you see?"

Tristan opens his mouth again to deny it, but realization dawns on him. "Are you saying..."

"Yeah, I am," I whisper. "Your wolf wants to mate with mine. *Has been* wanting to, ever since I landed in this damn town. That's why we can't control ourselves, that's what makes everything so much more complicated."

Tristan blinks once, twice, then shakes his head. "You lost me."

A tear escapes my eye, and I wipe it away furiously. "Your wolf may want me, Tristan, but it's not me *you* want. It's Izzy. It always has been."

Silence lingers between us, and his stare intensifies. I turn to walk away, but he reaches for me, grabbing my wrist and tugging me back to face him. Unlike last night, the movement's gentle, as if he's afraid to break me.

This time, he reaches for my cheek, cupping it in his hand. "Whatever my history with your sister, this has nothing to do with her. It's between you and me." He searches my gaze, then glances at my lips. "And for the record, that night had nothing to do with Izzy either."

"Then why?"

I take a step closer, wanting – needing – his answer. Tristan opens his mouth as if to speak, but closes it up once more. "I don't know."

Disgusted by his lack of an answer, I turn my head away, trying to flee his touch that makes me feel too much. But Tristan's stubborn, and not about to let go.

"No. Don't let this shit mean we can't... That you need to be in Cade's pack." His touch drops to my shoulder, eyes filled with pain. "Please don't. Everything else, we can fix. But Dani, if you go with them, you'll lose a part of yourself."

My gaze rises to his, more questions than ever in my head. I'm so tired of running, of no protection. Of being afraid, day in and day out.

As if reading my mind, Tristan adds, "We *can* protect you. Whatever's going on with your family, we can help. I promise, Dani."

The truth vibrates in his voice. And I know he means it – now. But can I trust him with my life? With my secrets? And what will happen when the truth comes to light? Finn's warning is loud in my head. *Tristan isn't one to forgive easily.*

I bite back the emotion before it leads to something else. Instead, I nod. "Okay. I'll come with you, and talk to Lucas. But it needs to be tonight."

Relief spreads on his features and Tristan pulls me into a fierce hug. His arms wrap around me, securing me against the world. And despite the agony in my heart, I hold onto him – because there is nothing else I can do.

When I pull back, Tristan hesitates to let me go. Those chocolate eyes dig into mine. "About the other thing, the wolf..."

I shake my head, biting the inside of my cheek to stop further tears. "Let's leave that at bay for now, please. It won't do us any good."

Tristan's hold tightens on me, then he nods, once, and lets me go. As we're leaving, Cade and his two wolves stand outside the barn.

Cade steps to me, narrowing his eyes. "Changed your mind so fast, darling?"

I shake my head. "My coming here was a mistake. Sorry to have wasted your time."

His smile is cold and chills me to the bone. "You're not yet. But you will be."

Tristan shifts, tugging on my wrist to pull me to his other side, effectively placing himself between us. Cade just laughs, then he steps aside and lets us leave.

As we near Tristan's car, a pickup pulls behind him. I tense, fearing more Reapers, but Tristan squeezes my hand. "It's my guys."

Sure enough, Dom and Finn step out of the pickup. They take us in, then Dom looks to the barn, frowning. "How bad is it?"

"Bad." Tristan shakes his head. "We need to see Lucas, no more dallying about."

Dom nods. "He's back in town, I was filling him on the phone. Follow us, and we'll take you to him."

It's the words I've been waiting to hear, but my attention is somewhere else. Namely, on the freaking raven perched on top of a branch, staring at us. At *me*.

"No," my soft whisper carries, and the raven blinks. With a seemingly innocent bird cry, it flies off. If only I could believe it's all a coincidence...

Tristan looks back at me, surprised at my rejection. "What gives? I want to stick by our deal, Dani."

I shake my head, not willing to risk it now. "Tomorrow morning is fine. I'd rather get some sleep tonight."

He hesitates a beat, then chances a glance to the guys. Whatever passes between them, Tristan nods. "Let's go back home, then."

Tristan

It took some convincing – and a near-fight between me and Dom – but Dani finally relented and came home with me. After we got home and ordered a pizza, she showered and went to sleep. I offered her the bed, and within moments she was passed out. If nothing else, that confirmed she didn't get much sleep the night before.

Watching her sleep, I have to clench my fists so I don't join her. Dani's sleeping in one of my old tank tops, hands tucked under chin and curled up. The bed looks like it's swallowing her whole, and my wolf whines, but I tell it to shut up.

"No can do, querida." My whisper lingers in the air for a breath, then drops to the forgetfulness of sleep.

Dani shivers under the blanket, and I move from my spot by the window to cover her up. The brilliance of the moon is enough to shine a faint glow on her face. And while it's an entrancing picture, my gaze is drawn from that beautiful image to something else – a mark on her shoulder.

Frowning, I move the cover off her, and look closer. My finger runs over the swollen flesh. At first I think it's a tattoo, but Dani whimpers under my touch, as if in pain. *What the hell?*

Still tracing the mark, I begin to get a picture of it in my head. It's a star, one of those pagan-looking ones, with a snake or some kind of reptile intertwined. I want to get a closer look, but fear waking Dani up.

"Tomorrow, querida, we have to talk," I whisper to her, then pull the cover to her chin. "Sweet dreams." I bend over and my lips linger on her forehead. Her whimpers quiet down, but my wolf is unsettled.

I pace back to the window, thinking of what she told me, about our wolves, and the mating ritual. It's something I should have picked up on earlier, but I've been so focused on her presence and trying to get through every night, that I missed it.

How could I?

My thoughts drift to Izabella. We'd been together since she was old enough to date. It didn't mean we'd been the only people in that relationship, though. On and off, it had all been as dramatic as only teenage love that morphs into young adult love can be. Izabella, for the most part, had an issue being monogamous. And when the relationship shattered, I thought I'd never love again.

My wolf, evidently, thinks otherwise. If he's been drawn to Dani, it'd be so easy to claim her. One more touch, one more night together, linking our minds... And it would be forever.

Yes...Let me choose, my wolf whispers. The idea sounds a little more appealing than I'd like.

Shaking my head, I snag myself a cozy spot in the armchair by the window, where I can keep staring at the moon. No matter what, I can't join Dani in bed. Not with everything left unsaid between us. If she's right – which, deep down, I know she is – and that's what our wolves are doing, then it's like trying to stop a train dead set on reaching its destination.

And I can't...There's no way in hell I'm going there. Not tonight. Not until she's safe and we can make decisions without it feeling like we're running out of time.

Aside from fearing our connection, there's another reason I don't want to be near Dani while asleep. Last time I'd been in bed with her, I'd fallen asleep. And by some miracle, it lasted the entire night. I can't run the risk that it won't, and I'll wake up like I always do – screaming.

Night is my least favorite time of day and nightmares.... Well, let's just say I'm better off awake.

So I bury myself in the armchair, stretching my legs on the rug, and stare at the moon. Hidden behind clouds, it casts enough brilliance in the room to light up Dani's face. She looks peaceful. All the anger is gone, leaving behind the girl I used to know.

Her soft sigh reminds of another, and my mind drifts back to Izabella....

"Stop it!" Isabella shrieks and tries to get away from my unmerciful fingers, but I'm having too much fun.

"Do you give up?"

She laughs again, burying her head in the pillow, but shakes her head.

"Brave woman." I tickle her harder until she's panting and begging for mercy.

Then those hazel eyes look up at me, the sensual mouth smiling. There's laughter in her gaze, and I drop my mouth to her lips.

My hands roam down, lower... Then the buzz of a cell breaks the spell. Izabella reaches over and glances at the text message. Already, she's distancing herself, pulling away from me both physically and emotionally.

She eases out of bed, pulling on a pair of designer jeans, her heels and jacket. At the door, she turns and blows me a kiss.

That was the day before I told her I was leaving for the Army. The day before all hell broke loose.

Daniela

It's the whine that wakes me up. Rising the hair at the back of my neck, it nudges my wolf awake. Who in turn stirs me up in a panic. I sit upright, aware of being alone in bed.

Then the sound comes again, and this time I look to the corner. Tristan's sprawled in an armchair, his massive frame jerking right and left. And the sound? It's coming from him, like a wounded animal.

I want to go to him, but I'm not sure what's going on. A part of me knew from the beginning that he has demons, but something tells me I'm about to find out just how bad they get.

The sounds grow in pitch, and he starts trashing in the armchair. His head moves right and left, his hands clenching in fists. Then he jumps in a crouch, snarling at the surroundings like he's seeing invisible demons. I curl into myself, pretending I'm still asleep. But I can't resist another peek past the covers.

Tristan's frozen, panting, his shirt soaked with sweat. His eyes take each inch of the place in, assessing risk and discarding it. I know, because with each movement he makes, I'm there with him, my wolf drawn despite it.

Finally, he breathes deep, and the connection breaks. Tristan stands, rubbing the back of his neck and stretching out his muscles.

I fall back asleep with his haunted eyes in my mind.

∞ ∞ ∞

CHAPTER SIX

∞ Segredos ∞

"There are no <u>secrets</u> that time does not reveal."

-Jean Racine-

Daniela

Morning finds me dead tired. Tristan actually has to shake me awake, and it's with loud grumbles and pulls that I finally get up and go shower. By the time I come out, he's nowhere to be seen, so I go about making coffee and sit on his couch to sip it.

I've only been there for about five minutes when I hear a croak outside. The cup slips out of my grip and shatters on the floor, coffee splashing everywhere. In the next breath, I move to the wall and glue myself to it, refusing to be seen again.

That damned raven sent me on a crazy quest last time, and there's no way I'm about to do it again. A wave of fear rises within me and morphs into something else. My hand becomes paw, claws digging into the wall. I cringe against the pain – too much.

"What's going on?"

I snap to and find Tristan at the entrance of the living room. He's sweaty, looking as if he just came back from a jog. His eyes are focused on my pitiful form plastered to the wall. I hide the morphed paw behind me, trying to control my breathing and pull the change back.

Tristan steps closer, frowning now as he takes the headphones out of his ears. "Dani? You okay?"

I nod a bit too eagerly, trying to keep him away. But he's still inching closer, and I know I'm about to lose it completely in front of him. *Shit. Shit. Shit.*

"No, you're not," he said softly, as if speaking to a doe. "What got you spooked?"

Questions shine in his eyes, but already I feel my hand returning. Flexing my fingers to make sure they're all there, I pull it out and use it to pin my hair in a ponytail.

"Nothing."

Despite my nonchalant attitude, when I try to move past him, Tristan grabs my hand in his. "Dani...talk to me."

I chance a glance outside – nothing. When I look back at Tristan, he's patiently waiting. "Thought there was someone on the balcony, is all. There wasn't. Just my mind playing tricks."

He peers over my shoulder, then his gaze falls back on my expression. "What about what you said yesterday, about our wolves wanting to mate?"

My body freezes. I hadn't expected this line of questioning, and something about having it in daylight makes me feel raw, exposed. I shake my head. "We're not talking about this right now."

Tristan shifts his stance, practically digging his feet into the floor. "Why not? It's a perfect time."

"I..." A sigh escapes me. "Just because our wolves want one thing, doesn't meant we have to give in. There, happy?"

"Not really."

His relaxed answer feels like an electric shock to my system. I have no choice now but to meet those chocolate eyes, trying to see where he's getting at. "What do you mean, *not really*?"

Tristan takes a step closer. "I'm not happy, Dani. You're making it seem easy, when we both know it's not. If we don't listen to our wolves, we'll never find the peace we seek. Not in a relationship, anyway."

At a loss on how to respond, I resort to defiance, tilting my chin in the air. "I'm perfectly fine with that."

He knows I'm lying, but I don't give him a chance to question me further. Moving away, I throw over a shoulder, "Going to get dressed, then we can go meet your alpha."

∞◆∞

Tall, dark and handsome just about describes Lucas. In his house out of town, buried in a forest, he's the epitome of a loner. His hard, angular features speak to aristocracy, and those onyx eyes grab mine from the moment I step through the door.

I want to turn back, and forget all about asking for protection. It feels like he's looking straight inside my soul, and if he sees everything...

"Going to tell me where you were?"

Lucas' eyes shift from me and assess Tristan. A single eyebrow lifts in the most arrogant way I've ever seen. "I wasn't aware I owe you explanations."

Cade's words ring in my ears. *It's not Tristan's pack.* As a Luna, I always knew I wouldn't be with another alpha, but the wolf inside me would want one. Something about this interaction should throw me off, make me feel more attracted to Lucas. Instead, my wolf wants nothing more than to cuddle with Tristan.

Well, shit.

Before I can voice anything out loud, Tristan rolls his eyes and says, "You don't, but it would've been nice to know when asked. Anyway, this is Daniela Da Silva, an old friend."

The alpha nods, his eyes still on me. After a long beat, he glances back at Tristan. "And the purpose of this is?"

"To ask for protection."

No surprise shows in his expression, but I could have sworn he tenses even further. "Leave us, Tristan. I will speak to her alone."

I open my mouth to dispute it, but a voice inside my head says, *I wouldn't if I were you. Not unless you want all your secrets laid bare before him.*

Masking my surprise, I squeeze back Tristan's hand. "I'll be okay."

He hesitates, then nods. "I'll wait in the car, whenever you're ready."

"No need, amico," Lucas cuts. "I will deliver her safe and sound to the shop after we're done here."

Tristan hesitates, seeking my agreement. I avoid his stare, not wanting him to see how scared I am. The Luna's blood in me rebels at the unknown sentiment, but it's not like I can control it.

By the time I snap out of my sulky thoughts, Tristan's stalking out, and then it's just us two. Lucas turns on his heels and walks further inside the house, and I follow grudgingly.

"Was that you, in my head?" I ask.

Lucas throws a look over his shoulder. "It was."

I gulp past my fear. If he can enter my head so easily, either he's very good at what he does, or I'm too weak to face off with an adversary like him. Either way, it doesn't bode well for the protection I seek.

We enter the living room, and he takes a seat on an old baroque couch, gesturing for me to join him. I head towards the opposite armchair, but Lucas growls. Yep, growls. Then he points right next to him.

Now I'm even more annoyed, but it wouldn't do to antagonize my next supposed leader. So instead of rolling my eyes, I shuffle over and sit gingerly on the edge.

Lucas' eyes are heavy on me. "Good. You know how to listen to orders."

My teeth clench so hard it hurts my jaw, but I try to push through. Then his next words completely unravel me.

"So, mind telling me what a witch is doing trying to get protection from my pack?"

If I thought I was afraid before, now I'm petrified. There's nothing warm in Lucas' expression, only the cold glint of steel and the hardest jaw.

Merda.

"I... Don't know what you mean."

He's on me in a flash, his hand on my throat, pressing me into the couch. I try to push him off, but his strength is inhumane. Then his grip on my throat tightens little by little, and air escapes me.

Next thing I know, my hand is pressing against his chest, and a blinding blood-red light escapes me. Lucas goes flying into a bookshelf, and everything tumbles down.

I get off the couch to run, but his laugh stops me. Slowly, I pivot on my heels, eyes narrowing on the alpha. He's on the floor, holding his stomach like he's having a blast.

Ignoring my confusion, he gets to his feet, and gestures for me to sit again. "Scuzi, cara. You've no need to fear me, I was only proving a point." He dusts himself off and then those searing eyes are on me again. "Now, if you wish protection, you'll have to tell me everything. Including the kind of trouble that had you run from your lobisomem pack into Tristan's arms."

Scowling, I sit back down. "I'm not a witch, Lucas. My family is made up of werewolves, just like Tristan. But..." My gaze drops to my hands and I start picking at the skin around my fingers. "Years ago, when my mother died killed by humans, my father was filled with grief and lost his mind. He became aware of his mortality – and ours, his children. My brother told him of a way to ensure we'd all be safe. So he made a deal with a witch. In exchange for powers to give us extra protection, he would allow his eldest daughter, and all eldest ones down the line, to be mated to darkness. That's what I'm escaping."

Lucas moves then, and it's enough to draw my gaze back up to him. His words, however, I didn't expect.

"I figured as much."

"You...what?" Nothing about this makes sense. *Unless he's with Thiago, and that means I'm in danger and –*

I look around, expecting my brother to pop out of nowhere. Or the ravens. Or someone. Lucas picks up on my agitation and lifts a hand, intending the gesture to calm me down. It doesn't. I flinch away, expecting a blow.

Lucas frowns then, leaning forward on his elbows. Contrary to before, this time he moves deliberately slow, as if to reassure me. "Cara, you can relax. I wouldn't hurt you. Earlier, it really was just to provoke the witch in you."

My mouth is dry. "Then what did you mean? Why do you seem unsurprised by all this?"

"Because I'm not. I knew the moment you stepped in town that there would be trouble. So I did what any alpha worth his salt does, and left to retrace your steps."

My agitation slows, to be replaced with dread. "You...went to Bow's Arrow?"

Lucas nods, once, and leans back against the sofa. "That same evening." I can't look at him anymore, so I stare at my hands instead. I've been picking at the skin around the nails for the last few minutes, and they're raw now, close to bleeding.

"I saw enough. Read enough scents to figure some parts out... And realize you're no threat. Still, having met you now, there's something about you. What is it you're not telling me, cara?"

I look back up then. "I never wanted these powers, and I refuse to use them. But they'll come after me, one way or another. Each female in my pack has to procreate. Me, even more so."

Lucas' gaze sharpens on me. "And why is that?"

"Because I'm their Luna – their last-standing leader."

Tristan

"Would you quit your gawking?" It comes off a tad sharper than intended, but their staring is getting on my nerves.

Since I burst into Claws Auto Shop and started furiously working on one of the cars, refusing help, Dom and Finn seem to think I'm ready to lose it. Which, come to think of it, isn't far off the mark.

Finn snickers and moves in my field of vision. "What's gotten into you, mate?"

I lift my head enough to glare at him, then go back to banging the bumper into place. Then I move under the car, but it's still not enough to push him away.

"You know what you did yesterday is reckless. Seems it's your flavor of the week since Daniela walked in." A pause. "Not that I blame you."

That sparks me. I step away from the car, baring my teeth. "Oh yeah? Why not?"

He backs off, hands held up. "Easy, mate. I've got no designs on your lady."

A car parking outside distracts us. Dani gets out, with Lucas following soon after. I can't read his expression, but hers is sad, downturned. Without thinking, I move forward and get in my alpha's face.

"What did you do to her?"

Lucas stares me down until my wolf relents and forces me back a step. He waits another beat, then says, "Nothing. I have taken her request under consideration."

A look to Dani, and she heads off, leaving me frowning. What the hell happened in the last two hours?

Then Lucas moves closer, his eyes narrowed. "You know I've respected your privacy all this time. Now I have to ask – what was your role in that pack?"

"Back off, Lucas." I try to head past him, but he blocks my way.

"No can do, amico. You nearly started a war with the Reapers. I think it's only fair I know."

I know what he's asking. Do I also have alpha blood in my veins like Dom does?

So I hold his gaze for a moment, then shake my head. "I'm no threat to you, and I'm not hiding some crazy lineage. Alpha isn't meant for me, plus that's not how my old pack ran. They go by the blood of the Luna. Izzy and Dani were daughters of the pack's Luna."

He frowns, as if the notion is new to him, but his words contradict it. "So they're led by the she-wolves?"

"In a way, yeah." My gaze is drawn to Dani again. "She's pack royalty, of sorts. Daughter of past Lunas. The leadership is meant to go to her sister, Izabella, as she's the eldest."

The name tastes like ashes on my lips now. Did I really lose as much as I thought when I left her, or was I only kidding myself? And the better question is, what if Dani's my redemption?

"Careful, amico. Your *cara* has secrets, and they will weigh heavy on you once you find out."

My gaze snaps to his. "What did she tell you?"

Lucas' eyes are inscrutable. "She said enough." He walks past me to his office, leaving me behind, confused. I can't stand still for long.

My feet walk me to Dani, interrupting whatever she's chatting with Luz about. "Ready to go?"

"Already?" She seems surprised.

"Yeah. Let's go grab a bite, then head home."

Luz touches my shoulder, drawing my attention away from Dani. "Just need a quick word before you take off."

I don't want to leave Dani alone after whatever happened with Lucas, but Lucrezia doesn't make it a habit to be so secretive.

"I'll wait outside," Dani says and steps away.

My eyes linger on her departing form, then I face Lucrezia once more. "What's so important?"

"Tristan, be careful with her." Before I can defend myself, Luz holds up a hand. "No, I don't want to hear whatever lie it is you're telling yourself. Fact is, I've watched you for the last months. Your nightmares, those demons you hold at bay, they've been getting worse, eating pieces of your soul. Then Dani stepped in, and now I don't see you with circles under your eyes." She smiles. "Not always, anyway. So, keep that in mind, whatever happens. Please."

Her words leave me feeling bereft, and like everyone's seeing something I'm not. But I nod, keeping my counsel. "Is that all?"

Luz waves me off, and I join Dani outside. Hand extended to her, I wait until she intertwines our fingers before heading off. Yet even with her by my side, I can sense the shadows weighing her down, and wish like hell I could wipe them away.

I figure bringing Dani to The Cave is better than interrogating her in my closed apartment. So I wait until the waitress brings us some coffee, sandwiches and cookies dipped in ice cream, then focus on Dani.

She picks up one of the sandwiches, gives it a quick sniff and bites in. For some reason, the gesture makes me smile – probably because it's so unlike Izabella.

Dani looks up then, and swallows her bite. "It is. Unlike her, I mean."

I try to hide my surprise, but it's hard. Her amber eyes hold mine for a moment longer, then she drops her attention back to the food. It's uncanny how easily she can read me. Our earlier conversation comes to mind, about our wolves.

Can we really fight this? Or should we just give in?

Dani's too skittish, so I don't bring it up. Instead, we eat in silence for a few moments, and I'm trying to find a way to broach the subject of her mark. Just as I'm about to say something, Dani's cup clatters on the table, and her gaze moves to the outside.

Fear radiates off her, setting me on edge. And while she's busy scanning the outside area for whatever spooked her, my heartbeat quickens. And quickens. And quickens some more.

My hand grips the edge of the table, and I try to stay in the present. Dani must feel my turmoil, because she drops whatever spooked her and focuses on me.

"Tristan?" Her voice is muted, and no matter how hard I try to focus, it's impossible. "Tristan, look at me."

I can't even do that. The bar around us starts fading – and then she grabs my hand in hers, tight, enough to hurt. The pain brings me back, and I meet her gaze.

"Focus on me. On my voice."

I shake my head "It won't be enough."

"Yes it will be. Breathe with me. Deep breaths, in and out." With her hand in mine, I manage that small feat. Once, twice.

Dani nods, and rewards with a small smile. "Good. Now look around and tell me five things you can see."

My eyes dart around the place, unable to focus on anything. Dani squeezes my hand again. "Anything, Tristan. It can be anything. Just say them out loud. And keep breathing."

I take another breath, then rattle out the first few things I can think of. "Sandwiches. Cash register. Door."

"Good." Another squeeze of my hand. "Take another breath. And give me two more."

"Coffee. Beer."

Dani nods, and slowly steps out of her booth to join me in mine. I move towards the window, then realize how bad of an idea this is. My heartbeat picks up again – then Dani grabs my shoulder.

"Breathe, Tristan. Now name four things you can touch."

I frown. "What the hell is this?"

"Just listen to me, please," she begs. "It'll help. Four things."

Shaking my head, I nonetheless do what she tells me, touching each as I go. "Table. Leather seat. Spoon." My hand lifts to her face, and she doesn't shy from my touch. "Your hair."

Another smile, this time so kind my heart leaps in my chest. "Now three things you can hear. And keep breathing, in and out."

This one requires more focus. And as I'm breathing in, trying to figure out what it is I can hear, I realize whatever Dani's been doing to me helps. The panic is slowly ebbing away.

"Doorbell. Oven. Your breathing."

Dani nods again, "Now tell me two things you can smell."

I take a deep whiff, and say, "Alcohol. Your scent."

She reaches for my hand again, breathing in sync with me. "And this last one. Name me one emotion you feel right now."

Love. I gulp, refusing to say the word aloud. Instead, I voice the second-best. "Gratitude."

Dani grins this time, "How do you feel?"

I take a moment to breathe, and realize it's gone. The panic, the need to fold unto myself, thhe unbearing feeling of losing control. I'm here, with Dani, and I'm not losing it. When I meet her gaze, my body automatically leans towards her. "Better. Thank you."

She doesn't move away, instead resting her forehead against mine. "You're welcome."

"What was that?"

She shrugs. "A trick I learned from Izzy. When we were kids, she used to have panic attacks. But she knew when they were coming, so she taught me to help her deal with them. This was one of the techniques."

I close my eyes. "That's what it was, then? Another panic attack?"

"Yeah," she whispers. "Tristan, I know you probably don't want to talk about it now, but if ever you do... I'm here. What you went through, when you went away, couldn't have been easy. And it doesn't take a genius to see your demons."

"So you've mentioned." My eyes open again, meeting her amber ones. "The same stands for me, Dani. Whenever you're ready to talk about that mark, I'm here."

She pulls away then, eyes widening. "What mark?"

"The swollen brand on your shoulder. I saw it last night, when you were whimpering in your sleep."

Dani looks away, and her shoulders fold inwards. She's shrinking in front of me, as if wishing to disappear. And I can't stand it. So I pull her in my arms, holding her for a long moment.

"Are you ready to go home?"

She nods against my chest.

Daniela

We enter Tristan's bachelor pad, and I head to the couch. I've no sooner stepped away, that Tristan tugs on my hand he still holds and makes me return to his arms. "I wasn't done, you know," he whispers.

Crap. I'd hoped he'd been, and wouldn't keep asking the hard questions. Judging by the look in his eyes, that was a foolish wish.

"I understand you may not feel ready to talk about the scar on your shoulder, but what about your chat with Lucas?"

My eyebrows go way up. "What about it?"

Tristan searches my expression, but I've no idea what for. "He alluded to secrets, stuff you told him. Care to share any of that with me?"

I wonder how much I can tell him, other than the obvious. In the end, I shrug. "Lucas has an odd way of interrogating, that's all. I explained to him the history that brought me here, and he seems willing to consider affording me protection."

"Hmm." Tristan waits a beat, two, and I bite the inside of my cheek to avoid blurting out the truth. "That's all?" When I still say nothing, he adds, "Okay, what about the wolf thing?"

This again. I try to pull my hand out of his grip, but he refuses to let go. His eyes flash, and his free arm wraps around my waist, tugging me closer. "Dani, talk to me."

I stop pushing against his chest long enough to glare at him. "What do you want from me, Tristan? 'Cause I seriously don't know."

His eyes narrow on me. "Alright, fine. You won't answer those two easy questions, then tell me this. What the hell were you thinking, going to the Reapers for protection?"

"I was thinking that I got so blinded by your wounded hero persona and all the history between us, that I forgot to care about myself. And that's not a mistake I'll make again, nor can anyone force me to."

His hold on me lessens, and he lets me go. Stunned chocolate eyes meet mine, and I ignore the hurt in them, turning away. Heading to the bedroom, I remove my clothes and crawl under the bed sheets, refusing to think about the sleeping arrangements.

Moments later, I feel his gaze on me at the entrance of the room. "I'd never ask you to forget about your needs, Dani. Whoever did is a fool."

I shut my eyes against the tears, refusing to let them fall. Instead, I let sleep claim me.

The noise wakes me again – and this time, I can't let it go. Slowly, I move off the bed, tiptoeing to the armchair Tristan is sleeping in. A sheen of sweat covers his body, and he feels feverish to my touch. I try to shake him awake, but nothing seems to snap him out of the nightmare.

Then I get the – albeit stupid – idea of using what I shouldn't. My hand rests on his chest. I don't expect anything to happen, after all I've been holding it all inside. Despite my ridiculous lack of faith, a slight vibration runs through my fingers. Before I can pull back, it leaves them and zaps into Tristan.

He jumps out of the chair, nearly smacking me to the side. I wisely move to the wall, giving him room to maneuver around. He's back in a crouch, his haunted eyes landing on me – then far away. I know he doesn't see me, but can he hear me?

"Tristan, it's me."

His head tilts to the side, and a whine escapes him. His hand is half-turned into a wolf paw, and I see the grimace of pain on his face at the rest of the change.

Tristan, I try again mentally. *Talk to me.*

There's a pause, followed by, "Izabella?"

I gulp past my throat choking, and nod. With a flicker of fingers behind my back, I undo my ponytail, letting my hair cascade around my face – just like hers used to.

Tristan turns to look at me, sniffing the air.

"It's me, Izzy. Come back to bed... It was just a bad dream."

His frown shows his confusion, but the paws have turned human once more. I inch closer to the edge of the bed, holding out my hand towards him.

"Come to me..."

He listens then, as if entranced, and meets my lips with a ravenous kiss. For tonight, I'll be what he needs. Whatever need is in him, it's in me too, and I couldn't ignore it if I tried.

So I'm with him touch for touch, removing piece of clothing in sync, until we're naked, in bed once more. His mouth moves over me, and with each kiss I feel myself falling deeper still.

Falling? I'm already fallen, period. Even before I came to this town. All my lies about being able to fight our wolves, about not mating... They're useless. Because the certainty is heavy in my blood, in my bones, in my soul.

I fell in love with this man years ago, and never stopped.

His touch stops my thinking, and then I push him on his back. Tristan's eyes roam over me, followed by his hands. I arch my back, pressing my breasts into his touch, then moan as I slide on him, taking him deep inside me.

Tristan blinks against the haze, then looks at me – *really* looks at me. He doesn't say anything, but lifts up on his elbows and buries himself deeper. His mouth is on my neck, biting, sucking, and I can't –

"Tristan..."

He hears my plea, flips us over, and dives into me deep. With each stroke, I feel like I'm taking him deeper – into my very soul. Then he completely shatters me when he touches my cheek and breathes, "Meu anjo."

My angel.

I soar to the sky, and he follows shortly after. When I fall asleep shortly after, it's in his arms. There's no more panic in him, and something tells me he'll sleep soundly.

∞ ∞ ∞

CHAPTER SEVEN

∞ Destino ∞

"It is not in the stars to hold our <u>destiny</u>, but in ourselves."

-William Shakespeare-

Daniela

I walk into the shop, my eyes scanning for Tristan. He wasn't there when I woke up this morning, and I'm afraid it'll be more of the same heartache when I see him. If nothing else, I'd like to be prepared.

Luz lifts her head behind the receptionist desk and smiles. "He's in the kitchen, making coffee."

Hesitation grips me, but I push past it and head inside. Tristan's massive form makes the place look tinier than it is. "Hey."

He turns around, and rather than the closed expression I'm used to seeing on him, it's open. His eyes light up when they fall on me, taking in my simple attire. Then he grins, and something in my stomach wobbles.

Before I can say anything, he crosses the distance separating us and drops his mouth over mine. I make a sound of half-surprise, half-moan, then I'm kissing back with all I've got. But Tristan doesn't stop there.

He moves me to the side, until I feel the fridge at my back. And still, he's kissing me, and one hand is going lower down my back until he sneaks in the back pocket of my sweatpants, and pulls me closer to him.

Really close.

I manage to pull away enough to catch his eye and breathe, "What's going on?"

He shrugs, dropping his lips to my neck now that my mouth is busy moving. And it's distracting as hell, sending tingles down my spine. Then the hand in my back pocket moves under my shirt, tracing my spine. I arch like a cat against his touch, craving more.

"Tristan..." I hate how breathless my voice is, and the puddle he's reduced me to. "Stop. Please."

To his credit, he stops moving, but his mouth stays glued to my neck. Almost as if he's trying to figure out if I'm serious or not. Then he lifts his head, meeting my gaze full-on. "Do you mean that?"

No. "Yes." My eyes narrow on him and I step to the side, watching as he drops his head to the fridge and takes in a shuddering breath. "Will you talk to me?"

"What's there to say?" He faces me again, puzzled. "I'd be stupid to ignore what's between us, Dani. And I know more than most how short life is. So, I'm trying to see what this is, and if it's more than chemistry."

My stomach knots. "And where does this new inspiration come from?"

"From waking up next to you this morning." He moves again towards me, the predatory glint back in his eyes. "Naked. And feeling extremely satisfied."

I gulp and break the stare, unable to hold it. My every nerve feels on fire, but something tells me now's a good time as any to get out of here.

"Luz needs, um, help. With, stuff." I jerk my thumb over my shoulder. "We can talk about this later, okay?"

Then I turned and rush off. Tristan's laughter follows me. When I erupt in the reception area, Luz looks up with an amused expression on her face.

"That took a while."

My cheeks flame, and I hold up my hands in prayer. "Please come with me."

"Where?"

"Anywhere! I told Tristan you need help with something."

Luz laughs, shaking her head. Then she stands and pulls on her thick winter jacket, following me out the door. I let her take lead, lost in thoughts of what just happened.

"They're stubborn, you know," Luz whispers.

I glance at her in surprise, noticing her wistful smile. "How so?"

"Besides their over packed hormonal bodies, I really think their wolf alter ego controls most – if not all – their reactions around their women. Very, err, primal."

A smile tugs at my lips. "I guess so." Then, noticing we're way down the street, I ask, "Where are we going?"

She shrugs. "Finn says sugar is the remedy to everything, so we're heading to a little bakery spot around here." A side-glance to me, then, "If you ever need to talk about Tristan, I'm here. I know we just met, but those guys are thick as thieves. We need to stick together, too."

A sigh escapes me and I dig my hands in my pockets. Not because I'm cold, rather to avoid picking at my fingers again. "He's just...confusing. And the history doesn't help."

"With your sister, you mean?"

I nod, staring at the snow and my sneakers crunching on it. "He used to date her, but she was a hard one. Made his life a living hell once he enlisted."

Luz is quiet for a while, and when I glance at her again, she has a peculiar look on her face. I replay the words in my head, not seeing what I said wrong.

Noticing my confusion, she says, "You said *was* a hard one. Is she...?"

I bite on my lip hard enough to draw blood, warring with myself. This is my one chance to come clean – if not to Tristan, at least to someone. Just as I'm about to spill, an arm wraps around my shoulders, pulling me close.

"What are you gorgeous ladies up to?"

We glance up at Finn, his green eyes filled with laughter. Luz holds my gaze for a second, and mouths, *Later*. I just hope there will be a later.

"Heading to get some sweets," Luz grins at Finn. "Want to come?"

There's something eager in her tone, and I clue in once we enter the bakery store. My mouth waters at the delicious aromas of vanilla, cinnamon and chocolate – and helluva load of others. Then I see the girl behind the counter, and can't help staring.

She's got brown wavy hair piled in a messy bun atop her head, and beautiful hazel eyes, wide and doe-eyed. Her refined features could be those of a princess, and I can't help but think of Cinderella when I see her apron filled with flour.

"Elle!" Luz waves, gathering her attention and we move closer. Or, at least, Luz and I do. Finn seems rooted to the spot, eyes wide and staring at Elle like she's a goddess on earth.

Which, judging by the scent emanating from him, his wolf definitely thinks she is. "Easy, tiger," I chuckle under my breath, knowing he'll hear me.

It snaps him out of his daze, at least enough so he moves to a small table and stares from there. Elle follows him with her eyes and blushes, making her even more endearing.

"Lucrezia," she says in a voice like a fairy, "what can I get you today?"

With a delighted sound, Luz starts pointing at everything in the window and Elle puts together a package for us. By the time we're done, Luz pulls out her wallet to pay. I want to help, but before either of us can, someone else hands over a card. "Let me."

Elle stares at the outstretched hand, then her gaze lifts to Finn. And I swear it's like a fairytale, because their connection fills the air. She stops breathing, and he can't take his eyes off her. They're in their own little bubble, completely unaware of how entranced they appear to the outside.

I throw Luz a look, and she smiles a secret little smile.

Then Elle snaps out of her daze and punches in the total on the machine. Finn takes it from her trembling hand and swipes his card. He's oddly quiet, focusing on the keypad like it has all the answers in the universe. Elle, too, busies herself with putting everything in bags.

I almost want to scream at them to stop, and Luz seems close to doing the same. But before we can, Elle hands over the bags to Luz and smiles. "Thank you."

Luz nods, then we're out the door, Finn trailing behind – and throwing glances over his shoulder, to no avail. His distraction gives me time to look around, and I notice a guy in the distance, facing the store. His stormy gaze is fixed on the bakery, and the girl within. When he notices me staring, he waves, a smirk playing on his lips.

I tear my gaze away, rushing to catch up with Luz and Finn. Once we're back in front of the auto shop, I elbow him. "Cat got your tongue?"

He mutters something under his breath and takes off, leaving me and Luz to break into chuckles. "Did you plan that?"

Luz grins. "Maaaybe."

I'm about to ask more, when I smell him. My body tenses, and before I can control myself, I'm bursting through the store.

Tristan

I narrow my eyes on the guy stepping in. He's dressed in casual clothes, but his scent screams wolf. It's a good thing Luz isn't here, but where the hell did they go? And are they safe?

"Hello," he says, noticing me hovering near the receptionist desk.

I nod at him. "Can I help you?"

"Yes, perhaps. I'm looking for Daniela Da Silva. I was given information she's in this town."

My eyes narrow on him. Everything about his statement is vague, but there's an eager look in his eyes. "Who gave you that information?"

"I don't believe that matters," he smiles. "Does she work here or not?"

Before I can say anything, Dani bursts in from the street. "What the hell are you doing here, Agostinho?"

She notices my gaze on them, and moves, making sure to keep him between her and Luz, who stepped behind. I gesture for Lucrezia to head to the back, and at least she listens. Though her curious look on us implies she's going to have questions after.

By the time my attention returns to them, Dani's now between me and this Agostinho, her every muscle tense. "What do you want?"

"You know what, carinho. They sent me to bring you home."

"You can tell them to fuck off, Agosti. I'm not coming back."

He grins, raising his hands as peaceful gesture. But it only spurs Dani on. "Get the hell out of here!"

She shoves him back, despite his raised hands. There's an aggressiveness to her movements, but it's not born out of rage. Rather, my wolf senses fear emanating from Dani in waves. *Fear, and shame.* I'm too busy staring at her to think about the guy, wondering what the hell I'm missing – again.

Dani's not done, though. She pushes him again, and Agostinho slams against the door to the shop, bursting through and outside in the snow. He looks up at her, making no move to stand up.

I'm afraid we have another Tommy situation on our hands, but something about his demeanor strikes me as odd. He claimed he's here to get her back, yet he's oddly subdued. Then it hits me – if Dani's a Luna, as is Izzy, why would a male wolf try to get her to do anything against her will?

"Dani?"

Her ponytail is coming undone and she's only got on a t-shirt. Barely enough to keep her warm. But her cheeks are flushed, and there's a glint in her eyes that brings me back in time.

It's another girl I see, with the same anger flashing – but at me. When I'd told Izabella I was heading to war, she hadn't been happy. Enough so that the same night, she'd slept with my best buddy to *show me what I was losing*.

But Dani – I shake my head and come back to the present, not realizing I've spoken my ex-lover's name aloud. Dani's eyes are on me, and hurt flashes across her face before she storms away.

I frown, until the guy gets up and dusts himself off. "You called her Izabella," he says softly.

A sigh escapes me and I rub the back of my neck. "Course I did. They're freaking–"

"–different," he finishes for me. Something about his tone really draws my attention. "No matter what you see, you must know they're *different*."

The urgency in his every word really draws me in. "Of course I know that. And my history with Izabella is done. It's been years since I last saw her, and whatever she's doing these days is her business. I don't appreciate you implying it's clouding my judgment."

The guy stares at where Dani disappeared, then back to me. "Has she not told you?"

I refuse to admit how little Dani confided in me, but it seems an answer is really not required. Agostinho shakes his head, answering his own question. "She didn't. So you have no idea Izabella is dead, do you?"

The ground shifts under me, but somehow I manage to remain standing. I stare at him, then at the spot Dani disappeared through. A single word escapes me. "How?"

"Suicide."

My narrowed gaze is enough to make him back up this time. "That's impossible."

"It's the truth."

I shake my head, pointing an accusing finger his way. "You've delivered your message, and stirred enough trouble. Now get your ass out of town before I kick it out."

Agostinho smiles, but it's sad. "I will leave, but they will send others. Daniela does not have much time."

I watch him skulk away, trying to control my tremors. *Izabella is dead. Suicide.* The thought goes on a loop in my head. How is that possible? The girl I knew, full of life... I shake my head. And this entire time Dani's been here, she lied. She had plenty of opportunity to tell me, and didn't.

Why?

That question burns its way to my chest, and I know I need to find her. A growl tears through my throat, and I stomp back inside. "Daniela, get your ass here right now!"

Nothing answers me, and Luz gets up from her spot at the reception. "She's gone, Tristan. Took off through the back."

No amount of cursing is enough to calm me down. And when I go to follow her scent, Luz steps in front of me.

"Get out of my way, Red."

She frowns at me. "You need to cool off. So how about you go for a run, or the gym, or whatever it is you do, and *then* try to talk to her? Doing so now will only lead to more issues."

Cursing under my breath, I take off – to the gym.

Daniela

I'm way past drunk at The Cave by the time the gang walks in. Luz makes a move my way, but Tristan steps in front of her and growls something. Everyone's staring, and something snaps in me.

I run out the bar into the fresh, crisp air, pulling desperate gulps into my aching lungs. Now I'm really out of options. And if Agostinho found me so easily, the rest will be sure to follow. Fear cripples me, but I can't move, can't run, can't hide. What else can I do, but take a stand and fight?

A door squeaks behind, and I'm not alone anymore. *He's* there. And I wish it didn't, but my body leans towards his heat.

"Why didn't you tell me?"

Tristan sounds less angry than I'd feared, and maybe that's a good thing. *If only I had such control.* All the guilt I've carried around with me since arriving here fills me, and I can't speak. Sobs choke me, and I gasp air in my lungs, trying to breathe – and failing.

Then Tristan's there, wrapping his arms around me, hugging me from behind. I don't know why he's so understanding. He shouldn't be.

"I'm not understanding," he whispers, hearing my thoughts. "The anger's in me, waiting to come to the surface. But I want to give you the benefit of the doubt, to trust you didn't lie because you wanted to screw me over. Not after everything we've shared."

"Everything we've shared?" I snort, moving out of his grip, but still refusing to face him. I can't stand those chocolate eyes filled with pain. "You must be delusional. All we have are lies between us. Your demons. Mine."

"You don't mean that." Now his tone is tauter, and I sense the anger less controlled. Good. The angrier he gets, the less I have to care.

"What's going on, Dani? Why are you acting like this?" His voice is soft, gruff – weird. It takes me a minute to realize it's filled with emotion, and that has me even more unwilling to turn towards him.

"Don't know what you're talking about," I mutter.

"Ven, beleza," he whispers, and I shiver at the words. He's calling me beautiful, when I feel anything but. "I know something deep must have pushed you here, into my arms, so what is it?"

A growl escapes me, and I whirl towards Tristan. "In your arms? Excuse you! Just who do you think you are, a wolf Adonis?"

He grins, and in the night it's so charming my heart twists. But I remember the same sideways grin aimed at my sister, and look where that got her. I harden my heart against him, unwilling to be another prey.

"I'm not going anywhere with you. Whatever you think you can re-enact with me, that you had with Izzy, you can forget about."

The grin fades away then, and his eyes flash. "Watch yourself, Dani. Some words, you can't take back."

"Oh yeah?" I take a step forward. "Tell me then that last night, when you were in bed, making love to me again, it was really me you were thinking of. Tell me it wasn't Izabella."

He stares at me for a beat, then shakes his head. "Why would you even think that? Of course it was you I was thinking about!"

"I don't believe you!" My shout echoes in the night, and by now tears are streaming down my cheeks. "You're lying, just like I did."

His jaw clenches, and he reaches to grab my chin, forcing me to look him in the eyes. "Don't do this, Dani. It won't get you anything but heartache. Let me help you, like I said I would. Stay and find out what this thing between us is."

"What for?" I sniffle, jerking out of his reach. "Only to find out I'm second choice? I don't think so. I'm here for the sole reason I said. Protection."

His eyes glint. "From who, Dani? From the people that gave you that mark? From your family? Who's the enemy here, exactly?"

I glare at him, thankful for my height for once. "Monsters. Creatures in the night. Does it matter?"

Silence lengthens between us as each tries to stare the other down. Then another voice interrupts.

"She's right, amico."

I recognize the Italian, and break Tristan's gaze to look over his shoulder. "You've already received my formal request for protection, Lucas. What will it be? Because there are others who can grant what I wish quicker."

His dark eyes are assessing in the night, and I know there's nothing easy about being submissive to a guy like that. But what other choice do I have?

Lucas nods. "I said I would take it under consideration, cara." A beat, then, "Tristan, a word. In private."

"No need, I was leaving." I push past Tristan, glaring at him one last time before taking off into the night. Before I know it, I'm jogging, running, and then I'm shedding my clothes and basking in the transformation – freedom.

Paws land on the ground rather than my human hands, and I take on a sprint. Anything to get away, even if for only a few moments.

∞ ∞ ∞

CHAPTER EIGHT

∞ Maldiçaõ ∞

"It is better to light one candle than to <u>curse</u> the darkness."

-Genghis Khan-

Tristan

I stare at Dani leaving, clenching my fists so I don't follow her.

"That went well."

Lucas' voice grates on my nerves. He knows shit I don't, and it's about time he starts sharing. So I turn to him and jab a finger in his chest. "You about to tell me what she shared with you?"

His onyx eyes glitter in the night. "No. Daniela spoke in confidence, and I don't see what use is betraying that to salvage your ego."

"Salvage my..." A growl tears through my throat, and I have to shake my head of my wolf. He's on edge, needing to be heard. A few deep breaths later, I look up at my alpha again.

"You shouldn't do that, you know," he says.

I pretend I don't know what he's talking about. "Do what?"

"Push your wolf down. Ignore his needs." His tone shifts, softening. "Especially with what you've been through, before coming here."

Soft is not what I'm used to from Lucas, so I revert to my best way of coping – anger. "My wolf is my business, Lucas. Now stop trying to deflect and tell me what's up with Dani."

His face hardens, those Italian lines rigid with tension. "Watch your tone, amico. And no, I won't."

I walk away in frustration, hitting the first thing I can get my hands on – a garbage bin. Then I run my hand over my face, throwing my head back and looking at the sky.

"If I tell you, you'll only make a bigger mess of things than you already have."

My eyes close, and I breathe deeply. "Then what the hell did you want to talk to me about?"

Lucas is silent for a few moments, long enough that it draws my attention. Once I'm facing him, he says, "I intend to afford Daniela my protection – and that of the pack. But before I do, I need your solemn vow that whatever happens between you two will not affect the rest of us."

I frown. What could be so bad that he'd need such a promise from me? My scattered mind goes back to Agostinho, and the reason for his presence here. What the hell's been going on in Bow's Arrow since I left?

When I'm silent for too long, Lucas' voice deepens. "And I need it now."

My wolf shies at the back of my head, responding to the alpha command. And I nod, bowing my head. "You have it." By the time I look back up, Lucas is gone, leaving me alone with my wayward thoughts.

Daniela

I must've ended up out of the city, because by the time I actually look around, I don't recognize anything. A weird scent fills the air, like sulfur mixed with... cinnamon? I realize it's what I've been following the last few minutes.

My paws slow down to a trot, and eventually I change back into human form. My fingertips tingle with the magic, but I can't – won't – use it. Not after what happened with Tristan, and especially not in the messed up state I'm in.

As I lean against a tree, curling into its embrace, a blast of wind hits me in the face. And some of that sulfur smell lingers. I look up and – no joke – see wings. Huge, flapping wings. And a tail in the shape of a diamond.

My jaw drops and I follow the creature, stumbling on wobbly legs. *It can't be what I think it is... Surely not.*

Yet when I emerge in a meadow, it's definitely a dragon my eyes settle on. It lands in all its rusted-colored beauty, and the ground shakes. He must be fifteen, twenty feet high, and easily twice as long. How in hell no one in town has seen him, is beyond me. The tail alone circles the full meadow, coming to rest by his front paw. And those claws – holy shit.

I'm too busy gaping to take cover. Especially when the dragon starts shining all burgundy, then disappears. In its spot is a man – naked. He glances over a shoulder, noticing me staring.

"Will you help me out, witch, or no?"

My jaw drops, and I have to lean further into the tree for fear of dropping to the ground. He chuckles darkly under his breath then lifts his hand. With his index, he traces something resembling a rune in the air. The air shimmers, then a veil drops onto him. Next thing I know, he's dressed in black jeans, a white t-shirt and a blazer, with shiny black shoes.

His head hangs back a moment, staring at the sky. Then he shakes it and turns to me. His eyes are stormy, the precise color of the sky in this moment. As he walks towards me, they fade to a pale grey.

"Will you speak, witch?" His voice is hoarse, guttural.

I gulp past my dry throat and try, "Why do you keep calling me witch? I'm not one."

He moves with disconcerting speed. One moment he's there, staring at me as if I'm stupid. The next, he's in my face, grasping my hand and holding it up for inspection. My fingers tingle again, and this time a zap hits his cheek.

He grimaces as if it hurts, then smirks. "See? Witch."

I shake my head, pulling my hand out of his grip. "I'm not."

Rolling his eyes, he walks past me, as if planning to leave me behind. "Wait!" I rush after him, but he doesn't slow down. I have to walk twice as fast to keep up. "What's your name?"

A smirk graces his lips. "Why are you females always interested in names?"

I try to think of a good reason, but instead find only questions. "Are you really a dragon? Here, in Rockland Creek?"

He stops then, and his gaze meets mine, rooting me to the spot. "And if I am? Who will you tell, little non-witch?"

It's my turn to grimace. "My name's Daniela – Dani Da Silva. And I'm not a witch or non-witch. I'm a wolf!"

He laughs then, but it gets darker and darker. When he's done, he notices my scowl and folded arms over my chest. His expression wavers between incredulity and anger. "Are you telling me you have no idea of your gift?"

It's probably the last straw, because I feel tears gather in my eyes. "Gift? I've exiled myself from my pack because they wish to sacrifice me to darkness to pay for these powers. I never wanted them. My father and brother took my will – my sister's will – and forced us into this blood pact. And you call it a *gift*?"

He's watching me closely now, no longer seeming like he's planning to run off. Then again, he's probably afraid I'm unhinged. I wave him off – or try to, anyway. I can barely see past my tears.

Then he holds out something white in front of my face. "Take it, it's a handkerchief."

After dabbing at my eyes and cleaning my mess of a face, I look at the piece of cloth. "Seriously? How old *are* you?"

A corner of his lips tugs in a half-smile. "Old." Then he waves me off when I try to hand it back. "Keep it."

He turns to leave again, and I whisper, "You haven't told me your name. I've made a complete fool of myself, and you've alluded to things you seem to know about me. Would you please share them?"

Though tense, he nods to the forest and faces me again. "Very well. I sensed you following me from above, perks of being a dragon. Only I'm not what you think. I'm a zmeu."

I frown. "A what?"

"Romanian dragon, if you will. We have the bulk of regular dragons, but also magic – most of it intended to influence the weather." He sounds impatient now, so I keep further questions to myself. "Rather, *I* have this. Considering I am the last of my race."

He narrows his eyes, giving me his full attention. "Whichever way you've gained your gift, it is not to be ignored. The more you do so, the more it eats at you. You will die if you don't learn to use it, and control it, within a fortnight." He gestures to my hands. "You already are."

I'm thankful for the tree still at my back at his uncouth declaration. "That's impossible."

"No, it is not." He shrugs. "Whoever gave it to you knew what they were doing."

I shake my head. "There has to be a way to undo it."

"There is not." A speculative glint appears in his eyes. "Unless you can reach the witch who gave it to you..."

My eyes drop to my hands. "It's not possible. And I can't use this magic, either. That'd mean giving up my wolf part."

He shrugs. "Not my problem, is it?"

I glare at him. "You can't just drop this all on me and not answer my questions."

He raises his eyes to the skies. "Little wolf, I don't have time for this. There are much more pressing matters to attend to."

"Please." I hate the weakness in my voice. "I have no one to go to."

His gaze turns speculative. "What of the wolf whose scent is on you?"

I avert my eyes, refusing to let the pain show. "He's not... It's complicated."

A snort draws my attention back to the dragon. "Well, you had best un-complicate it. The longer you wait, the worse it gets."

I risk a step closer. "Will you help me, then? Show me how to control it."

"And in exchange?"

What could a dragon want? I think back to his change in the meadow, his allusion that he's the last of his race. Knowing this world and everything in it, if he gets found out, it would lead to annihilation of his race. "I won't tell anyone what you told me."

His eyes glitter then and he takes one step closer. "You won't, because you won't remember." I'm too slow, and don't on to his meaning until it's too late.

Then he raises his hand, and a breeze blows into me. A flurry of snowflakes masks my vision. By the time they're gone, I'm left alone – and wondering what the hell I'm doing so far away from the main square.

Shoulders slouched, I make my way back to town. I've nowhere left to go, least of all the Reapers. The only place for me is back with Tristan, waiting for Lucas' decision. I just hope he won't kick me out.

Tristan

My feet are rooted to the ground as I stare at Dani in my bed. I didn't think she'd come back after the way we left things. After my anger at her.

Yet despite knowing how I felt, she returned, risking that I'd throw her out. Seeing her like this, sleeping peacefully, I know I'd never be able to. And while the rage still simmers underneath the surface, it's tamed by her presence here.

The whole thing leaves me confused. Izzy and I had our problems. We also had history. History that should've been respected enough by her sister to tell me the truth. Shouldn't it?

It's still something I can't wrap my head around. Nor can I sleep. Especially not when Lucas implied there's more she's hiding, and it could be enough to tear us apart. If I can't even let go of this, how will I stomach whatever else there is?

Fuck.

My feet carry me back to the living room before I lose it and shake Dani awake or join her in bed – and it won't be to sleep, or talk. My wolf demands something else, and I know he can't be denied. Not when I bet her wolf craves the same thing.

I'm busy staring out the window, trying to get my thoughts under control. Night seems to go on forever, and the last thing I want are more bad dreams. But the only person who can keep them at bay is in the next room over, and I can't bring myself to go near her.

Then a glow behind me catches my eye. I spin, ready to shift and defend my territory, but my gaze lands on the most impossible apparition.

Eyes like the sun, flawless skin, wavy hair that looks alive... She smells of spring and freshness and flowers, and my jaw drops. "You..."

"I am Ileana, wolf. You can call me your pack's godmother," her eyes twinkle, "though in truth, I am only meant to be Dominic's."

A faint exotic accent flows through her words and something Finn said a while back runs through my mind. "You're the one who kicked Finn's ass."

Her eyes twinkle in amusement, and she laughs – a sound like crystalline water. It dawns on me then that she wouldn't be paying me a visit unless something was up. My thoughts go back to my pack mates, and Dom and Luz.

"What..." I clear my throat. "Is something wrong?"

"Yes, there is." The laughter dies out of her expression, replaced by a sadness so pure it seems to echo within me. "You need to let go of your anger."

And just like that, my fascination is gone. "Go butt into Dom's life, not mine." I turn to walk away, but run smack into an invisible force. "What the hell?"

I bang my hand on it, to no avail. When I turn to her, Ileana's smiling. "Hear me out, then you may leave."

"Lady..."

She holds up her hand, and this time I really can't get any words out. So I settle for glaring, though it's hard when she looks so...nice.

"Hear me, wolf. You have anger inside you, but it has nothing to do with what was omitted from you. The woman in your bed is not the one you are upset with. So before you ruin what can possibly be your salvation, it would be best you take a look inside. And find what really upsets you."

A wave of her hand, and I can speak again. "So, what, you're saying I'm mad at Izzy, not Dani?"

Ileana inclines her head and floats closer to me. The smell of wildflowers hits my nostrils, and they flare in appreciation. She smiles. "The heart is complicated, even more so when one loves as deeply as you do. This is your chance, wolf."

When she floats past me, I call out. "Why bother coming to tell me this?"

"There is much awry with this world, and much more hurt and pain coming your way. This is something I can affect, and I choose to. The rest, well... That, my dear wolf, is entirely up to you."

Then she's gone like I've dreamt her. Only the scent of wildflowers lingering behind tells me it was all real. I stare out the window for a long, long time, thinking about Ileana's words. And while it's true what she said, there is something else I've been ignoring about Dani, too. Or rather, about her wolf. And mine. And it's about damn time to deal with it.

Determined, I make my way to the bedroom.

Daniela

"Dani, wake up."

A hand is shaking me gently. It takes a while, but Tristan's voice finally penetrates my brain and I jump up. In the darkness, my eyes land on his, and I sit upright.

"Sorry, I..." Glancing around, I'm wondering where the hell I threw my sweater. "I know you're mad," I whisper to the air, refusing to meet his gaze. "But I don't have anywhere else to go, Tristan."

He says nothing for the longest time. And it's the silence that forces me to finally look at him. I still can't make out his intention, but he doesn't seem ready to kick me out. Yet.

Then something shifts in him, and he sighs. "I'm not planning to kick you out, Dani." He turns away, dropping his head in his hands. "I've really made a mess of this, haven't I?"

Unsure what to say, I stay quiet. Tristan takes deep breaths in, then out, before speaking again. "Answer me one thing. Why didn't you tell me about Izabella?"

I bite my lip. "You want the truth?"

"Yes."

I wish I could see his face, but I'll have to take what I can get. "At first, it was because I was afraid you'd turn me away if I reminded you of something so painful. And then, the more you started treating me like me, not Izzy's sister, I didn't want to bring her back to your mind." A deep breath, then, "I was there, you know, and saw the after-effects of her acts."

He raises his head from his hands, but still doesn't look at me. "You were the one who waved me off at the airport, when I left."

I gulp. "Yeah."

"But you pretended you were Izzy. Why?"

One shoulder lifts in a shrug. "It was what you needed to go off and do your thing. I didn't want you upset."

He shakes his head then. "I've been such a fool." When his gaze finally collides with mine, it's soft and filled with – my throat closes.

"Tristan?" It's a fearful whisper, but he doesn't care.

He moves over the bed, cupping my cheek and dropping his forehead to mine. "I know what you did that night, Dani.

When I woke up in the middle of my nightmare, not knowing what planet I was on. You pretended, again, and gave me what I needed. But that's not what I want, or need, anymore. It hasn't been since you walked into this town. It's just... Just you." His lips hover above mine. "Can you give me that?"

Is that even a question? I push past my tears, and breathe, "Yes."

It's all the approval he needs before his lips crush against mine. Tristan's a good kisser – he's a great kisser. But damn, the way he makes me go from zero to hot in just a few seconds is insane. When I moan in the kiss, trying to pull him closer, he slides one hand under my tank top, up my spine and rests it at the top of my back.

A delicious shiver runs through me as his heat permeates my skin, washing my doubts away. Maybe we can do this. Maybe we can move past, and be together. And maybe I was meant to come here, to find him.

Tristan pulls away from the kiss then, sighs, and rests his forehead against mine. "You were, beleza. We were both meant to find each other, I think. But I need one more answer, and I need it to be honest."

I close my eyes, and a shudder runs through me. Are we really so close to airing everything between us?

"Lucas implied there's more you're hiding, and I need us to be fully truthful with each other, Dani. Open your eyes." I listen and stare into his, waiting. "What is this?"

His fingers, splayed on my spine, move to touch the mark on my shoulder. I gulp, an irrational fear taking hold of me. Tristan doesn't let me get spooked, instead kisses my cheeks, then nose, then forehead. "Talk to me, Dani. Please."

It's that last pleading that gets through to me, and I force the words past my throat. "After Izabella died, dad wasn't the same anymore. He'd been slowly giving the reins to Thiago–"

"Your older brother?"

I nod. "Yeah, and moving away from having Lunas in power. This one night we were celebrating the summer equinox, Thiago decreed that all females in age of breeding and not mated were to be branded, so the males would know who they were and have their pick. None of us were quick enough to fight. He... They overpowered us. And branded us like cattle within the hour."

That horrible night drifts through my head, and I don't tell Tristan the rest. That the brand is meant to mark me with magic, to make me easier to track – and more likely to submit, at least according to Thiago.

"Is he still in Bow's Arrow?"

I snap out of my thoughts and look up at Tristan. Only then do I notice the murderous intent in his eyes, in the clenching of his jaw, the tightness of his muscles. "*No*, Tristan. You can't go there."

He drops his mouth to mine for a soft kiss, so at odds with his contained rage, then pulls away before it gets heated. "Meu anjo, answer me. Is he still there?"

"Yes," I whisper, looking away. "Thiago owns the entire town, now. That's why I left. It was...getting worse, and worse."

Tristan grits his teeth, his free hand digging into the mattress by my side. Then his mouth to my neck. "Turn over."

I do as he asks, silent and wondering what the hell he's about to do. He tugs the strap of the tank top aside, exposing my mark fully. Then his lips drop to it, and he kisses every inch.

"Dani, I swear to you," he says in a hoarse voice, "Thiago will pay for this. Once I know Lucas affords you the protection of the pack, and you're here, safe, I will go and find him. And he will pay. Mark my words, querida, he will *pay*."

Then his kisses move lower, and he's pulling off my shorts and underwear. And under his expert fingers, I stop thinking about the past, or the future. And all I know is Tristan's mastery of my body, until we're tumbling back into the world of dreams and fairytales.

∞ ∞ ∞

CHAPTER NINE

∞ Verdade ∞

"Everything we hear is an opinion, not a fact. Everything we see is a perspective, not the <u>truth</u>."

-Marcus Aurelius-

Tristan

In the morning, I wake up and stare at her face for the longest time. It could be another by my side, but it's not Izabella's presence I miss. Dani looks vulnerable like this, with the moon on her face. As I shift, she reaches out for me, her smaller hand resting on my chest, right over my heartbeat. It's an unconscious movement, one she'll never remember.

Something swells in my heart, and I get now what Dom's been trying to say. When you know, you know. The wolf in me wants more than this – more than a quick fuck. It wants Dani at any cost. And the thought she's been through so much is something I can't reconcile with. I won't let her run off, no matter how scared she gets.

Not if I can help it.

I bend over and nuzzle her neck, until she rolls to her back with a soft sigh. Eyes closed, she opens her arms and breathes my name. "Tristan."

My name is pure heaven on her lips, and I bend down for a taste, and another. Before I know it, I can't stop. And we come together, joined, and those eyes open and look at me – my entire world stops.

Later, when she's back asleep in my arms, I whisper words she doesn't hear – won't, until she's ready.

"Meu anjo, you're mine. No more running."

∞ ♦ ∞

In the morning, I wake up to the smell of food. When I enter the kitchen, Dani's there, cooking us breakfast. I sneak behind her and kiss her neck. She moves her head to the side, allowing me better access.

It feels right. It feels....

And then the room closes in on me. I don't know what it is, but I step back from her, unable to catch my breath. Dani turns around, forgetting the food. Her expression is filled with worry, and she reaches for me, saying something.

I can't – I see blood. ***Women murdered. Creatures
everywhere. And the smell of charred skin.***

Something swells in my throat and I gag. *Won't make it to the
bathroom.* I rush to the sink just as my stomach empties out
its contents.

It doesn't stop there. I'm dry heaving for so long – the smell
in my nostrils, in my hair, on my skin. I can't see the sink in
front of me, barely feel the counter I'm almost snapping in
my half.

Then fresh air coats my face, and everything clears. I slump
to the ground, holding on the cabinet with one
white-knuckled fist. A shudder runs through me.

Soft hands touch my head, caressing slowly. "It's okay," Dani
whispers. "It's okay. You're safe."

She keeps repeating that, keeping her voice low and soft.
Then something wet touches my face, and I jerk, hitting the
cupboard with the back of my head. Dani grabs my chin in
her hand, catching my panicked gaze.

"It's just me. Wet compress."

I shudder again, then nod. She runs it over my face, wiping
me as a mom would her newborn.

Shame runs through me and I turn my head away. I'm calmer
now. Enough to look around and realize it was the charred
smell of meat that had triggered me. And Dani – dear, sweet

Dani – somehow realized it and opened the window. It's all but gone now.

Even calmer now, I stand. She rises with me, holding out a hand, but I shake my head and walk away to the bathroom. After brushing my teeth and wiping my face, I make my way back. Each step feels heavier, yet somehow lighter.

This is the worst she's seen me, and she's still here. Cleaning the sink – wiping my mess. I lean against the wall this time, simply watching her. Then I clear my throat and Dani turns to me.

Her expression softens, but there's no pity in her eyes. No horror. No disgust. Just worry and understanding. "How are you feeling?"

"Better." I look behind her to the sink, now fully clean. "I could have done that, you know."

"I didn't mind," she whispers, then walks closer.

When I don't move away, she wraps her arms around my waist and tucks her head under my chin. "I'm sorry. Was it the smell?"

I nod. "Flashbacks. Bad times." It's the most I can say.

She tightens her hold on me, then says, "Will you tell me about it, someday? It might help to talk about it."

I sigh, remembering Luz's similar offer. "Dani, I..."

"Just try me."

So I nod, and disengage to start pacing. "I need to keep moving for this, so if I get agitated, just...be careful. I don't want to hurt you."

Dani only leans against the wall, watching me. I look away, and draw in a deep breath. "It's not just one experience that triggers me. There are too many. When I left for war, I thought I'd be fighting human bad guys. But about three months in, my commanding officer pulled me aside. He was a wolf too, you see, but from Greece. He had the ability to hide his scent to others, which is why I didn't pick up on it."

"Was he much different than you?"

I shrug. "In a way, yeah. His changes were fully controlled by the full moon. He couldn't shift like you or me, let alone change his form once shifted. He lost all sight of himself."

Memories bounce around in my head then, trying to pull me back in. Dani must feel it, as she raises her voice a tad. "Tristan, keep pacing. And focus on me. What happened then?"

My feet start moving of their own accord. "Turns out my CO had sniffed out a couple more wolves in adjoining units. He ended up introducing us to each other. We were five in all, six with my CO. And he started taking riskier assignments that were designed to test our skills."

Dani frowns at that. "How so?"

"Our missions took us to various parts of the world. Turns out, it's not just enemy combatants you need to be afraid of. There are...*creatures*...everywhere." I shake my head, trying to shrug off a shudder. "Some more ghoulish than others. Over the two years I was out there, that's what I saw. What I fought. They belong in my nightmares only now, but... I've seen horrors I can't describe, Dani."

"It's okay," she takes a step closer, and I can tell she's trying hard to give me my space to move. "Answer me one thing... Have you ever been able to make it stop?"

I shake my head, bitterness flowing out of me. "You don't get it. Don't you think I'd stop it if I could? It's not the past. It's not the future. It's my every day, and it's not going away. Those monsters in the night you fear as a kid? Well, they're every-fucking-where for me. And they're never leaving, trust me."

Dani raises her hands and approaches me slowly, keeping her voice soft. "I get it, Tristan. Not...entirely, you're right. And I probably never will to the extent you've experienced everything. But I want you to know you *can* talk to me. Whenever. Wherever. You don't have to, unless you want to, but I'm here."

At her open expression, all bitterness flows out of me. *She's still here.* I gulp past my dry throat. "Maybe someday...if you feel up for it. If you don't find it too heavy."

Dani touches my shoulder then. "If I want to be with you, it's not."

A slow smile stretches my lips. "Okay."

"Okay," she repeats, then rises on her tiptoes and kisses me.

Forever. The word is imprinted in my head like a brand, but I don't say it out loud. Not yet.

Daniela

I heard him, clear as day in my head. And Tristan's words are enough to send me in a rising panic. What brought me here, hiding, is still very much a menace. And if he's willing to love me, that means he'll be in danger alongside with me.

I had my chance, and I didn't tell him everything. And now it's too late. Can I really be his, forever, when I'm living a lie? When I can't even trust myself to lose control around him?

Unable to calm down, I wait until he's called on pack business, then go outside, hoping a walk will help.

It doesn't.

The air is crisp, still in the midst of winter, and I relish its bite against my cheeks. What if this is all a mistake? What if I hurt him, like Izabella did? What if he won't forgive me?

Maybe I'm his second choice, after all.

The thought is so sudden, so harsh, that I bend over, unable to catch my breath. It's my deepest fear, because with each passing day, each moment in his presence, I fall deeper. And the more I do, the less I'll be able to think on my own, to escape if I need to.

My hand morphs, my wolf detecting my uneasiness. I stare at it, panting hard, my breath coming in puffs of white.

"Dani?"

It takes me a second, but I recognize the female voice behind me. When I turn, Luz is standing a few feet away, bundled up better than a tortilla. A faint smile cracks her lips, and I respond in kind. Then her eyes take in my hand, and I try to hide it.

"Sorry," I mutter. "You caught me at a bad time."

Luz tilts her head to the side, the mass of red curls bouncing off a shoulder. "I'd say. Tristan's got you all worked up, huh?"

"I–" The lie dies on my lips. I don't deserve to be here. Maybe I should have listened to Agostinho and gone back to Bow's Arrow. I'm irrational, pushed by panic, but no amount of logic seems to penetrate right now.

Luz takes a step closer, frowning. "Are you okay?"

I shake my head, and to my horror, tears fill my eyes. By the time I snap to and try to wipe them away, they're coating my cheeks and being frozen by the wind.

Luz's blurry form draws nearer, and she touches my shoulder. "Dani, you're not okay."

It takes me a minute, but I manage to get hold of my emotions. After a shuddering breath, I wipe at my face and say, "No, but I will be."

Something about my tone sets her off. "You're not about to do something silly again, are you?"

I snort, recalling my idiot attempt to join the Reapers. "No, I'm not. It's just, Tristan, he... This bond between us, it lets us hear each other's thoughts."

"That's pretty neat!"

"Not when what I hear is him promising me forever."

A sparkle of amusement lights her green eyes, then she jerks her head to The Cave. "Drinks? Looks like you could use one."

After a hesitation, I nod. It's almost noon, so why the hell not?

∞ ◆ ∞

Hours later, The Cave is starting to get busy. Me and Luz are past tipsy, now just plain giggling like schoolgirls. And it feels good to let it out, to act normal.

"I can't believe Dom tried that with Lucas," I chuckle, referring to how she and Dom got together. "Does he have a death wish?"

She grins. "I used to think so. I'm glad they're at peace now. Somewhat."

I snort. "Somewhat. Wonder if that'll ever happen with me and Lucas."

"What do you mean?"

I forget sometimes she's human, and how new all this is for her. "My lobisomens pack, they're more matriarchal. Go by Luna's blood rather than the alpha. And my mom and grandmother were Lunas. So," I shrug, taking another shot, "I was supposed to follow in their footsteps once Izzy died."

"That's pretty cool," she whispers. "Why didn't you?"

"Cause my family's psycho." Somehow, that sends us into another fit of giggles.

Luz takes another sip of her drink, then her expression changes, growing pained. "Is that why you didn't tell me about your sister?"

A sigh escapes me, and I end up twirling my index around the now empty glass. "Yeah. I almost did, once..."

"Before we went to the bakery with Finn," she whispers.

I'm surprised she remembers so clearly, what with the alcohol we just consumed. But then again, it shouldn't surprise me. She's a vârcolac's mate, after all.

Lost in the alcohol, good times and conversation, I'm too distracted to smell them right away. It's only when I feel eyes on us that I look around – and see the Reapers. Luz follows my gaze.

"This isn't good," she whispers.

"It's worse than you think," I whisper back, throwing her a warning look. "You need to leave before they do something."

"They wouldn't," she argues, eyes flashing. "Dom warned them off me last time."

"And yet, they're here without their alpha."

We stare at each other, then Luz nods. I stand, blocking her, and she manages to slide past me. Then the blasted door opens, and the wind picks up everywhere. The Reapers at the bar freeze, noses up in the air, then look towards us.

I recognize Cade. And by the looks of it, he remembers me – and his promise. Anger flashes in his eyes, and when he looks to his buddies, I know there's only one option left for us.

"Run."

Luz grabs my hand and takes off out the door, and I trail behind. Chairs scrape behind and I know we're being followed. As we run through the streets I curse Lucas taking his sweet ass time to give me protection. Had I been in the pack, I could have called for help.

As it is, Luz and I are on our own, heading deeper into the town. And by the sound of crunching snow behind us, we're being chased.

A glance over my shoulder confirms Cade and four of his men are there, and they're gaining on us fast. In front of my eyes, two of them morph into wolves and speed up.

"Shit, shit, *SHIT*!" I mutter under my breath.

Then I realize something. Luz is in more danger than I am. Tristan filled me in on their reputation, and I've seen the worst of it. Hell if I'm going to let these guys get to her when the only reason she's around me is because she was trying to be nice.

So I rip my hand out of hers, slowing down. Luz turns to me, eyes wide and mouth gaping open.

"Go!" I shout. "I'll hold them back."

"Dani, no!"

"I said *GO*!"

I push her away, and she stumbles away. Undecided, her eyes flicker between me and the wolves gaining on us. I shake my head at her. "Get help, Luz! Call out to them, or something, and find a spot to hide!"

Once I see her getting away, I run full force to Cade and jump. Midair, I morph into my wolf form – and land on his chest. We tumble on the ground, rolling in hard ice. I manage to bite into his shoulder before he backhands me off him.

At least I land into another Reaper and manage to scratch his face off. As he howls in pain, I jump on another.

Cade and the two others in wolf form are running still – heading for Luz. I can't be in two places at once, not like this. But there is something that can save her.

I never would have thought to use it. Never have in a battle, never wanted to. But in that moment, with my friend's life on the line and the certainty that if I don't something, she's dead meat, I know I have to.

There's not much time to debate semantics. Cade is catching up, the other two lagging behind. I finish the Reaper under my paws and morph back to human form. The magic is tingling at my fingertips, like it always has.

When I focus on it, narrowing my eyes and straining, my hand turns into a wolf paw. Claws emerge, and a faint reddish light surrounds them, like a halo. *Am I really about to do this?*

Yep, I really am, I answer myself. This time, I don't hold it back.

"Do what you will," I mutter, and aim my palm towards the building next to the two Reapers. Like before with Tristan, the power I've been holding up escapes in a blast. A jet of burgundy light unfurls, hitting brick, and it explodes into pieces.

Pieces of the building crumble all around, and a domino's effect starts. On and on, the magic flows out of my hand, like an unstoppable river. *I can't control this. Shit.* Yet as if hearing me, the jet stops, leaving me panting and my palm tingling.

Half of the building buried the last two Reapers, leaving only Cade and Luz to face me. As the dust settles around them, I notice their wide eyes on me. And they're not the only ones.

High up in the sky, a raven circles above us. Its dark wings are unmistakable, as are the curious moonshine eyes. He circles a few more times, then flies off in the distance. I force myself to focus on Cade, and my captive friend. Ravens – and the problems they'll bring – will have to wait.

Cade's expression is unreadable, but his tone implies he's considering something. "Interesting. How long have you had this power?"

"None of your fucking business," I hiss, and move closer.

"Ah ah," he says and tightens his hold on Luz.

It's enough to make me pause in my attempt to get closer. Luz struggles against Cade, but her hands are frozen by the cold and completely ineffective against his bulk.

Did she get a chance to call out for help? Did the guys hear her? I wish I could ask, but don't want to alert the Reaper in case someone is coming.

Cade seems completely unaffected by Luz's struggles, instead focusing on me. "I could use one such as you. What's this human's life worth?"

I step closer. "Don't do this, Cade. It's war if you hurt her, and you know it."

He snorts. "She's a pet. Insignificant." Then his gaze turns speculative. "Unless I turn her. Bind her to us." He forces Luz to face him. "Would you like that, scum?"

She glares at him. "Fuck you. If you think I'll cower in front of you, you got another thing coming."

Cade pulls his hand back to hit her, but Luz manages to duck and knee him in the balls. He lets go of her arm for a millisecond. Then his other hand snakes out and grabs her throat.

I can't let this happen. "Stop!" Walking towards him, I hold up my hands. "I'll do whatever you say."

"Dani, no!"

The shout isn't from Luz. It's coming from behind. I close my eyes, then dare to glance over my shoulder. Tristan and Dom are at the end of the street, running towards us.

She did it. And I could wait until they're here, and they rescue Luz. But Cade is unhinged and the chances he won't snap are thin. Something's up with this guy, and the way he keeps making decisions on his own, without an alpha.

I can't trust that he won't hurt her. And with the way his eyes take in Dom and Tristan's approaching forms, and his sneer, I know there's no time. If I wait until they're here, Luz is dead.

What I have to do is so clear – as are the consequences. So I walk closer still, until I'm a foot away. "Luz," I speak to her directly. "I need you to *bow* out of this."

I stress the word, and her eyes widen. There's confusion in there, but I hope she picked up on my meaning. Then I take another step.

"Close enough," Cade says. His gaze shifts to Tristan and Dom again, whom I feel getting closer.

"It is," I grin. Then my other hand shoots out and blasts a ray at the ice stalactite above his head. It drops down, embedding itself in his shoulder.

Cade howls in pain and Luz ducks out of the way – just as more of the ice picks fall. Then the entire building follows. *Oops.* I lunge forward and grab Luz's hand, pulling her away to safety.

Only then do I look back at Cade. Most of the massive icicles missed him, but the last one runs straight through his foot, pinning him to the ground. He struggles against both, then his hateful eyes land on me.

"This isn't over, witch."

"I'm not a witch," I whisper, but he doesn't hear me.

With an agonized howl, he grabs the icicle in his shoulder with both hands and yanks it out. Then he does the same to the one in his foot. The bloody ice picks land on the ground, and Cade shifts.

Before long, he's limping away in wolf form, and I can breathe freely. His acolytes have disappeared as well, most likely seeking refuge in their territory.

I squeeze Luz's hand, and face her, half afraid of her reaction. Her relieved expression is all I see, but our peace doesn't last long.

"Que porra...."

Gulping, I turn to Tristan – and the betrayal in his eyes.

∞ ∞ ∞

SHAPTER TEN

∞ Traiçaõ ∞

"Each <u>betrayal</u> begins with trust."

-Martin Luther-

Daniela

I see the shock in his eyes, and bite back my tears. It was bound to happen, I knew it from the moment we got close. And now that he's seen me for what I really am, he's staring at me exactly like I'd been afraid he would. Like I'm a freak.

Then Luz tugs on my arm, whispering, "You saved my life, Dani."

She hugs me, barely reaching my shoulder, and I force myself to smile. It's a small blessing that she's safe and sound, away from Cade's clutches.

Then she's ripped from my arms and into Dom's. He buries his head in her neck, breathing her in, then kisses her like there's no tomorrow.

The purity of their embrace is too much to behold. I look away – and meet Tristan's glare. I take a step forward, wanting to explain. "Tristan, it's not what it looks like."

"Really?" He snorts. "Cause from where I'm standing it looks like you lied all along. You don't need protection, you're a damn witch!" He shakes his head in disgust. "And to think I fell for those pretty eyes and fake smile."

My heart clenches, but I still try to reach out for him. He brushes me off, side-stepping me. "Don't fucking touch me." His voice his filled with hate. "I've seen your kind – they do nothing but serve their own selfish purposes."

The worst part is, he's right. My brother's only in this for his selfish reasons, as is the rest of my family. Only *I* never wanted it. How can I explain that, when he's just seen me use magic?

"Tristan, please. Let me explain." Tears stream down my cheeks, and I can only hope he takes pity on my miserable expression. Maybe it's that or the last shred of patience he finds within himself, but he nods.

"Fine, but make it quick. The sooner we finish this, the better."

I take a deep breath, aware of Dom and Luz's eyes on us. "Before I dive in, Lucas knows. I had to be honest with him when I asked him for protection. He kind of knew already."

Tristan's face closes further. "Wonderful. So you could share this second massive secret with your new alpha, a complete stranger, but not the guy you've been screwing."

I gulp past my dry throat, forcing myself to keep meeting his burning glare. "I get you're hurt, Tristan, but please hear me out. This happened before Izabella died. After you left, our lobisomens pack was weak. Izzy and you were supposed to mate, carry on the lineage. My parents fought – a lot. Then mom died on a raid, and my father lost it. Thiago took advantage."

"He always was a little weasel," Tristan mutters. He notices my hopeful look and his expression shutters again. "Go on."

"Thiago told our father there's a way to make us more powerful so no one else dies. They forced us – me and Izzy – to partake. A witch performed a ritual and next thing we knew, we had powers. Magic." The last comes out in a whisper. "I never wanted it. It comes with a price – the eldest daughter has to be sacrificed to the darkness. Izzy was it, that's why she committed suicide. There was no other way to get out of it. Then it was my turn and... I came here."

Tristan watches me, something flickering in his eyes. Then his nostrils flare. "And is it a coincidence I smell the zmeu's scent on you, querida?"

"The what?" I frown. Something about that word is familiar, but I can't place it. "I don't know what you're talking about."

"Enough!" Tristan shouts, shaking his head. "I'm done with the lies. With you. You have protection, you've lied from the beginning. I don't know what the hell your purpose here is, but—"

"Enough."

Dom steps by my side, frowning at his friend. "Don't say something you'll regret, Tristan. Take the night to cool off."

Luz joins him. Her green eyes dart to Tristan, then she grabs my hand in hers and says, "Dani's staying with us tonight."

Tristan finally snaps out of his daze. "Like hell she is. We're not done talking."

Luz drops my hand, to place both her hands on her hips and glare at him. "Hell yes, you are! I said it, so it's happening. If you have a problem with that, take it up with Dom."

Without waiting for a reply, she's dragging me out of there. Dom tosses her his car keys, then steps to block Tristan's path. And I have no choice but to follow Luz. I'm still on a high from the magic, but that look in Tristan's eyes...

Fuck. Why did I use it?

The redhead ahead of me is the answer. I couldn't let Cade hurt her, not when I see what she's got with Dom.

We hop in Dom's pickup, and Luz drives us in the silence to the bungalow they live in. She marches to the kitchen and pulls out a bottle of wine. Her nose wrinkles, then she puts it back in the fridge and heads to the antique hutch in a corner. After rummaging through, she comes up with a bottle of what looks like tequila.

Luz pours us shots and pushes one towards me. Without blinking, I throw it back – and cough as it tears through my throat. "This isn't tequila!"

Luz laughs. "Nope, it's țuică." The word is unfamiliar, and she pronounces the "t" like a "tsch", but the liquid is burning fire in my stomach.

She shrugs. "Call it Romanian vodka, if you will. Dom's secret stash. Now, sip."

Luz pours another shot, and I drink it. And another. And another. By the fifth, I'm wobbly on my feet and then she pulls the wine from the fridge, pouring us both a large glass. She motions to the stool by the island, and serves us both.

"Now, talk to me. What was all that?"

I bite my lip, feeling emotional. "Told you everything already." The semi-lie only serves to make me teary-eyed. *Merda*. Must be the freaking drink.

"You kinda haven't." She sits on the stool next to me, leaning forward and holding my hand. "There's more, isn't there? Than what you told Tristan. You don't strike me as the type of wolf to run and leave a pack behind, regardless of how crazy your brother is."

I shake my head, unable to push the words past my clogged throat. Luz doesn't give up, though, instead softens her tone. "You need to talk to someone, Dani. And if it won't be Tristan, then it might as well be me."

Tears stream down my cheeks, and before long I'm blubbering like a baby.

Tristan

I acted like a dick. There's no way about it, no excuse. *But fuck it, how...* Clenching my fists, I turn away from Dom and pace the width of the street. The pile of rubble in the distance didn't attract anyone, and I think it's probably lucky the area is abandoned.

Despite my anger, I can't help but be impressed by Dani's powers. To think she could do all this and stand up to an unsanctioned assault from the Reapers deserves my respect, if not my forgiveness.

"So... I take it you didn't know about any of this?"

I glare at Dom and he lifts his hands up. "Relax, buddy. I just meant you've been getting close to her, but you didn't feel anything?" He must read something in my expression, because he walks away and starts inspecting the ruins more closely.

Then he pulls out his cell, and I know he's calling the rest of our pack here. I focus back on pacing, and trying not to hit anything. No matter how much I might feel the urge to.

Everything starts making sense. Do I feel betrayed? Fuck yeah. Dani had too many opportunities to tell me the truth, and didn't take any. Obviously she doesn't trust me – first going to the Reapers, now this.

Fuck. Fuck. *Fuck.*

I run a hand through my hair, turning on my heels and hitting the wall closest to me. Screw control. What has it ever gotten me? My knuckles bruise, but hell if I care. My wolf is at the surface again, and a shudder runs through me. I need to shift.

Then a hand is on my shoulder, and Dom's there. "You need to cool it, buddy."

Before I can tell him to back off, Lucas' Hummer pulls up, and he steps out with Finn. They take one look around, then Lucas motions for Dom to join him. As they edge away, presumably filling our alpha in on what happened, I glance down at my bruised knuckles again.

And I remember Dani helping me with my panic attack, with my triggers. Yeah, everything makes sense now, including each piece of the puzzle she revealed before, and why she hasn't said everything since. But it doesn't make it any easier to swallow.

I didn't lie when I said I've seen witches be selfish. In my travels, my team had tried enlisting some to help us out. But in the end, they only served their own self interests. The thought she's like that, and it's all been a play...

The wall becomes my focus, the target of my punches. I don't even feel it when my knuckles crack and start bleeding.

Dom finally pulls me back, placing himself between me and the wall. I'm panting hard then, struggling to see past the rage.

Lucas' voice is what finally grounds me. "Tristan, enough!"

I lower my arms, and finally face my alpha. His eyes are narrowed on my bleeding hands, and I shrug. "They'll heal. So?"

"So, what?"

"Did Dom fill you in?"

He nods, and I notice the speculation in his eyes. "And this doesn't make you second guess her request for protection?"

"*Daniela* deserves consideration, still," he emphasizes her name like I don't know it.

It's my turn to glare. "Not when she lied her way into your good graces."

Lucas shakes his head, looking to Dom for help. "Talk some sense into him. We don't have time for his bruised ego when we need to move on to more important things. Like Cade pulling a stunt like this, in *our* territory, on our pack."

"Dani is *not* our pack!"

Dom throws me a look. "No, but Luz is. And the Reapers had no business going after her. The only reason she's still alive is thanks to your girl."

"She's not mine," I scowl at them in turn. "You're bewitched, all of you."

Lucas snorts. "Hardly. From tonight, we need to run constant patrols, ready for protection. And tomorrow, I need two of you to head into Reaper territory and see if you pick up any waves. I'll make a formal meet request to Jared to talk about this."

He looks at us, then his gaze drops on me. "You're with me for the meet. Finn, you and Dom can scout the Reapers' territory."

My eyes narrow on him. "I'm not the most diplomatic wolf you got, Lucas. Finn's your guy for this."

"Watch yourself, amico. That almost sounded like you're contesting your alpha."

The hardness in his eyes makes my wolf respond, and I take a step back. "Not the intent."

Finn pulls up next to him, defusing the situation. "So, a witch werewolf, eh?" His eyes are glinting with humor, but

I see nothing to laugh about. "Seems about right, especially for a lobisomem."

"What the hell are you going on about?"

Finn shrugs, waving his hand in the air. "Never mind. How do you plan on fixing this, mate?"

That's a good question if I ever heard one.

Lucas, surprisingly, provides the answer. "With a lot of booze. And then, we can talk about next steps."

∞ ◆ ∞

They've plied me with alcohol. But nothing takes away the sting of betrayal. How could I have slept by her, believed in her, and missed the mark so bad?

"You didn't."

I glare at Finn. He's relaxed at the end of the booth, his too-knowing eyes on me. "Get out of my head."

"Then stop projecting." He drinks his single malt, then throws a look at Lucas. He's by the bar, chatting up a pretty brunette. "He will offer her protection, you know."

"Lucas wouldn't," I scowl. "Dani's done nothing but lie since she got here."

"And is that really what upsets you the most?" Finn leans forward. "Or is it the zmeu's scent on her? Bringing back memories?"

I move without wanting to. One hand grips his throat, the other's up in a fist, ready to make contact.

Basta.

I shudder against the command, but listen to my alpha. Then Dom's there, prying me off Finn. "Let's take you home."

Shrugging out of his reach, I stomp outside. Dom's relentless, following me. "You need to get yourself under control."

"Like hell I do."

Without a word, I climb in his pickup. Once he drops me at my apartment, I head for the liquor cabinet. There's no way I can go near the bedroom – not with *her* scent all over the place.

Daniela

I turn from the window when the door opens and Dom walks in. His eyes take in my bedraggled appearance and he smiles, albeit sadly. "Sorry I missed the party." He looks around. "Luz okay?"

I nod. "She's sleeping. I got her hydrated. Thank you... for allowing me to spend the night. I realize it puts you in an odd spot with Tristan."

Rather than go to his mate, Dom shrugs out of his coat and heads towards me. "It's the least I can do, considering everything you risked to save her life." He frowns then. "Why did you?"

I shrug. "Luz is special. I've never had a friend like her, so accepting and...warm. I see what you two have, and I couldn't have lived with myself if anything happened to her, not while I could stop it."

Dom reaches for my shoulder. "Tristan will come around."

"I doubt that." My whisper carries to the moon, and I can't help asking, "How is he?"

Dom shrugs. "Drunk. Probably about to get drunk-er."

With one last squeeze, he heads to his mate. And I need fresh air, so I step into the backyard for a minute.

Moments later, the fence creaks as it opens and I feel a presence. The voice behind me is ice cold. "I will offer this once, and once only, cara."

My eyes stay fixed on the moon, even as Lucas walks around me. His presence is intimating, but I've seen his kind before – fought them, too.

A side-glance to him confirms that while he's tense, Lucas is not here for a fight.

"Offer what?" It's barely a whisper in the quiet night, but he tilts his head to the sky as if listening for an answer.

Then his dark eyes settle on me, and he nods. "My protection, if you still wish it."

I think back to Tristan, to the betrayal in his eyes. Is that why Lucas is finally coming around? And am I ready to submit to an alpha like him? The power lying dormant in him is something else.

When I look up in his eyes, trying to see the man behind the leader, I find no malice. Only understanding and regret.

"Yes," I say before I can change my mind. "I still need it."

Lucas inclines his head then, and blows out a breath. "But is it something you wish?"

I think back to my freedom – and can't lie. "No. But it's what I need."

He nods then. "I'll let the guys and Lucrezia know in the morning."

Tristan

I groan against the sunlight. Glancing at the kitchen clock, I notice it's past ten in the morning. *Shit.* I doubt Lucas will be lenient considering last night, but fuck it. Something tells me it's already going to be a shit day.

Can't be worse than last night.

Despite the bottle I consumed, I still didn't get much sleep. Whenever I closed my eyes, it was Dani I smelled, felt under my hands, heard moaning in my ears. It was the worst kind of torture, so I forced myself to stay awake through the night. Obviously, that didn't work.

Grunting, I get off the couch and drag myself to shower. An hour later, I finally make my way in the auto shop, and stop dead in my tracks. Dani's scent is all over the place – fresh.

I look through the translucent doors to the garage and notice her chatting with Finn and Dom. Luz is leaning against her boyfriend, and Lucas is in a corner, watching over them.

Tell me he fucking didn't.

Before I can take a breath to calm down, I burst through, pointing an accusing finger towards Dani. "What the hell is *she* doing here?"

Dani flinches under my angry gaze and I feel the pack's protective stance shift towards her. Luz moves first, glaring at me and stepping next to Dani. Finn arches an eyebrow, and Dom looks at the ceiling for help.

Thanks for the help, guys. Looks like I'm on my own.

Dead silence lingers in the air, until Lucas speaks. "I've awarded Daniela protection."

I seethe. "Seriously? Do you know she's in league with the zmeu?"

"I'm not —" Dani stops, shaking her head and curling her shoulders inward, as if realizing it's useless to fight my accusations.

Lucas narrows his eyes on me. "I know everything there is to know, amico. Believe me, she is not in the wrong."

I look at all of them, and it's too much. The one place I thought I could escape this, escape her, and now I can't even do that. "Fuck this."

Shaking my head, I turn on my heels and walk out, ignoring their calls to me. I step on the gas and take the main road – out of town.

Land passes by, but I'm not even focused on it. I just drive, and drive some more. Dani's stricken expression keeps running through my mind and guilt swirls in my gut. It gets worse, to the point of physical pain, until I have to pull over and hurl my breakfast all over the side of the highway.

I try to write it off to the alcohol I consumed, but I know it's not that. And as I stand up in the middle of nowhere, surrounded by mountains and nothing else, I admit the truth to myself.

I've been a dick. And whether she lied or not, Dani is still the woman I've fallen in love with. The one I swore to protect, even if she's unaware of it. And because of that, and how much she's done for me, I need to try to mend things.

Apologies will be in order, but not yet. Before I do anything else, there's someplace else I need to visit. I get back in my truck and step on the gas, hoping to get there before nightfall. After all, if I'm going to be there for Dani, I need to deal with my demons first – and one of them is Izabella.

And while I'm there, another promise needs to be kept. Not that long ago, I swore to Dani I would hunt down her brother and make him pay for branding her. Alone or not, now's as good a time as any to do it.

Hours later, as the sun paints the sky blood red, I pass the beaten down sign welcoming me to Bow's Arrow. Rather than take the main route into town, I turn right at the first intersection and head to a deserted-looking hill.

Tires crunch on gravel – the snow's melted here. *Odd.* After I get out of the truck, my feet take me up, following the names on the tombstones. They're in order of death years, and it doesn't take me long to end up in front of her grave.

I kneel next to it, then lift a hand and touch the headstone. Her laugh, her scent... The wind picks up and it's as if she's right there, next to me.

"Izzy..."

∞ ∞ ∞

∞ Memória ∞

"Memory…is the diary that we all carry about with us."

-Oscar Wilde-

Daniela

Hours have gone by since Tristan took off. I haven't been hiding, exactly, but I sought refuge in Lucas' office. So it's no surprise when he walks in with a demanding air about him.

"It's time I teach you a bit about our little town. Free my seat, cara."

I roll my eyes and stand, moving to the small sofa on the side. "Is there a reason you keep calling me darling in Italian?"

He chuckles. "Only for my own amusement." Then his expression grows serious. "Dom told me it was Cade who attacked you. But I need to hear it from your pretty lips. Everything. From the beginning."

With a sigh, I slouch into the chair and start going through the story. I tell him how we were at the bar, the Reapers noticed us, and Cade chased after us.

"And none of this was provoked? You didn't do anything with your magic?"

I scowl at him. "No, I didn't."

"It wasn't meant as offense, cara. I'm going to bat with Jared in an hour, so it's imperative I'm informed of all the details."

His explanation and tone get to me, and I settle. I'm too on edge. Using that magic is like a drug, and now I'm even more aware of it at the tip of my fingers.

"What do you think?"

I snap out of my thoughts, aware I've missed the last of Lucas' words. "Sorry, what?"

He smirks. "Since Tristan took off, and he was meant to come with me, you'll take his place. But no matter what happens, I'll need you to keep your mouth shut. Understood?"

Part of me wants to refuse. Yet with the protection he's awarded me, I feel indebted, especially considering Tristan is gone because of me. So I nod, and stand to follow Lucas out the door. I can only hope there'll be no ravens around this time.

∞ ♦ ∞

Turns out the meeting is taking place at The Cave. I expected a forest and us in wolf form, but I guess things are done differently in Rockland Creek. So I join Lucas in a secluded booth, leaving the opposite bench free for Jared and whoever he brings along.

My wolf is settled, having not seen any ravens about, so it makes it easier to focus on what's about to happen.

We don't have to wait long. A few minutes after we sit, the door opens. Lucas straightens from his slouch, and hisses, "Remember, keep quiet."

Then Jared shows up, flanked by a guy I've never met. He has bleached, cropped hair and blank eyes. A perfect follower, by the looks of it.

Jared sits opposite Lucas, and folds his hands behind his head like he's at the beach. "So, what gives?"

My nostrils flare, catching their scent. *They've just hunted.* And judging by the odor, it wasn't an animal.

Lucas doesn't move, but something tells me he smells it as well. "For starters, why did one of your men attack two of my females?"

Jared snorts. "Don't know what you're talking about." But his eyes flicker betrayingly to me, and it's the proof Lucas needs.

He leans forward, elbows on the table and body tense. "We've co-existed well, you and I, for a reason. Should that reason become...obsolete...then you would find the full strength of our attack aimed towards you. And we both know how that ended last time, if you recall."

Jared's eyes flash, and he stands, practically kicking the other guy out of the booth. "I've heard enough."

As he stalks off, Lucas doesn't drop it. He doesn't turn, doesn't go after him, doesn't yell. Yet his voice still carries in the empty enclosure. "Watch your back, Jared."

After they're gone, I turn to him. "Now what?"

"This little meet should have given Dom and Finn enough time to gather some intel. We'll regroup tomorrow."

Morning finds me on Dom's couch. I stretch, then sniff the air. The smell of bacon and eggs assails my senses, enough to jostle me up. With the open-concept kitchen, I can see Luz cook food in there.

Dom is waiting patiently at the table, his eyes glued to his mate, tracking her every movement. He must hear noise on my end, as he spares me a glance and a smile. "Awake yet?"

"Mmm. That smells delicious!"

Luz grins over her shoulder. "Thought you'd need some after last night's party. Dom offered to cook, but I was already in the mood."

It's then I notice Dom's sharpened look on me. "What?"

He hesitates a beat, then admits, "We haven't heard anything from Tristan."

I look away, trying to pretend – and failing – that it's not affecting me. Even though my stomach clenches in pain, and my chest feels as if it's being ripped apart. The fact he left town the moment he heard I was in his pack is telling enough about our relationship, and I don't know if we'll be able to recover. If he'll be able to forgive me.

"Do you know where he could have gone?" Dom pushes.

I run a hand through my hair, wincing at the tangled mess. "No. But I'll think on it. Can I use your shower?"

He nods, and I walk away with my backpack. Just before I go in the bathroom, I turn to them. "Did you find anything, last night? When you went with Finn."

Dom shakes his head. "Not much. There's trouble in the Reapers pack, that's a given. Could be Cade is causing it, but whatever it is, feels like there are two separate factions of the Reapers now."

"Shit."

He gives me a look that echoes the sentiment, and I go inside the bathroom. As the water cascades down my back, I think about his question, about Tristan – *really* think about it. There's only place he'd go in anger.

Where it all started.

My eyes snap open at the realization, and my stomach plummets. I get out of the bathroom and dress in a rush, piling my hair atop my head in a messy bun. Then I practically run through the hallway and emerge in the kitchen.

"I know where he went!"

Only, no one reacts. Their attention is already occupied by the dark-haired man standing in the living room. He turns at the sound of my voice, and his stormy grey eyes twinkle. "Hello, little wolf."

Tristan

My breath hitches, eyes filling with tears. The hand touching Izzy's headstone trembles and a shudder runs through me. "How did it all get so fucked up?"

Then other memories assail me – her with my best friend, legs tangled, moaning at his touch... I shake my head to push it away. "You always knew how to push my buttons. But Dani... Fuck, Izzy. How can I love two women so much?"

I don't know what brought me here, of all places. What kind of closure do I expect from a grave, when I didn't get it of Izzy's living? Worse still, what did I leave behind, in my stubbornness?

My gut clenches, and I bend over, trying to gulp air. Breathing becomes harder, like the air is being ripped from my lungs. Next thing I know, I pass out.

"You're a fool, Tristan Cayne."

I stand from the grave, looking around. My jaw drops when it lands on Izzy. She's got the same blue streaks in her hair I'd last seen her in. Only, she's wearing a quasi-virginal white dress that comes up to her knees.

Noticing my surprise, she smirks in a very Izzy way. "I know, it's not really me. How about this?" She moves her hand in front of her body, and now she's clad in a form-fitting, red dress.

"Better, yeah?"

I stand without answering her. Instead, I look around. My truck is a few feet away, parked on the road. And I'm definitely still in cemetery. But I know it can't be real.

"Depends on your definition of real, I suppose."

My eyes settle on Izzy. "You can hear my thoughts?"

She shrugs. "We were pretty close, remember? It doesn't go away just because I'm dead."

"If you're dead, then what...What is this?"

A delicate shoulder lifts in another shrug, and she steps closer to me. She's barefoot, which is also new, since the Izzy I knew was always in heels.

She rolls her eyes at my thoughts. "You can't have it all, Tristan."

I shake my head, then pin her with my stare. "What the hell is this?"

"Not sure, to be honest. I'm well and truly dead, don't worry. But..." Her gaze roams the land, wistful and nostalgic. "I guess I needed to see you for a minute."

I cross my arms at that. "And why?"

Izzy notices my stance and laughs. "A minute ago, you were ready to cry over my grave." She shakes her head. "You're a complicated man, Tristan. Makes sense only Dani could get through to you."

Rather than jealousy, it's amusement I notice in her expression. "You... You're okay with that?"

"As okay as I can be," she whispers, stepping closer. "I'm sorry, Tristan. For the hurt I caused you, for not waiting for you. You deserved better than that, and I failed when it mattered."

The past lingers between us, a constant reminder of our history. Yet in that moment, looking into her eyes, it hurts less. Her betrayal, the memories, the abandonment she gifted me with when I left for the army. Those wounds have healed, and though the realization is new, I know exactly who's to credit for this.

That's a topic for another time. In that moment, I'm finally able to give my former lover what I wasn't able to before. "I forgive you, Izzy. You shouldn't be losing eternal sleep over this."

She chuckles. "Oh, I don't know about that."

"Why did you..." I clear my throat, trying again. "What made you choose to end it like that?"

"It wasn't conscious, you know. I was mad at them – Dad, Thiago. I left the house in a rush, drove while angry in bad weather, and lost control of the car." Another shrug. "It must've been fate, because I died on impact."

"Earlier, you said I was a fool. What gives?"

Her gaze sharpens on me then. "Dani loves you, and you love her. There's no loving two women, silly. It's been her for you, all along. I don't doubt you loved me at some point, but not anymore. So whatever guilt you're convinced you feel, let it go. Be happy." She reaches for my chest. "Go back to her."

Another glance around. "Leave this place, before all it is taints you too."

Then she rises on her tiptoes and kisses me softly.

I blink, and I'm back on the ground, facing her grave. A dream, a hallucination... It could have been either. *Doesn't make it any less true.*

Izabella is gone for good, as is the burden of our relationship I've been carrying around. Those last cobwebs of the past evaporate with the rising light. And somehow, having seen her at peace makes me realize I can't fix everything. Maybe if I'd been here when Thiago went crazy, I could have made things better. Or maybe not. We'll never know.

What I'm certain of, however, is that I can affect things now. Dani makes me the best version of me I can be, and the promise I made to her is crystal-clear in my head. With the sun rising, I have my closure, and the only thing it enhanced is the certitude I want to go back home – back to Dani.

On firm legs this time, I stand and move to my truck. My exhilaration overtakes my senses, making me blind to the surroundings. Or maybe it's more than that, some type of magic. Either way, I'm completely taken unawares when a shadow moves behind me and hits me over the head.

The ground draws closer, and all I see is darkness.

Daniela

"I know you," I frown. "But...I don't."

Dom glances between us, and I notice he's positioned himself half in front of Luz, as if protecting her.

The stranger throws them a glance, then steps towards me. "Let's talk, you and I."

More out of a desire to get him out of the house than anything else, I nod and head to the backyard. He follows me out, then closes the French patio doors behind us. I see Luz and Dom talking, but my attention is drawn again to him.

"Who are you?"

He sighs and lifts a hand in front of my face. With his index finger, he writes something in the air. It sizzles, smoke escaping it, then a thin ribbon escapes the icon he's drawn and wraps around my head. I try to shake it off, but it's already in me.

There's a sharp flash of pain, enough to make me yelp. My temples throb, and a flow of images hits me. I shake my head, then look at him again. "You're the dragon from the forest."

He grins. "My name is Tytus."

Dom steps through at that point, having heard my yelp. "I only agreed to let you in because you helped Luz once upon a time. Doesn't give you the right to harm one of my pack."

Tytus looks at me. "Did I harm you?"

"I..." My eyes dart between him and Dom, and I sigh. Curiosity wins over anything else. "No, he didn't harm me. I'm okay."

After a hesitation, Dom moves back inside. Luz smiles at Tytus, and I notice for the first time his expression softens. Then the doors close, and it's just him and me, and the bitter cold.

Tytus tilts his head to the side. Rather than charming, the gesture seems more predatory. "Your magic left traces everywhere."

I cross my arms over my chest. "And?"

"You used it," he says matter-of-factly. "What changed your mind?"

I scowl, recalling what he'd erased from my mind. "I didn't really have a choice. Luz was in danger, and I wasn't about to let the Reapers harm her."

"Hmm," Tytus moves away, paces for a bit, then faces me once more. "And your wolf couldn't have handled that?"

"No."

His eyes flash. "You know what I think?"

"I have a feeling you'll tell me anyway."

Tytus laughs a booming bark, then meets my gaze. "You're lying, little wolf. The magic has wanted to be unleashed for a while, and you finally gave in. And relished it. Because you used it again and again."

Denial is on the tip of my tongue, but the tingle in my fingers says otherwise. As if reading my mind, Tytus' smirk grows and he looks down at my clenched fists. "Having a hard time not using it again, aren't you?"

I cross my arms over my chest, refusing to give in. "So what if I do?"

Something akin to satisfaction spreads on his features. "Then it's time I teach you a few things. The Reapers are not the only ones you need to fear, now that you accept your true nature."

Tristan

I blink against the unnatural brightness. My head throbs, painfully so, and the damn light isn't helping things. All I see past it are lines indicating I'm in some type of building.

By the time I take in my surroundings, shadows at the back move closer. One speaks first, his words tainted with a Portuguese accent. "He wakes."

My eyes fall on the intruder. Blonde hair to mid-shoulder, dressed in a business suit, eyes the color of amber – but colder than Dani's. "Thiago."

It comes out as a croak and I clear my throat. "What the hell are you doing?"

"Getting some answers, meu amigo." He crouches in front of me. "Where is my sister?"

"Dead, didn't you hear?"

Thiago scowls and takes another step closer. "You really want to play foolish games?"

I stare back, refusing to give an inch. Then his hand shoots out, grabbing my neck. Little by little, he squeezes. "You know which sister I mean. Where is Daniela?"

Rather than answer, I tilt my chin, giving him better access. "Go on, then. Do it. See how much you get out of a dead body."

I glare, knowing full well he's not going to kill me. My brain is going haywire, assessing, preparing to escape. I've been trained in these situations. There has to be a way out – there always is.

And if I was the soldier I'd been when I first went to war, that would be enough to reassure me. But I'm not. And being tied, the scents around here, anything could trigger me. If that happens, I'm fucked. Thiago needs only one trace of weakness to bite down. And I can't give that to him.

So long as I can keep my damn panic attacks at bay, I'll be good. *Guys?* The call goes unanswered in my head. I must be out of range, or Thiago's magic blocks me. And if that's the case, he must be way more versed in it than Dani. *Shit.*

Seeing he's not getting anywhere, Thiago drops my throat and moves back. "You will speak, eventually. Even if I have to pull you apart fingernail by fingernail."

A cough escapes me, and I pull more air into my lungs. "Be my guest." I attempt a shrug, but the bindings make it hard. My vision is getting better though, and despite the light I can see past him. He has three wolves in here with us, but are there many more on the outside?

I need to gain time. "What do you want with Dani?"

Thiago smirks. "Family business. One you have no stake in, Tristan. You left long ago, and I had to clean up your mess."

"Huh?" I rack my brain trying to see what he's getting at, and come up empty. "What the hell are you talking about?"

Fury flashes in his eyes, then his expression grows calm. "Your leaving is what caused my mother's death, *perro*. Once the opposite packs out here found out there was no marriage, no surviving legacy, they threatened to attack. My mother went out to stop them – and never came back."

"You're overreaching, *idiota*. What happened to your family is no fault of mine. And losing your mother is definitely no excuse to treat your sisters as you did – branding them like cattle."

"You've seen the mark, then?" He laughs, as if it's the funniest – not most fucked up – thing he's ever done. "Too bad you weren't here for the auction."

My breath rushes out in a gust of air. "The...what?"

Thiago laughs, shaking his head at my befuddled expression. "Come now, how do you think the eligible men of the pack would have otherwise found the females? We had to brand them, yes, but also make sure they could find their scents. See which one spoke best to the males."

Blood rushes to my temples, and it's all I hear. Fury rises like a tidal wave within me. "You put your own sisters for auction, you fucking bastard?" I jump in my seat, making it rattle.

Thiago steps back, but keeps grinning. "I also won them."

His admission makes everything stop. There's only one thing I know, and I have no problem voicing it out loud. "When I get out of here – and I *will* – I will rip you apart, piece by miserable piece. You deserve nothing less for treating them like that."

Thiago sneers in my face, then turns to the men behind him. "Our friend is being very uncooperative. Bring the ravens."

In front of my stunned eyes, they bring two cages filled with black ravens. Thiago opens them, and waves one hand. Like good little soldiers, the birds fly out and land around me. Then two move forward, followed by another two.

When their beaks dig into my thighs and my hands, I grit my teeth against the pain. And Thiago, crazy sonofabitch that he is, watches on.

∞ ∞ ∞

∞ Medo ∞

"Courage is resistance to <u>fear</u>, mastery of fear, not absence of fear."

-Mark Twain-

Daniela

I'm panting, ducking yet another blast from Tytus. "Would you let me catch my breath?"

He snorts. "No time, little wolf. Now, catch." He throws me one of those blasts he's so great at. Of course, unlike me, he's had a lifetime and then some to practice. So he draws the rune in the air, and a ball of fire emerges from the design.

Yeah. Like in a damn sci-fi movie. And once more I miss catching it and fly into the fence, then drop to the snow.

Its iciness drips down my spine, coating my already soaked clothes. Inside the house, Dom shakes his head and steps out once more. I explained to him that Tytus wanted to teach me, and he offered his backyard as the grounds for it. I'm pretty sure he's regretting it now.

"If something happens to you, Tristan will have my hide," he says, and his glare settles on Tytus. "You know she hasn't had much time to practice by the sounds of it. You could go easy on her."

"No, he won't," I scowl at the first part of his lecture. "Tristan couldn't care less."

"And we don't have time for easy," Tytus sneers. "If you can't stand to watch her in pain, then go back inside to your mate."

Dom bristles, uncrossing his arms and clenching his fists. He takes a step forward, but Luz saunters from the house and grabs onto his arm, holding him back. I watch with some measure of envy as he practically melts at her touch, his expression softening and focusing on her.

"You don't mean that," Luz says to me. "Tristan's in pain, Dani, but he'll come around."

I shake my head. "So you all keep saying. But you know what? Tytus is right. There's no such thing as a fairytale. The best thing I can do for myself is learn how to protect myself."

They share a look, but I turn my back to them and face Tytus. "Let's go, dragão."

Tytus' eyes flash when I call him a dragon in Portuguese. I probably shouldn't have. Without mercy, he blasts me again, and I go back flying.

Growling, I pick myself up and dust the snow off. For the first time, I'm starting to feel cold. *Guess not even wolf heat is a match for a dragon's idea of a magic boot camp.*

"What am I doing wrong?" My whine rings in the air, not that my teacher cares.

He shrugs. Big help, he is, did I mention that already? Then his stormy gaze looks around the backyard and finally settles back on me. "You're overthinking it, little wolf. Trying to catch fire with wolf instincts won't get you very far."

"How about throwing it, then?" I scowl. "Show me how to do that instead."

Tytus snorts. "You have to learn to walk before you can run, witch."

This time, my eyes narrow on him. "Which is it, then? Little wolf or witch?"

He crosses his arms over his chest, and the way he's clenching his jaw tells me I'm on thin ice. "You tell me. All you've done since I offered to teach you is whine and switch between your two identities. Pick one and stick to it, Daniela."

It's the first time he uses my name, and maybe that's why it makes his words even more ultimate. "I don't want to choose."

Dom and Luz have been watching this, but at least he's had the foresight to pull them both to the side of the house. I'm thankful they're out of the way when Tytus throws another blast of energy my way and I end up on my ass – again.

Tytus towers over me this time, his expression as stormy as his eyes. "You don't have a choice. Your magic won't work like this."

We stare at each other, and I'm on the verge of tears. "What's the point of even trying, then? I might as well let it kill me."

Before Tytus can say anything, Dom steps in my field of vision and sticks out his hand. He pulls me to my feet, and his eyes are gentle on mine. "I think what Tytus means is not that you have to discount one part of you. More that when you choose your magic, you need to think like a witch. And when you're in wolf form, be a wolf."

He throws a look over his shoulder at Tytus, who shrugs. "Isn't that what I've been saying?"

"No, it *wasn't*!" I march forward and shove my palms against his chest. He doesn't move, instead seems amused. "All this time, you've been saying I need to choose."

"And you do." His nostrils flare. "Make no mistake, wolf-witch. You cannot be both at the same time. So when I next throw you a blast of energy, you need to catch."

He walks away, putting a few feet of distance between us. Dom joins Luz by the side of the house again, and I pull in a deep breath. *Think like a witch.* Easy for him to say.

Nonetheless, I watch Tytus draw the rune, sense the energy vibrate as he pulls it and fashions it into a weapon.

Then it's swinging in the air, aimed towards me. Larger and closer it grows, and I hold my hands out, fingers curled as if getting ready to catch a ball being thrown. Only this one can burn me to hell and beyond.

My fingers tremble, but it doesn't seem to matter as the ball lands between them. I clench them around the orb, surprised to feel its squishy texture, rather than the heat I'd been expecting.

Luz cheers on the sidelines, but I'm petrified, staring at Tytus in a panic. "What now?"

"Use it. Throw it back at me."

I do as he instructs, fumbling with it. The damn thing keeps vibrating in my hands, and I'm afraid I'll drop it and set fire to the house. By the time I finally launch it, all Tytus does is lift his index, then blows. The whole thing dissipates in a flash.

Now I'm scowling. "What the hell was the point of all this, then?"

"We're done for today," he says instead of answering me. "Much bigger things await."

"Tytus..." I growl, unable to hold back. "I'm not some pet you play with whenever the hell you want. You promised me!"

He gets in my face, surprising me with his anger. "And I am holding that promise. But unless you want your mate to die, it would be best we stop this and go practice on the real enemies."

My knees wobble, but I manage to remain standing. Barely. "What?"

Dom and Luz see my consternation and come closer. "What's going on?"

Tytus looks at each of us in turn with an almost bored expression. "Your pack member, Tristan? He's been captured. And he needs your help."

Dom snaps out of it first. "How the hell do you know this?" He makes the mistake to move closer to Tytus, who draws up to his full height.

"Watch yourself, vârcolac. You've no business challenging me."

While they stare at each other, Luz nudges me. "Dani. Dani! You okay?"

It's enough to snap me out of it. I stalk to Tytus, shoving him backwards. "*Where* is he?"

He glares at me. "You know where. In your old town, with your brother."

"Shit." I turn to Dom and Luz, trying to fix my dismayed expression. "We're going to need back-up." *I'm nowhere near ready for this.*

Dom throws another look to Tytus, then nods and heads into the house, pulling out his cellphone and making calls. Tytus is still here, though.

"Will you help?" It's but a whisper, but I need to know if I can count on him.

"Yes, but not for the reasons you think. There is something I need from your old town, something your father and brother guard. Once I have it, I'm gone."

I nod, uncaring of his price. "Whatever you want. I only ask you stick around long enough so they'll see you in dragon form."

His eyes narrow on me, and I fear he might decline. Surprisingly, he nods and takes off, leaving me and Luz alone.

"Why did you want him in dragon form?" she asks.

"Because it's the only thing that'll scare my brother senseless." At her confused look, I add, "Since getting magic, Thiago thinks he's unbeatable. The witch warned us long ago that a dragon's fire will kill us, regardless of whatever other protections we may try. It burns through everything with its eternal flame." My eyes linger on Tytus' departing form. "Thiago thought it was a myth, but he'll remember that warning, as have I."

Dom exits at that point, waving me over. "Finn and Lucas are coming. Let's grab my truck." He goes to Luz and kisses her, but she pushes him back.

"I'm coming with you."

"No, you're not."

"Yes, I *am*! Tristan's my friend too."

"Lucrezia..." His jaw is tense. "If anything happens to you, I won't be able to live with myself."

"Nothing will," she says, touching his hand. "Please, Dom. I held my ground against Jared, didn't I? And you know I'm not some helpless princess."

Dom's expression softens then, and he drops his forehead to hers in a gesture so similar to Tristan, that I have to look away. I miss the rest of their exchange, but when it looks like she's nowhere convincing him, I step in.

"There's another thing to consider... If you leave Luz here alone, what if Reapers come calling? None of us will be around to provide backup."

Dom's eyes flare as he recalls Luz's last interaction with them. He glances at his mate one more time, then kisses her forehead. "Fine, iubirea mea. You win."

Tristan

"Ready to talk yet?"

Everything hurts. Scratch that – everything feels like it's being ripped from me. And in a way, it is. Thiago's magic stops me from turning and healing myself, and the ravens are picking at my skin. Bloody bits of it already cover the ground underneath my chair, but the damned birds keep going.

"You're still here?" I snort, though it takes everything in me not to give in to sleepiness. "I told you I'm not talking."

The only thing that keeps me going is the knowledge I'll eventually be free, and will have the chance to rip him apart. I can only imagine what Izzy and Dani went through with a psycho like him for a brother. Being marked, put up for auction... No wonder Izzy tried to run away. No wonder it all ended so badly.

Guilt fills me anew. Had I been here, could I have stopped his craziness? It's one thing to know the full story, now. How come I didn't feel any of this, if Dani's my mate, if Izzy was my lover?

The answer dawns on me when I watch Thiago pacing, growing increasingly agitated. My call to my pack didn't go through, and I'm bonded to the werewolves. Within our small troop, Luz was able to call out to us when she and Dom were fighting Radu and his vyrkolakas. And she wasn't even in our pack back then, but the connection was strong.

Me being unable to do so means Thiago must be blocking my link. Maybe even the entire town. It explains why Dani had to leave, and why she's been dreading to come back here – or be dragged back here.

Yet if it's true he's able to block these links, then there's a strong possibility Thiago's lobisomens are disconnected when in wolf form. I file the little piece of information away for future use. If ever we end up in full conflict with them, then maybe it'll turn out useful.

My eyes focus on Thiago. He's staring at me like I'm some insect, and I have a feeling these ravens aren't all the pain he's prepared for me.

"Why?" he asks, moving behind the light.

I don't like not seeing him, so I blink, trying to locate the bastard by his voice. He steps into the light.

"Why protect her? Izabella only broke your heart. You owe them nothing."

A hoarse laugh escapes me then. "You're such an idiot, Thiago. Guess your mom wasn't around to teach you the power of love, huh?"

Anger flashes across his face, and the minute after he's pummeling me into my seat.

Daniela

I don't know if I'm ready for this. I ran away to escape them. Now I'm running towards them to save Tristan. Dom drives at the speed of lightning, while Finn and Lucas are following in a Hummer behind us.

Yet through the entire drive, I'm biting my nails, picking at my skin, wondering if Tristan's okay – wondering if he'll hate me even more after this.

There's no doubt in my mind that Thiago knew the minute he crossed the town line. While Izzy and I fought our magic, wanting to preserve our lobisomens over the witches we had become, he learned to use it. Perfected it. He got so good, he even imprisoned the witch who originally gave us the powers, keeping her for his use whenever he wanted to.

Thoughts of him weigh heavy on me. And when we cross the barrier to my old town, it all hits me. I should've expected this, knowing he blocks everything in there. Nausea rises in my throat, pain tingles down my arms, and I gasp. Then moan in pain. Try gritting my teeth against it, to no avail.

"Dani!" Luz turns in the front seat, noticing my reaction. "What's going on?"

"M-magic," I manage, closing my eyes. "T-Tristan..."

"She must have reconnected with his wolf," Dom whispers. "As a mate to Tristan, she must feel his lobisomem's – wolf's – pain." Louder, he asks me, "Can you lead us to him, Dani?"

I nod and point my index in the air. "Go left."

With painful directions, each more agonizing than the last, we finally make it past the cemetery where my sister is buried. Tristan's truck is there, I recognize it sure as water. And now that we're closer, I'm even less likely to move.

My vârcolac friend is right. This isn't my pain I feel. It's Tristan's. Which means not only is he here, but Thiago must have him. My eyes shut against the newfound agony. *Tristan...*

Dom pulls the car to the side. I try to get out, but he shakes his head. "Stop. I got Finn and Lucas, we can win this. Just watch over Luz."

He's out before I can disagree. Before I can warn him that four werewolves – no matter how great they are – are no match for my psychotic brother and the pack of lobisomens that follows him.

Tristan

I can't see anymore, but Thiago's still panting above me. His knuckles are bloody – I only know because of the smell.

Then I hear what sounds like an altercation happening outside. The walls of the building shake as if someone's been slammed into it. And the scents coming to me make me sigh in relief.

"Your pack is here?" Thiago snorts. "More food for us."

When the sounds of the fight draw closer, I manage to crack one eye open. Dom's in full werewolf mode, Finn by his side. They're tearing everything apart while Lucas is cutting a path towards me. But there are more wolves in the darkness, and Thiago lifts his hand.

Magic.

Watch out! I scream mentally to my comrades, but it's too late. A blast hits them full-front, blowing them back outside.

Something else grabs my attention. The tightness holding me prisoner is gone. Thiago's attention is elsewhere, meaning I can finally shift. I close my eyes, letting the change roll over me. The cub shape lets me out of my binds, then I morph my form to a larger one.

I'm still wobbly, even on four paws. But I make it outside where my pack is fighting to help me out. They're losing, surrounded by more wolves than I can count. And they're all lobisomens like me, able to shift and change their forms at will. Not even my paltry attempt to defend them will help when we're outnumbered ten to one.

Just as I'm about to ask Lucas to retreat and leave me behind, all hell breaks. A whoosh of air moves above us. It's strong enough to make the closest of us move backwards a few steps. Stunned, I glance up to see where it's coming from, and my jaw drops.

A burgundy dragon is flying over, roaring and blowing fire. He hits half of Thiago's lobisomens, but the bastard's there to send a gust of air into the fire, making it move to Dom's truck.

I look around for my friend, and his howl pierces my ears a few feet away. The white stripe on his back is easy to recognize, as is his bulk. His agitation is plain, and he tears into a wolf with renewed enthusiasm. Then he catches sight of red hair in the distance, closer to my truck.

His relief is palpable, and so is mine – until I see a flash of dirty blonde. *Dani.* I want to head to her, apologize for everything, protect her from Thiago.

Unfortunately, I'm not the only one who spotted her. "Come out, come out, *irmãzinha*. My darling *little sister*, home at last. Time for your reckoning."

To my surprise, Dani doesn't cower or even take a moment to gather herself. Instead, she stands and comes out. Hatred replaces any fear in her expression, as she takes each step closer. "Não, brother. It's time for yours."

The dragon reappears above her head, roaring fire. I want to scream a warning, afraid she'll get burned. But instead of being burned alive, Dani lifts her palms and picks at the fire, holding it in her hands. Without wasting a breath, she throws it at Thiago.

Make your way to me.

I'm too busy being stunned by her abilities to clue in. A few seconds later, I realize she's talking to me. Our eyes meet across the distance, for a brief second. It's enough. Inch by inch, I move towards her, trying to drag my pained body. And still the dragon breathes fire, circling back to Dani, using her to channel his flames.

She throws each one towards her brother, aiming them into specific attacks designed to isolate him. With each hit, Thiago moves further and further from us. The lobisomens pull back in the opposite direction, confused as to what's happening.

A glance around shows me Lucas and Dom working together, helping Finn with the last of Thiago's pack mates. They're easy picking, which confirms my theory that they're not connected when in wolf form.

The dragon returns for one more spin. He looks below, watching us closely. Then his gaze is drawn elsewhere, and he hovers mid-air, undecided. Dani lifts her palms, waiting for him to send another gust of fire her way.

Only, the dragon takes off – leaving her hanging. She gapes after him, and Thiago watches the entire scene. A deep laugh escapes him.

"Now, let's see what you can do without that creature holding your hand." His foolish mistake is he underestimates Dani, throwing a blast of burgundy light towards her.

My darling mate, rather than cower away, digs her heels in and manages to grab the energy. Then she screams, throwing it back at Thiago, watching as it slams him into a building.

"Run!" she screams, and Lucas, Finn and Dom morph to human form, heading to the cars.

Dani heads for me, bent as if in pain. I whine, but she pets my head. "You'll be okay, Tristan. Just breathe."

The ground vibrates under my feet, then I'm being picked up in a man's arms. Before I know it, everything goes dark.

∞ ◆ ∞

I've never seen the back of my truck. Seems weird to say, but I'm always driving it. Now that I'm here, I'm aware of how cramped my legs are, and the fact the back is piled with a bunch of shit I should've thrown out a while ago. I wonder what Dani thinks about all of this.

Dani....

The thought of her is enough to snap me out of my head. My eyes open and I stare at the back of Finn's head, driving my truck. Luz is next to him at the front, Dom with me at the back.

"Finally awake, huh?"

I try to shake my head but a massive headache tears through without mercy. "Where's Dani?"

Dom and Luz share a look. "She's riding with Lucas."

"Why?"

"Because she didn't think you'd want to see her."

My heart lurches. "Stop the car."

Finn looks in the rear view mirror. "You need to see a doctor, mate."

"Since when have we gone to doctors? Stop the freaking car!"

He jerks it to the side, causing Dom to release some curses in Romanian under his breath. Before he's done parking, I hop out and limp into the incoming path of Lucas' car.

It's only as I stare at the approaching headlights that I realize my precarious position. A blanket is wrapped around my shoulders, but underneath it, I'm completely naked. Meaning there's no armor to protect me – from any kind of wounds. And my body still feels sore from Thiago's ravens.

Like an idiot, I don't move though. The car stops in a screech of tires and I step closer, smacking my fist on the tinted window. Lucas rolls it down, but there's no Dani. "Where is she?" I roar.

Then the back door opens and I see her ponytail, and she comes around the car to face me. Her expression is shuttered, her eyes wary as hell. And I can't take it.

"What do you want, Tristan?"

I move closer before she can say anything else and with one tug on her wrist, she's in my arms. Then I tilt her chin and drop my mouth to hers – without hesitation, without mercy.

She's mine and she better damn well start getting used to it.

∞ ∞ ∞

∞ Salvaçaõ ∞

"Work out your own <u>salvation</u>. Do not depend on others."

-Buddha-

Daniela

I don't have time to react before Tristan's kissing me, and all my senses go haywire. But something nags at the back of my mind, and I know we can't do this – not like this. Not until we deal with everything.

So I press my hands against his chest. He makes an appreciative noise at the back of his throat, until he realizes I'm, in fact, pushing him away. Then he listens, unlocking our lips. His chocolate eyes scan my features with a slight frown.

"Dani..."

"Not here," I whisper. "There's too much to talk about, and the middle of the road isn't the place for it."

His frown deepens, his hold on me growing tighter as if he doesn't want to let go. "But..."

I shake my head, extricating myself from his embrace. Then I look around, noticing Lucas not far off. "See you back at the shop," I murmur, then step back to the car.

We drive off, and I'm glad for the tint that keeps me hidden from Tristan's eyes. He's grateful now, because I just saved his life. Still, something in me says it won't be long before he goes back to despising me.

Yet even as we drive away, he's watching us leave, and his unmoving shape is the last thing I see before we turn around a corner.

Lucas is quiet for a long time. "You okay?"

I throw him a surprised look. "Wouldn't have pegged you for the sensitive type."

"I'm not, cara," he snorts. "But you are part of my pack, and being a leader means sometimes having to ask the hard questions. No matter how uncomfortable that makes me."

A quiet laugh escapes me. His features are pained, as if it's taking all his might to say these words. It's only fair I actually give him an honest answer. "I'll be fine," I say. "Once I talk to Tristan."

His eyes meet mine in the rear view mirror. "The pack is still here for you, regardless of what happens between you two. And he gave me his oath."

"Oath?"

"That he will be okay with you here, despite anything that might happen."

I gulp past the lump in my throat. "Good to know."

Silence grows again in the car, and the drive lengthens. It must be an hour later when we come to a crossroads. Lucas glances at me again. "Still need time to think?"

I nod, not knowing where he's going with it. "Yeah, if possible."

"Long way it is, then," he says and turns to the right. It's only then I realize we're not going back the same way we came.

"You did well," he adds. "It can't have been easy facing your brother like that."

No, it wasn't. Knowing how much Lucas values loyalty, though, I don't say it out loud. Instead, I pick at the skin around my nails to distract me. "It was bound to happen."

"Hmm." Lucas drives on for a bit longer, then asks, "I didn't see your father anywhere. Now, or the last time I was there. Is he..."

"Dead?" I finish for him, then shake my head. "Thiago's had him in isolation for a while, so he can't intervene when my brother does something stupid. I'm not sure exactly where he is being kept right now."

Lucas throws me a look out of the corner of his eye. "It'll come to you, like the magic did. You surprised me, cara. Considering you're a newborn witch and all."

I snort, relishing the praise yet embarrassed by it at the same time. "Yeah, well, I had help."

As if on cue, Lucas slams on the brakes, cursing under his breath. I peer around the driver's seat, my jaw dropping. A very familiar dragon is blocking our way, smack in the middle of the road. And by the looks of it, he's not happy.

"Che cazzo..." Lucas murmurs.

I'm tempted to agree. *What the hell?*

Tristan

Dom ends up having to drag me back in the car, much against my protests. The minute we're in, I tap Finn on the shoulder. "What's going on with Dani?"

He looks at me, narrowing his eyes. It's the first time I've directly asked him to share something he's picked up on via his gifts. And to my surprise, he shakes his head. "Sorry, mate."

"Are you shitting me right now, Finn?" A scowl takes over. "The one time I ask you for information and you deny it?"

Finn's normally warm eyes go cold. "Watch yourself, mate. I'm not your psychic-on-command."

My teeth clench with enough force to snap. "No, but I thought you were my friend."

"Enough!" Luz whispers, frowning at both of us. "This is hardly the time to fight like a pair of children. Have you forgotten what just happened?" She points at me, and the blanket around my shoulders. "You were picked apart by ravens, Tristan. Healing is in order, and *after* that, you can talk to Dani." She glances between me and Finn. "As for whatever Finn picked up on, don't you think that's a bit unfair? Dani has a right to the privacy of her own thoughts. If you want to know why she pushed you away, then ask her." She leans back in her seat. "Once you're back home, and all."

A heavy silence falls in the car, and we're all staring at her. She arches an eyebrow. "What? Are we going to sit here all night until Dani's old pack of lobisomens comes after us? Let's get a move on." She snaps her fingers, and Finn starts the car.

Dom settles into the backseat with me, a smug grin on his face. *Bastard.*

He throws me a look. *I heard that.*

Shaking my head, I curl into my seat and let sleep claim me once more. What else can I do, besides stress over something I can't change?

∞ ◆ ∞

What feels like hours later, someone nudges me. I'm in that half-drowsy state, slowly slugging out of dreams – when it hits me. And rather than jerk awake, I fall deeper into the nightmare.

Thiago's taunting me, his ravens picking at me. Only I realize the pain is more intense, more than what I endured. I look down and it's my intestines they're eating, like damn Prometheus.

A blood-curling scream escapes my lips, and I trash against the restraints. Then Thiago's there, choking me. His claws around my neck. In the distance, I see one of his men with Dani. He's ripping at her body, tearing her insides out.

My wolf goes crazy. I lose it. The restrains snap, and my hands come around Thiago's neck. I'm squeezing, choking, refusing to let go. Someone's yelling at me to stop, but I can't – not until he's dead. Not until Dani –

"Tristan, *STOP*!"

Someone's pulling at me, then two pairs of arms are dragging me away. A resounding slap echoes around, and I blink – staring into Luz's furious green eyes. My cheek stings, and feels hot to my touch.

"What..." I look around, noticing Dom on the ground, holding onto his neck.

"Are you okay?" My gaze shifts back to Luz, noticing now her worried expression. "What happened?"

Dom gets up, still rubbing at his neck. After a roll of his shoulders, he heads closer. His brow is furrowed, as if he's assessing me. The reason becomes apparent shortly. "You tried to choke me to death, that's what."

"Shit." I go to take a step, only to realize then I'm still restrained – by Finn. My head turns to the side enough to say, "Don't let me go, whatever you do. I'm not sure if it's gone yet."

"If *what* is gone?" Dom frowns.

I can't answer him. They'll see me as weak – weaker than ever. I know they're aware of my demons, but they've never witnessed anything like this. I've been careful around them, specifically because being in a pack keeps me together. But showing this side of me, fully...

Fuck, why did I have to fall asleep?

A weak wolf is no good. I'm about to shake my head, but Luz answers for me. "The nightmare."

My gaze meets hers, and instead of pity I only read acceptance. "What can we do to help, Tristan?"

Her green eyes are wide and trusting, despite me having nearly choked her boyfriend to death. Only Luz could be capable of such kindness. And just as she's there for Dom, there's only one person who can help me. "Dani."

Luz stares at me for a beat, then slowly nods. After a glance to Dom, she moves away and pulls out a cellphone.

Daniela

Lucas gets out of the car first, and I follow. My steps are hesitant, not knowing if the dragon's about to blow fire at us, or what. We get a bit closer, and he shifts. After the burgundy haze is gone, Tytus is facing us, his expression stormy. The smell of sulfur and cinnamon still fills the air.

"Is there a particular reason that pack is still alive?" he growls.

I stop dead in my tracks, feeling his anger directed at me. "I..."

"You were supposed to eradicate them," he spits, moving closer. "What possessed you not to?"

"*Eradicate* them?" I choke. "Since when? You were teaching me how to use my magic! Not once did you say what it was for."

"I didn't think I had to." His reply roots me to the ground, and I turn to my alpha in shock.

Lucas side-steps him, blocking his way before Tytus can reach me. Which is just as well, because he appears ready to throttle me.

"Easy, amico." Lucas lifts a palm in a peaceful gesture. There's nothing calm about him, rather his body is tense as hell. "I don't believe we've had the pleasure of being introduced."

Tytus clenches his teeth and moves his gaze off me. "I'm the zmeu owning your city, alpha boy. Now move out of my way."

Lucas snorts. "I think not."

Before my stunned eyes, Tytus seems to grow in size. His shoulders widen, his expression darkens. I don't know if it's a trick of the mind or the real thing, but he's definitely *changing*.

Lucas still doesn't move. So I do, stepping closer and putting a hand on his shoulder. "Hang on, I want to hear what he has to say."

Then I turn my gaze to Tytus. "Not that I have to explain myself to you, but Thiago is still my family, and last of my line aside from our father. I can't be the one to wipe that."

Tytus' eyes flicker with anger. "Then I have misjudged you, and you have wasted my time. Those lobisomens need a firm hand – a ruler – to bring them back in the fold of a Luna. You are neither."

Though his words sting, I don't bend under their weight. I've heard worse before. Instead, I raise my chin. "Maybe, but at least I'm not a coward."

Tytus takes another step, getting up in my face. "What did you just call me?"

"You heard me. Or was there a legitimate reason you took off rather than eradicate them yourself?"

His stormy eyes glow like embers. "Watch yourself, little wolf. You're close to crossing the line."

"That line was crossed when you presumed I'd wipe out the rest of my family for you! I'm no one's bitch, so if you want them dead, you'll have to do it yourself."

He scowls. "Apparently so, since I wasn't even able to find the one thing I was there for."

"And what exactly was that, amico?" Lucas asks.

I'm curious of the answer, and something nags at the back of my mind. I may have an idea of what he's looking for, but why, is another question altogether.

Tytus growls at Lucas. "It matters not. It was not there." Then his stormy eyes land on mine again. "You will have to make harder decisions before this is over, little wolf. Might as well be ready."

Then he takes off in a puff of smoke, leaving no trace behind. I'm left staring at the sky, wondering about his words. Then Lucas' cellphone rings. He picks up the call, listens for a second, and his eyes shift to me.

My stomach plummets and I taste bile. "What is it?"

He nods into the phone, and says, "On our way." Once he hangs up, Lucas heads back to the car, gesturing for me to hurry up. "It's Tristan."

Tristan

Finn walks into the shop, still restraining me. Dom and Luz follow behind, looking around. But there's no Dani to be found. I'm calmer now, but can I really be sure I won't lose it again?

Never.

So I don't strain against my friend's grip, nor try to engage them in a conversation. Instead, I retreat deep within myself. Trying to focus on what Dani taught me. *What was it again? Five things to see, four to touch, three to...hear, two to smell, and one emotion.*

Emotion. *Huh.* I have hell more than one running through me. And none of them are good. I close my eyes in an attempt to break through. And I do...just not in the way I want. The shop fades out of my vision, replaced by blackness.

Next thing I know, Finn's grip is tightening on me and he's yelling in my ear. "Cut it out, Tristan!"

My eyes snap open, and I look around. Luz and Dom are staring at us – at me. I glance down and see my hands have turned to claws, and they're bloody. I've ripped through my shirt, cut through skin. Finn's gripping my elbows, but his hold isn't strong enough to keep me safe.

"What the hell?" My whisper goes unanswered.

The door to the shop opens, and Lucas walks in, followed by Dani. My eyes drink her in as if I haven't seen her in days. So many words are on the tip of my tongue, but they stay there. Her presence soothes me and I relax in Finn's arms, and my wolf does, too. My claws retract, my hands go back to human.

Finn feels it, but keeps his grip strong on me. Then Dani moves closer, taking us in. "What happened?"

Her question could have been for anyone, but it's Luz who answers. "Tristan had an...episode. I think it was triggered by a nightmare. He wanted to see you."

"It was a bit more than that, by the looks of it," Lucas says. His eyes are narrowed on us. "I warned you about holding your wolf back, Tristan."

I look away, unable to hold his gaze. This is what I had feared. I don't want his disappointment.

Then his feet come in my field of vision and he touches my shoulder. "I'm worried for you, amico. With what you have seen, you're more sensitive in ways that even Finn is not. We are more than friends, we're family. All here if you need us. But I know it's another you need right now."

He steps to the side, and Dani inches closer instead. She looks over my shoulder at Finn. "You can let him go. I'll take him home."

"You sure?" This comes from Dom, who's frowning and rubbing his neck. "He has quite a grip when he's mad."

"Yeah," Dani smiles. "Tristan won't hurt me." Then she finally meets my gaze, and her expression softens. She holds out her hand, and Finn releases me. "Come on."

∞ ♦ ∞

Once we walk into my apartment, Dani settles us on the couch and sits opposite me. Her hair's fallen out of its ponytail, framing her face.

And I suddenly can't keep the words in any longer. "Meu anjo, I'm so sorry."

She shakes her head. "You were hurt, and you had every reason to. I should have been honest from the beginning, or at the very least once you found out about Izzy. But..." She looks away. "I was afraid you'd hate what I've become, and then it just seemed easier to hold it in."

I reach out for her hand, and she doesn't pull away. "Nothing about you repels me, Dani. It never could."

"Then why did you take off like that? And to Bow's Arrow, to boot?"

It's my turn to be silent. Her amber eyes are waiting for an answer, and the only thing I can give her is the truth. "I went there...for closure, in a way. After seeing what you could do, I was mad, yes. At you for lying, despite having so many chances to tell me the truth. Before I knew it, I was there, and thinking of Izzy."

She takes a shuddering breath, closing her eyes. I grab her hand in mine, squeezing it. "It's not what you think, querida. I went there for closure, but I stayed because I wanted to keep my promise to you." When she looks at me in confusion, I reach for her shoulder, and the mark hidden under her jacket. "I swore to you that once you have protection of my pack, I would hunt down Thiago and make him pay."

Her bottom lip trembles, and I drop my hold on her shoulder. "Granted, it didn't quite work out as it should have. Izzy came to me. I must have passed out, because it felt like a dream, but it wasn't one. She said she's happy for us, and that you were always meant to be the mate for me."

My free hand rises to cup her cheek, and my thumb traces her bottom lip. "I knew that. I've known that since the first night you slept here. Lucas is right, I've been keeping my wolf at bay. Afraid to let him loose, to become a monster like those creatures I've seen. But you... quiet him. Always have, Dani. You're everything for me, for *us*. And if you'll have me, I'd like to be your everything, too."

Tears shine in her eyes when she meets my earnest gaze. There is much more to say, to be heard, to air out. But I don't care. Because when my lips meet hers, it's heaven on earth. And I'm finally, *finally* where I belong.

Then Dani's in my lap, kissing me. Her hands trace down my abdomen, and I hiss in pain. She glances down, at the still open wounds on my stomach. With a secret smile, she kneels before me and removes the tatters of my shirt.

Her lips touch my skin with butterfly kisses, and a groan escapes me. I have to dig my hands into the sofa so I don't move. Then Dani's tongue snakes out, licking each wound from beginning to end. By the time she's done, I'm panting, and I've ripped through the cushions. My cuts have healed.

Dani grins at me from her spot, and I lose it. My arms move to her waist, and I lift her up in one movement, groaning when her heat connects to my painful hard-on. Lips to her neck, I pull her closer.

Clothes are an obstacle and they're removed quickly, impatiently. This time, when we come together, there's no doubt, no other feelings. Only love.

It shines in Dani's eyes as she watches me slide inside her. It's in my every touch as I worship her body until she begs for more. And finally, it's there when our gazes lock, and we drop the last of the barriers.

Our minds, separate before, merge into one. Our wolves purr, and pure, unconditional love vibrates between us. I grip her tighter, she claws me deeper... That last climax is more than either of our bodies can withstand, and we black out.

Later, I wait until she stirs against me, her breathing evening out. My hand traces circles on her back, and she presses tighter. We ended up in my bed at some point, and I relish the comfort of the sheets, but only because Dani's there with me.

Thoughts race in my head, refusing to allow me sleep. In the end, I know there's no other option than to let them out, airing the remaining shadows between us.

"Will you tell me, now?" It comes out as a whisper, but still not subtle enough. "Everything that's still left unsaid. From the beginning."

Dani freezes against me, and I can feel her shutting down before I even tighten my grip around her. She tries to move off me, but I shift in bed, pinning her with my leg over hers, my body over hers.

She lets out a breath that sounds like a sob against my shoulder, and I sigh. Mouth on her temple, I shush her. "Breathe, querida. I'm not mad, but I need to know."

Dani pulls back then, her eyes filled with shadows. "Does it really matter?"

I know what she's asking. It's right there in the amber gaze that had me from the beginning.

Does Izabella still matter?

My knuckles graze her cheek and I bend over for a kiss. "Yes, but not for the reasons you think. It matters because it's hurting you and I need to take that burden off you. Thiago talked – a lot. I know most of it. But I need to hear it from your lips, meu anjo."

She's still tense, like a bow ready to snap. Then my breathing syncs with hers, and that connection – our wolves – snaps into place. Dani sinks into the bed, closing her eyes – and then the waterworks start. Between sobs, she chokes out one thing, and it freezes the blood in my veins.

"I'm dying, Tristan."

∞ ∞ ∞

∞ Decisão ∞

"A good <u>decision</u> is based on knowledge and not on numbers."

-Plato-

Tristan

"What do you mean?" I try to quiet the panic in my heart, but it's thudding a mile a minute. Dani's too much of a mess to say anything.

Each moment she's sobbing makes it harder and harder to see past the despair. I can't lose her now. Not after everything. I've never been the type of guy to believe in forever but she makes me want to. *Fuck.*

The last thing I want to do is push her, but I need to hear the rest of it. Finally, long moments later, she quiets down enough to speak and raises a tear-stained face towards me.

"Tytus warned me," she whispers.

"Warned...." I frown, trying to control my thoughts wanting to jump on that. I'd never gotten the scent of the zmeu out of my mind.

Dani notices my distraction. "What is it?"

"Nothing, just.... Remember when I first saw you use magic?" She nods, and I continue, "I accused you of having the zmeu's scent on you."

Dani thinks about it for a second, then her expression clears. "The handkerchief."

"What?"

"Earlier that day, I'd run into Tytus in the forest. Only, our first convo didn't go exactly to plan. He got mad and spelled me to forget everything. Including the fact I had his damn handkerchief, because I'd been crying."

"That son of a...." A few dozen ways of making him pay run through my head, each more tempting than the last.

Dani intertwines our fingers, guessing at my thoughts. "I don't think aggravating a dragon is a good idea."

"Probably right."

"Plus, it's old news now. Well, sorta."

"What do you mean?"

Dani sighs, then pushes me to my back. She scrambles on top of me, placing one hand on my chest to hold herself up. I'm acutely aware of the bed sheet's thin material separating us.

"Okay, when Lucas was bringing me back, we ran into Tytus. Here's the thing. We wouldn't have known you were taken if not for him. So in exchange for his help, I agreed he could take whatever it was he's after."

"And what's that?"

Dani shrugs. "No idea. But it has to do with my family, or at least my town. Either way, he held his word…. sorta. Once I got to you, he disappeared. We could've been attacked or captured and he wasn't around. So I told him off. Tytus didn't like that."

My hand moves to her hip, squeezing it to ground us both. "Which brings us to…."

"Tytus won't be joining further fights. If he can't get what he wants, then we're done."

Her words sound like a death sentence, yet relief spreads through me. Dani notices it, or perhaps feels it through our bond, and tilts her head to the side. "What is it?"

"I was just thinking it's just as well, because he seems to really put Finn on edge."

"And Lucas."

I snort. "Everything puts Lucas on edge these days." Shaking off thoughts of my alpha, I go back to the original topic at hand. "So what did Tytus warn you about?"

Dani's expression grows wary again. "The magic in me, I've been repressing it for months. It'll combust if I don't use it."

A small measure of relief rolls through me. "So there's hope?"

Dani looks at me, biting her lip. New tears emerge, raining down her cheeks. I pull her against me, unable to hide my joy. "Merda, Dani, you scared the hell out of me!"

"You don't get it," she tries to temper my happiness. "To survive, I have to use magic, Tristan. Always."

"So what?" I shrug, tucking a strand of messy hair behind her ear.

Her amber eyes are wary. "That means you haven't mated with a wolf, Tristan. But with a witch."

A laugh bubbles out of me, but she doesn't seem to appreciate it. I try to rein it in. "And you think that makes a difference to me?"

"It should," she scowls.

"Well, it doesn't." I take a deep breath. "I love you, Daniela Da Silva. On some level, I think I always have, but was too blinded by other things to realize it." My forehead rests against hers, and she closes her eyes. "I'll be here, no matter what. If you can accept my faults and all the baggage I come with, there's no reason I can't accept some magic."

My hands tighten against her waist, and I bury my head in her neck. "I just can't lose *you*."

Before she can think of something to say and ruin this, I bite her neck, then soothe the sting with my tongue. Dani moans, arching against me and tilting her head to give me better access. Then I'm moving the blanket off her shoulders, and reveling in her nakedness once more.

Lips trace skin, hands move against body, and I'm inside her again, groaning my release to the heavens.

Daniela

I'm deep in a dream when the ring of my cell wakes me up. Tristan rolls over, pinning me under him. There's enough free movement left to grab the damned thing and answer. "Yeah?"

"Had a good fuck, irmãzinha?"

The last cobwebs of sleep evaporate at the sound of his voice, a shiver running through me. "Thiago." Then his words register, and I slide out of bed, hastily pulling on clothes. "What the hell do you want?"

"Meet me at the edge of your town. Dad wants to talk to you."

Then he hangs up, and I'm left standing in the middle of the bedroom, staring at my cellphone. As if sensing my agitation, Tristan sits up in bed, rubbing his face. "What is it, meu anjo?"

I want to smile at his calling me an angel, but I can't. Instead, I'm trembling, wondering what I should do. Tristan picks up on this and moves off the bed.

"Dani?"

I finally look at him, unable to get the lie past my lips. Instead, the truth comes out. "Thiago just called. Wants to meet me outside town."

His eyes flash in the night. "You can't be thinking of going."

"I wouldn't," I whisper. "Except he says our father wants to talk to me."

"Could be a trap."

"I know." Chewing my lip doesn't ease my anxiety, so I move to my thumb nail. Tristan reaches out for my hand, stopping me mid-way.

"I'll come."

A new type of panic arises in me. I remember seeing him all cut into, weak, and can't deal with that again. "You can't!"

"Relax, meu amore. They won't see me."

I frown at his assured tone. "How do you mean?"

"You're going to cloak me."

My jaw drops. "Tristan, I've barely started using this magic. I don't... I can't even... I don't know if it's possible."

He thinks for a bit, then says, "But there is someone who would know?"

I bite my lip, this time hard enough to draw blood. "Tytus."

"Then we go see him."

As if it's the easiest thing, Tristan lets go of me and pulls on a pair of boxers and sweatpants. My wolf is too busy drooling at his abs, and my reaction is a bit delayed.

"Did you forget everything I just told you?"

Tristan grins my way. "I didn't. But I fully intend to make him listen."

Tristan pulls up in front of a beat-down bar. I exit the car, staring at the half-on neon sign. "What is this place?"

He shrugs. "Dom told me this is where Luz found him." At my curious gaze, he sighs. "Before you got here, Dom got kicked out of the pack because he kept crossing paths with Lucas. When he did, he ended up here – as a way to bury himself into booze and forget. Luz found him."

"And what does this have to do with Tytus?"

Tristan makes a face. "He's the one who brought Luz here, and seemed to know the place. So I'm thinking, we may find him here." He sniffs the air. "Plus, his scent's all over the place."

He grabs my hand in his, holding it tight. "Just stick around me, will you?"

I nod and we head in. It takes a few moments, but in a dark corner I spot him. Tytus is leaning against a wall, nursing a dark of amber liquid and surveying the crowd. His eyes flash when they land on us. Any hesitations disappear and I hurry over, dragging Tristan after me.

"Little wolf."

"Hey." I shift on the balls of my feet, meeting his gaze and looking away.

After a dead beat, Tytus asks in a bored voice, "What brings you here?"

"A question about magic."

He looks away, disinterested. "I've taught you all I want to."

"But you haven't. Please. My brother's at the edge of town, and I need to know if it's possible to use this *magia* to cloak someone."

Tytus keeps avoiding my gaze, then finally looks at me. "It is possible, yes." A pause, then, "But you cannot do it."

"Why not?"

He sighs, pinching the bridge of his nose. "Because you refuse to listen to the *magic*."

"That's changed," Tristan butts in. "She'll listen now, I swear it." When I glare at him, he shrugs. "Sorry, meu amor. But I'm not about to let you die."

A spark of interest enters Tytus' eyes. His eyes dart between us. "Is the wolf correct? You're ready to listen?"

At a loss, I nod. There's more than just me to think of now, and I owe it to Tristan to try.

Satisfied with my answer, Tytys pushes off the wall. "Very well. Watch me."

I look around, keenly aware of all the humans, some only a few feet away. "Here?"

He shrugs. "What better spot?" Then he motions to his hand, and my eyes fall on it. He moves his thumb to the center of his palm, rubbing it in a triangle pattern.

Tytus does it once, twice, three times. The third time, a thin line of smoke appears, and he lets out a hiss. "It will hurt, I should mention. If you're doing it in front of someone, you need to keep your expression neutral."

Then the smoke lifts in a wisp, and surrounds Tristan. Before my very eyes, he blurs, then disappears. I can still smell him, though. When I point that out to Tytus, he smirks and rubs more around his palm. Another jet of smoke appears, and this time Tristan is truly gone.

I gulp. "And to bring him back?"

Rather than show me, Tytus leans back against the wall. "A price, first."

"Are you serious right now?" I glare at him. "Or else, what, you won't give me my boyfriend back?"

"I'm still here, Dani," Tristan whispers so close to me, I jump.

"And I can't see you!" My shout is a bit too loud, and a couple nearby turns to me. Blushing, I glance away, and turn my glare back to Tytus. This time, I whisper. "What's your price?"

"While I do not understand your misplaced loyalty to your family, I can understand some of your hesitation in killing them. Even if it won't do you any good, in the end."

I open my mouth to retort, but Tytus lifts his hand in a gesture to shut me up. "Don't argue with me, little wolf. So this is my price. If anything happens to your father when you see him tonight, grab the pendant around his neck and bring it to me."

"How did you know–"

"Nothing happens in this town without me being aware of it," Tytus cuts me off. His tone leaves no room for contesting or asking questions. "Now, swear it."

"Not until you tell me what it's for!"

Tytus's eyes narrow to thin slits. "You've already made me lose out on one prized possession. I will not forfeit the second. This is nonnegotiable." He pushes off the wall as if to leave, and I break. Not seeing Tristan is too much.

"Wait! Fine, I swear it. The pendant will be yours. *Now* can you bring Tristan back?"

Tytus doesn't answer. Instead, he lifts the opposite hand, and a waft of air breathes over Tristan. Next thing I know, he's standing next to me once more, fully visible. Relief spreads through me, and I hug him tight.

By the time we pull apart, Tytus is gone.

"Let's go to Thiago," Tristan whispers. His faith in me gives me wings, almost making me believe I can do this. Almost.

As we drive away from the bar, I'm left wondering what the hell I'm going to find in the darkness of the woods.

Tristan

We're near the edge of town, so I pull the car over and park it under a tree. We step back out, and I kiss Dani swiftly, lingering a little longer. When I pull back, she clings to me, her eyes wide and wary.

"You can do this, meu anjo. Thiago may be psychotic, but you're way smarter and quicker. Just don't let him get into your head."

She closes her eyes, her grip tightening on my shoulders for a second, then nods. "Let's do this."

Stepping back, Dani follows Tytus' instructions. The first set of smoke envelops me, and my hands and feet disappear. Then the second does the same, and it feels like I'm wrapped in a very warm blanket.

I can still see everything around me, but it's like I'm peering through a waterfall. "Can you smell me?"

Dani turns her nose in the air, walks around where she'd last seen me, then shakes her head. "Nothing. Let's hope my brother won't, either." She starts heading off the beaten path, and I follow.

"I'll be right behind you," I say.

It's not long before we cross the border, the last of Lucas' territory, and end up in complete wilderness. It's a dark moon night – no moon, for the humans. Which means we're surrounded by pitch darkness. But there's another layer to it that could work in Thiago's favor.

As if thinking of him conjured him, the devil steps out of the darkness. Behind him, two of the guards from before help carry an elder man. It takes me a minute to recognize him as Dani's dad, and she seems just as shocked.

Cristovao Da Silva used to be a proud man, with the body of a Roman warrior. Now he's bent over, looking a hundred years old instead of his sixty. His face is saggy, cheeks hollow, eyes staring blankly – blind. If the wind picks up, I'm afraid it might carry him away.

Dani's whirling emotions drag my attention away from him. She takes a step closer to Thiago, clenching her fist. "What the hell did you to do him?"

He snorts, sparing their father a glance. "Nothing. But the fool refused to use magic after Izzy went and killed herself. This is the result."

Dani shudders, but doesn't back down. Her gaze is locked on Cristovao's feeble form. Then Thiago delivers his ultimatum. "Come home with me, little sister. Or our father dies here, tonight."

A gasp escapes her, and I know why. A death on a night like this for her pack, for a lobisomem, means never finding their resting place in the afterlife.

Shit.

"You wouldn't," Dani whispers.

Thiago holds her gaze for a moment, then turns to his acolytes and nods. They push Cristovao to his knees, and one pulls a hunting knife with a jagged edge from his coat. He sets it at the old man's throat.

Cristovao does nothing, only stares out with unseeing eyes.

Dani, on the other hand, takes another step closer to them. "Stop it, Thiago!" she cries, and it takes all my strength not to rush to hold her. "You can't do this to dad!"

"Come home, then." I know the sadistic look in his eyes, and I'm not about to let Dani bear the brunt of this decision.

As she sways, eyes narrowed and trying to decide, the knife digs into Cristovao's neck. A trickle of blood comes out, causing a sob to rise out of Dani. I want nothing more than to wrap my arms around her, take her away from this shit.

The blood, though... Its scent lingers in the air, and all I can focus on is the burgundy liquid staining his shirt. My vision narrows, the ground shifts under me. *Fuck it, not now!*

It doesn't matter. No matter how I try to struggle against it, my breathing picks up.

The snow under my hands and knees turns to grass. The biting air is warmer – but filled with charred flesh.

I raise my eyes and see not Thiago, not Cristovao, but a pile of humans. Each mauled, organs out. Their intestines are on the ground, on their bodies, everywhere. Bile rises in my throat. The vrykolakas did this, in the mountains...

A growl starts, and one of the yellow-eyed monsters walks around the pile. His jaw is opened wide, his rotting scent wafting to my nose. It's putrid, and I want to move, but I'm frozen to the ground.

I've never seen a creature like this, or such carnage. And its yellow eyes, tinged with red, are fixed on me.

My wolf rebels against the memory, and its claws dig into snow. I'm half in the memory, half in the reality. Half-human, half shifted into my lobisomem form. Vaguely, I'm aware Dani is pleading with Thiago, her cries wrenching at my heart.

Let me out. My wolf demands, it doesn't ask. *Protect your mate.*

Lucas' words ring in my ears. My hands become paws, but still I struggle. If I let him out, if I let him fully loose, without control, who's to say I'll be able to hold on to sanity?

You are me. I am you. We are one. Stop fighting it.

With one last shudder, I give in, letting the change course through me. And for the first time, it doesn't hurt. It's smooth, like swimming through a cold lake. And when I'm on the other side, fully wolf, I'm still me.

Told you.

I let me my wolf take over, and move stealthily towards the two lobisomens holding Cristovao. Then I pounce on one, ripping his head off. My wolf relishes the blood, the surprise. The other man turns to me, eyes wide as he finds nothing to attack. The knife is in his hand, and I lunge at it.

Tearing his hand from the rest of his body, I spit it out and he collapses on his knees. Jets of blood spurt out of the wound, staining the snow. Dani's eyes are on us, as are Thiago's.

"So, you learned tricks, have you?" There's nothing good about his tone, and I see the rune he draws with one hand behind his back.

Dani!

The blast hits her full front, and she goes slamming into a tree. Then Thiago turns in my general direction, blasting air towards me. The waterfall around me ripples, then is gone, and I know I'm visible once more.

"Should've known she brought her boy toy to this meet." He lifts his hand to presumably blast more magic at me, but all hell breaks loose.

Wolves emerge – from everywhere. There must be twenty or so of them, and I recognize their scent. *Reapers.* This is no welcoming committee, that's for sure.

At their front, Jared steps up. He's in human form, eyes narrowed on Thiago. "What are you doing on our territory?"

Thiago smirks. He whistles once, and the rest of his lobisomens emerge to fight. As they move, his wolves shift their forms, some growing larger, others smaller for agility. Then we're left staring at two lines of predators, each ready to attack the other.

My eyes land on Dani, apart from them. At the base of the tree, she groans, shaking her head and slowly crawling on her knees. Then she raises her eyes and they widen when they fall on the scene.

The moment after, Thiago lifts his hands. A jet of magic escapes them, blasting through half the Reapers. Jared yells something to his men, then morphs and attacks.

Dani!

∞ ∞ ∞

∞ Família ∞

**"Without a <u>family</u>, man, alone in the world, trembles
with the cold."**

-André Maurois-

Daniela

Shit.

Well, this got out of control pretty damn fast. My head is still
ringing, but I manage to crawl to the bushes, where Tristan's
dragged my dad over. Or what's left of him.

The change automatically gave me back clothes, but Tristan's
naked now. Since I figure he may need to shift again, I don't
worry about it. So we kneel next to my dad, but Tristan's eyes
keep darting around, keeping an eye on the situation.

My brother's insane taking on this entire pack. And trying to
kill our dying father. *What the freaking hell is going on?*

My eyes fall to the pendant around my dad's neck. Tytus said he wants it, and I know I promised it. But he's not dead yet, and I can't make myself do it. Even if it means attracting the ire of the dragon again.

"Izabella?"

My father's raspy voice draws my attention. I reach out for his feeble hand, holding it into both of mine. "No, it's Daniela, pai."

His smile is weak at my use of his nickname – daddy – and his grip trembles in mine. "Why did you leave, minha filha?"

It's been a long time since he's called me his daughter. Even before I left, Thiago kept him apart, not allowing me to see him. Especially after Izzy died.

"Where's Thiago? He'll be happy to see you."

I gulp past the lump in my throat. "No, he won't. He hurt me, pai. A lot."

"Nonsense," he whispers, squeezing my hand. "He's family. He wouldn't hurt you, or Izabella."

The tears stream down my cheeks now, silent. "Dad, Thiago's a monster. He kept you imprisoned so you wouldn't see what he did. How he took the witch, forced her into his slavery and treated all the women of the pack like cattle."

Tristan's gaze meets mine, and his expression softens. He brings his hand to his heart, touching it twice, and I get his meaning. It's spiritual support he's offering, while knowing I need to do this on my own. He says nothing out loud, instead keeping guard. My heart swells for his understanding, and it takes a moment to focus back on the painful task at hand.

"Forgive him. He knows not what he does."

I stare at my father in shock, then shake my head. "Really? He doesn't?" I pull the shirt off my shoulder, then force his hand to meet my skin, touching the mark. "Do you feel it, pai? *This* is what your precious son did to me. And Izabella. He held an auction – an *auction*! – to sell us to the highest bidder in the pack. Is it such a wonder Izzy tried to run off, and ended up killing herself in the process?"

My father's breathing is raspy, and he's shaking his head. "No, Thiago wouldn't…"

Tears rise to my eyes but this time I don't let them fall. "You always defended him, pai. But he's past reason now. I cannot allow him to continue."

My father frowns, and I let go of his hand. "I love you," I whisper, kissing his cheek.

Then I take a step pack, fixing my t-shirt. Tristan stands from his crouch. "It's a blood bath out there, Dani. Thiago's lobisomens have the advantage over the Reapers. We should get out of here."

I peek past the bushes, seeing exactly what he described. My brother's wolf form stands out in middle, and I know I can't leave. He's the size of a grizzly bear, sandy-colored like me. But worst of all, his claws seem to still shoot out magic.

"Thiago can use *magia* as a wolf," I whisper.

Tristan moves by my side, trying to see what I mean. His eyes narrow on something further in the distance. "And it looks like Jared's getting ready to attack him."

I glance back to my dad, and sigh. "I can't leave here, Tristan. Thiago needs to be stopped, and there's no one but me to do it."

Cries of ravens interrupt me, and we both look up. A swarm of the birds moves over the wolves. They seem suspended in mid-air, as if awaiting a signal. Thiago howls – once – and they fall on the Reapers like carnivorous birds.

Their beaks attack their eyes, their claws dig into their backs. Whines and howls of pain echo around us, and I move through the bushes. Tristan grabs my hand.

"Dani..."

"I know they're not your friends. But I can't let Thiago decimate them like this."

His expression softens. "I know. That's why I called for help."

As if on cue, a car pulls up in the distance and I smell our pack. To my side, I sense a shift, and I turn back to find my mate in wolf form. "You called them?"

He nods, and I shake my head. "Damn, Tristan! They'll only get hurt!"

His glare tells me different, but I'm scared for them. Lucas, Dom and Finn move past the trees, and take the scene in stride. Lucas meets my gaze across the distance, and nods. Then he shifts, launching himself in their midst. He seems to be heading towards Jared – to coordinate attacks, I'm guessing.

Tristan throws me one last look, whines, then takes off, joining Dom and Finn in the fray. I glance behind at my dad one more time. There's no way I can babysit him and help everyone. So I walk away, but don't shift.

Tytus' words echo in my mind. *There is a time to choose witch, and a time to choose wolf.* Tonight, it's the former for me.

So I keep myself to the edge of the clearing, eyeing Thiago. Tytus didn't get a chance to teach me everything, but the few tricks he did, I can use in my favor. I etch the rune in my palm, cringing at the pain. Then smoke envelops me, and the battlefield before me looks like it's behind a waterfall.

A croak to the side draws my attention. It's a raven, head tilted to the side and looking straight at me. I frown. "You can see me?"

The raven keeps staring, not joining the fray. I remember all the times I've feared these creatures. The countless nights they've kept me awake. And how Thiago's using them. What if there's a way for me to do the same? *And if there is, how do I go about it?*

A piece of the puzzle floats in my mind, and realization dawns on me. *By spying on Thiago, that's how!*

So I let my hand turn into a claw, just in case I need to protect myself, and move closer. My intent is on my brother, determined to see what his trick is. He's too busy tearing into Reapers to pay attention, so it's easy for me to observe him.

Then I remember how our pack used to be tied together. Once he took over, those ties eroded and we couldn't talk amongst ourselves once in wolf form. Which explains the disorganized way in which his people are fighting.

Maybe I can still breach it. I focus on the back of his head, trying to think like him. The thrill of the kill, the sadistic enjoyment of taking a life. Turns out, it's not hard when you're in the middle of a battle.

I reach out with my mind, and then I'm in Thiago's. Only, it feels alien, lonely...empty. At least until I hear a command. *Atáca-los! Don't you freaking stop attacking them!*

Could it really be as simple as a Portuguese command of *attack*?

Before I can dig further, Thiago looks around, and his gaze seems to burn right through me. *Shit.* I turn tail and run back to my dad. As I pass a few lobisomens, I notice Finn fighting one, while another of Thiago's men is drawing closer to his back. Before he can attack from behind, I let my claws sink into his back, digging deep and tearing into him.

He howls, moving away, swatting at empty air. Taking advantage of my invisibility, I help out right and left as I retreat. By the time I'm back to my original spot, I realize Thiago's nowhere to be seen.

"Daddy!" *Merda!* I run past the bushes, only to find my old man still on the ground. Removing my invisibility, I kneel by his side, but he's still breathing.

Then the voice behind me freezes me. "Well now, dear sister, what is your answer?"

I get up from my father's side, facing Thiago. He's filled with blood, naked and looking more ghoulish than I'd care to admit.

"I'm not going anywhere with you."

He snorts. "Should've known." Thiago's hand starts glowing blood-red and he aims it towards me. I really wish I'd stuck with Tytus to learn more, but as it is, I'll have to take my chances.

I throw out my consciousness and yell, *Atáca-lo!*

Nothing happens at first. Then two things take place, almost in slow motion. First, Tristan jumps over the bushes, placing himself right in front of me. Then, three ravens circle above our heads. They look between me and Thiago, and I yell again, *Atáca-lo!*

Tristan makes a move to lunge, but Thiago blasts him into a tree. I focus back on the ravens, pushing my conscience towards them. They rise in mid-air, their moonshine eyes focused on me. At my nod, the ravens descend on my brother with a vengeance, picking at his skin. They're me, I'm them. We're one conscience, pushing through.

And while Thiago's busy trying to regain control and swatting them away, I focus on Tristan.

He's shaking his head, getting up and shifting his form to a larger one. Thiago's managed to get rid of two ravens, and he snaps the neck of the third. Then he narrows his eyes on us, hand raised. I see the blast and jump in front of it, taking the brunt as it sends me flying into a tree's embrace.

"Tsk, irmãzinha, don't be stupid." He rolls his shoulders and cracks his neck, then those cold eyes settle on me. "I need you in one piece, so you can mate with me."

For a second, I think I misheard with the ringing in my ears. "You....what?"

Then Tristan snarls, baring his teeth, and I know I haven't. His anger pulsates in the air and he lunges at Thiago. As they grapple in front of me, I stare in shock. Blood pounds in my ears, and my palms have become sweaty.

In a daze, I crawl over to my father. My throat is dry, the words hard to formulate. But I owe it to myself, to Izzy, to know the truth.

"Pai, is this true? Is this why Izabella ran away? It's *Thiago*, the darkness we're supposed to mate?"

Blind eyes seek my voice, and a feeble hand lifts, searching mine. He smiles the same way he used to when I was a young kid, and he'd tuck me into bed and read me stories. Only this time, his words cut what's left of my innocent belief in family. "The pack...must prevail. It was the only way."

I look at the man I used to admire, whose love for my mother I hoped to achieve in my own mate. And I shake my head, wiping at the tears.

Then someone grabs my hair, pulling me to my feet.

"I've tried to be nice," Thiago hisses in my ear. "But enough is enough. You're coming home – *now*."

"No, I'm not." I let what I've been fighting rise out of me. The magic tingles on my skin, vibrating underneath and over it. The ravens cry, stopping their attack and staring at me.

Thiago lets go of me as if burned. When I turn to face him, my expression is blank, and a burgundy glow surrounds my hands. "I'm not going to let you bully me like you did Izzy. Her death is on your hands – both of you."

Thiago snorts. "Well, since I have no use for the old man." He makes a slashing motion with his hand and a ray of burgundy goes for my father's neck. Then blood seeps out, and his eyes close forever.

I wish I could say I feel something in that moment. Sadness, despair, anything. But I don't. I'm too angry at what they've done, tearing our family apart, to feel sorry for being an orphan.

"Do you honestly think our mother would have approved?" I try to reason with him, knowing it's useless.

Thiago confirms as much with his shrug. "Do I care? She only ever had time for you two. The precious *princesas* of the pack."

His tone is scathing, and it's in that moment I realize this wasn't just some act of craziness. My brother planned this – the whole thing. From beginning...to now.

"Must have taken you years to come up with this," I whisper. *Is this the sibling I grew up with, the one I taught to read and play catch?*

Thiago's eyes glint in appreciation. "Hell, yes. But it's all been worth it." He takes a step closer. "And you won't stop me."

I clench my fists, standing my ground. Magic, I may not fully be versed in. But it looks like this is going to become a wolf fight.

Before Thiago can reach me, his eyes flicker over my shoulder and widen. Whatever he sees, it's enough to make him go pale. Then he's stepping back, smoke arises from his palm, and he's gone in a puff of smoke.

I whirl, trying to see what spooked him, and notice only my fellow pack members trying to help out the Reapers. Before I can help out, there's something else I have to do. As stealthily as I can, I move to my father, and reach inside his shirt for the pendant Tytus wants. With one snap of my wrist, it comes undone, and I pocket it.

Then I look around, trying to locate everyone. Finn and Dom are grappling with some ravens, trying to free Jared. Lucas is fighting two lobisomens by himself. My feet step closer, intending to go to his aid, until Tristan's voice echoes in my head. *Dani, stay back!*

He's grappling with a wolf of his own.

Then the woods gape open and more wolves come out. They're Reapers, and I've never seen so many in one spot. Their numbers are intimidating, and I finally start to hope. Maybe we can finally outnumber Thiago's pack, despite their ability to change their forms.

Only, nothing works as we hope. Rather than attack the ravens, the new Reapers jump on their own members. The realization is slow to dawn on me, but it's inevitable. This is a coup, and there's no way in hell I'm letting my friends fight this alone.

My hand clenches then morphs into a paw, and I hear the ravens' cry behind and above me. Their consciousness surrounds me like a blanket. A look to the sky confirms they're there – waiting. With Thiago gone, they only need a little prod in the right direction.

A second wave of bloodthirsty Reapers comes out of the woods, and Lucas moves forward. Dom and Finn are by his side, Tristan ahead of me, protecting me. We hadn't expected this – any of us.

And I'm not about to let my new pack go without backup. *Atáca-los!* The ravens descend on the new Reapers, and continue their attack on the remaining lobisomens who are loyal to Thiago.

A shudder runs through me and then I'm wolf, scenting, feeling. Everything hits me at once, but one scent above all raises my hackles.

Tristan, watch out!

The dark wolf pouncing out from behind is too fast, and I recognize Cade. He and Tristan roll on the ground, pawing and trying to get a bite in on each other's throats.

I want to throw myself in the mix, but one voice thunders over them – *Enough!*

Everyone looks in surprise to the new wolf entering the premises. The Reapers stand back slightly to let him pass. It's the wolf Lucas went to earlier, the Reapers' leader – Jared.

He overlooks his pack, then ours. *I need a minute.*

Lucas gets the message and motions for us to slowly step backwards. But as the distance between us and the Reapers increases, I can't help looking back at them. Something's wrong. And sure enough, I'm about to be proven right.

While Jared is pacing in front of the other wolves, snarling and evidently lecturing them, one particular wolf steps out of line. His dark fur had just been intertwined with my mate's, and the murdering intent in his eyes is still evident.

None of us have time to yell out a warning. And none of the Reapers do, either. Before our stunned gazes, Cade lunges at Jared, and they roll in the snow. Cade ends up on top, and lifts his paw, claws extended. One swat towards Jared's throat, and it's ripped to pieces, gaping open. Cade digs into it, his growls echoing in the silent night.

With bloody jaws, Cade then moves back in front of the pack, and throws his head back. A hair-rising howl escapes him, echoing all around. There's a stupefied silence, then one by one, the wolves howl in sync with him.

The Reapers just got a new alpha.

Tristan

Fuck.

Did that just happen? It's Finn who turns to look at us. Dom and Lucas share a look, and our alpha shakes his head.

Don't.

Dom takes a step forward. *Are you sure?*

Not now. Not like this. Lucas glances around, taking in the bloody scene. *I know what I said, that if this comes to pass we have to intervene. But we're in a weakened position, with no understanding of why this happened. And there is Lucrezia to think of, she is without protection.*

Dom moves forward, whining. Lucas nods, showing he hears him, and turns to Dani. His eyes linger on her sandy blonde wolf form, and the ravens perched in a tree nearby.

Can you control them? She inclines her head. *Good. Send them over, I want to hear what's being said.*

Then he steps backwards towards the tree line. We follow, albeit grudgingly. My every instinct is telling me to move closer rather than away, but alpha's orders supersede that.

I wait by the edge as Dani orders her ravens about, then comes to join me. Nuzzling her neck, I shoot to her alone. *Where did Thiago take off to?*

Hell if I know, she growls, looking around as if expecting him to show up. *Something spooked him.*

What do you think it was?

Before she can answer, two ravens return. Dani focuses on them, and I catch some kind of undercurrent entering our bond.

I jerk back at the unfamiliar sensation, and her eyes sharpen on me. *You okay?*

Yeah. Can't really tell her it's freaking me out, so I keep it to myself. It'll just be one more thing to get used to.

After another moment of listening to her birds, Dani snorts towards them, and the ravens disperse. Then she heads to Lucas and I trail behind, watching her back.

Cade prepared this coup a while back. Seems it was part two of a plan he'd started with someone named Aiden. Ring a bell?

A growl escapes Dom. *Freaking yeah.*

So, what now? Finn asks.

While we retreat further into the woods and try to think this through, Lucas growls. *No sense in starting a fight we may not have to.*

We follow him out of the clearing, and when he shifts to human form, we do as well. Dani takes care of clothing me, while Dom throws spare clothes from his truck to Lucas and Finn.

"I'm going to check on Luz. We can debrief at your place, or the shop?"

Lucas mulls it over for a second. "The shop."

Dom nods and tears out of the forest, eager to get back to his mate. I don't blame him, considering what we just witnessed with Cade.

Lucas heads over to his truck, but a voice stops him. "Bad idea, letting this problem fester."

We all turn to face the newcomer. He pushes away from the tree he'd been glued to, and walks towards us, hands in the pocket of his slacks. *No wonder we didn't feel him.*

"Tytus," Finn greets, and there's a hint of a warning in his tone.

I glance at Dani, but she shrugs, as surprised as I am. "What are you doing here?"

The zmeu rolls his eyes. "Cleaning messes that are not mine, witch. This new development with the Reapers does not suit me."

Lucas takes a step closer, clenching his fists. "I couldn't care less if it suits you or not, dragon."

Tytus sighs, pinching the bridge of his nose. "Need I make myself clear? Again?"

Lucas opens his mouth, but Dani steps in front of him. "No!" Her vehement denial takes me by surprise, until I catch her thought.

They can't be fighting, not when we need both to defeat my crazy-ass brother.

"Lucas..." At my warning tone, Dani throws me a pleading look. I shake my head her way, hoping she'll stay silent. "Let's not antagonize anyone, shall we?"

Lucas frowns, then something eases in his expression. He pushes past Dani until he's nose to nose with Tytus. "You want to throw magic around? Be my fucking guest. But don't act like some savior when we all know you're not."

Tytus' eyes flash. "What?"

"I know what you hide here," Lucas seethes. "And unless you cooperate, I'll make sure she's in a less perfect state than when you last saw her."

I expect some sort of retort, but Tytus seems shaken. His eyes narrow on Lucas, then on each of us. "You couldn't..."

"You're not the only one able to keep tabs, amico," Lucas says. "Shall you call my bluff?"

Tytus says nothing, his silence indicative enough. Then Lucas waves me and Finn onwards. "Grab him and bring him to the shop. I think it's about time we find out exactly why our zmeu friend has been so great at popping up in unexpected places."

Finn and I share a look, and he shrugs. I know the meaning – we don't have a choice. He heads over to the car and comes back with some rope. His green eyes assess Tytus to see if he'll struggle, but the zmeu continues to stare at Lucas, unflinching.

"This is a mistake," he tells our alpha.

"Sure it is." Lucas nods at us, and Finn wraps the rope around Tytus' hands. Then we each grab one of his elbows and push him towards Lucas' car.

Dani slinks back to my car, and I feel her disappointment rolling in waves. By the time we drive to the shop, Dom has filled Luz in on the fight. They both turn to us when we walk in with Tytus, his hands tied behind his back.

Luz moves out of Dom's embrace, her green eyes flashing. "What the hell?"

Dani sighs, "Seems our fearsome pack leader thinks the dragon's a problem."

∞ ∞ ∞

∞Erro ∞

"<u>Mistakes</u> are always forgivable, if one has the courage to admit them."

-Bruce Lee-

Daniela

Dom's eyes narrow on the captive Tytus, then shift to Lucas. "Seriously? *This* is your solution?"

Finn shakes his head and grabs Tytus, pulling him to the back in Lucas's office. Luz watches him go, then her gaze travels over each remaining wolf in turn.

"Is that why you've all been acting so weird, because he's a dragon?" Luz frowns. "It wasn't a shock to my system finding out you're all werewolves, why the hell would this be any different?"

I look from Lucas to the guys, then Luz, feeling like I've just put my foot in my mouth. "She didn't know?"

No one answers me.

"Dani?" Luz presses when her question goes ignored, too. I open my mouth to answer, but Lucas beats me to it.

"Si, cara. He's a dragon, and stuffing his nose where it doesn't belong."

Dom intervenes then. "Why's he bound?"

"He showed up when we were leaving," I say, "and said something about the Reapers' situation not being his ideal."

"That's no reason to treat him like a criminal!" Luz cries.

Lucas' expression darkens. "It is when he's been showing up all places, offering help where it suits him and he's the only thing Thiago seems to fear. Seems a bit too coincidental."

Tristan steps by my side and holds my hand in his. To Luz, he says, "Long story short, Tytus got into it with Lucas." Then he whispers to me, "Come with me."

I duck into the garage with him, and he pulls us out of sight. Once there, his eyes roam me up and down. "Are you okay?"

"Why wouldn't I be?"

"Dani..." His chocolate eyes are soft, and I see where he's going with it. But I can't cry about my father – I won't.

"He got what was coming to him already. I don't want to talk about it, not now." A few feet away, I hear Luz's voice predictably increasing, followed by Dom's attempts to calm her down.

"Why's Luz so angry for Tytus?"

He shrugs. "Remember how I told you he helped her find Dom? I think there's some weird bond between them, or something. Plus, Lucrezia tends to see the good in everyone."

I sigh, and my body shifts of its own accord. My head drops on his shoulder, and I inhale his scent. "It just doesn't feel like something he'd do, Tristan. Why would Tytus join my brother?"

He shrugs. "Who knows? But it's amusing how both you and Luz defend him, without really knowing him."

Disagreeing with him is useless, so I simply burrow deeper in his chest, seeking his heat and reassurance. Tristan wraps his arms around me, holding me. He doesn't talk, doesn't offer empty comforting words. And it's more healing than he'll ever know.

After long moments, I pull back and meet his gaze. "Let's go back before Luz goes overboard."

He chuckles and we open the door, just in time to catch the end of their conversation.

"You're being irrational, Lucas! Nothing of what you said gives you reason to bind him!"

I'm surprised Luz will take this tone with Lucas, but while he's annoyed, he's also amused. "He's been in the right time one too many times, Lucrezia. After a while, it becomes suspicious."

I think Luz will back down, but instead she places a hand on her hip and tilts her head, glaring at him. "And he still saved my ass. I think that warrants some respect, not imprisonment."

Lucas' jaw clenches and he looks at Dom, who shrugs. Uninterested as he seems, he still takes a step closer and wraps an arm around Luz's shoulders. "Draga mea, let Lucas handle this."

She looks at Tristan, then at me, before meeting Lucas' glare once more. "Fine, be your usual stubborn self. But I want five minutes with Tytus."

Lucas pinches the bridge of his nose, exhaling loud enough we can all feel it. Tension builds up in the room, all eyes on him. After a few moments of silence, he nods.

Luz doesn't wait until he changes his mind. She darts past him, dragging me with her.

In Lucas' office, Tytus is exactly what I picture. Huffing and puffing like he's ready to blow the place down. Only he's tied to a chair, and Finn looks ready to kill him.

Tristan

We've moved into the garage while the girls have their five minutes with Tytus. Finn's not back yet, so it's just me, Dom and Lucas.

"You're sure about this?"

Lucas arches an eyebrow in my direction. "Sure about what?"

"Tytus and his involvement." Okay, so maybe Dani's conviction might've gotten through to me. At the same time, I feel like Lucas jumped the gun with the dragon.

I'm nowhere near reassured when Lucas simply shrugs. "Maybe, maybe not. I can't tell, amico. All I know is he's keeping something from us. And Dom himself said Jared had a deal with a zmeu. Now that Jared is dead, the Reapers are under Cade's leadership and the zmeu just so happens to be around?"

Dom's silent so I prod him. "What do you think?"

He rubs his jaw, then shakes his head. "I don't know. Tytus helped Luz a while back. Why would he do that, and then turn against us? It makes no sense."

"Right you are, godson."

We all turn around to see Ileana. Lucas' eyes flash and I get the feeling it's not the first he's seen of her. His next words confirm that.

"What are you doing on my territory – again?"

Ileana floats closer, and this time her expression is hard. "I knew you were stubborn, but not to this extent. You have the wrong man imprisoned and it will cost you."

"Spare me," Lucas snorts and tries to walk away.

Tries, because the minute he takes a step, Ileana raises one pale hand and he finds himself two inches above ground, unable to move. A snort escapes me, but I stifle it. It's hard not to take satisfaction when someone else is being tortured with her tricks, as I have.

"I grow tired of your attitude, wolf. And you have no right to threaten the zmeu with something you know he cares deeply for."

Lucas glares at her. "I have every right. This is my territory and since he's appeared on it, chaos has reigned. Come to think of it, your appearance has not helped, either."

Ileana rolls her eyes. "It is not his appearance that causes chaos, nor mine." Her eyes flick to Dom. "I told you before, more than one thing will come to pass."

"Release me now, witch."

Dom shakes his head and takes a step closer to his godmother, using her title in Romanian. "Nașă, all due respect, antagonizing Lucas won't get you what you want."

"It is not about what I want. Your leader feels threatened because there is another in town he cannot control." Her eyes flash again. "That fear leads him to make stupid choices. Do not be the idiot who follows him onto this path."

Then she releases Lucas and he lands on his feet. Her otherworldly eyes find each of us in turn, and a shiver runs through me at her next words.

"You will be attacked past midnight. Do not lose sight of what you hold dear."

She disappears before we can say anything, and my gut clenches. "What we hold dear? Does she mean Dani?"

"And Luz?"

Our questions go unanswered by Lucas. He's staring at the ground, eyes narrowed as if it would provide the answers he seeks. When he looks back up, his expression is hard. "The five minutes are up. Time to talk to the dragon."

Daniela

Finn turns to us when we enter and it's the angriest I've ever seen him. Nostrils flaring, fists clenched, it looks like he's shooting fire through his eyes.

"What's going on?"

Tytus shrugs, relaxing into the chair. "Seems your pack member has a prejudice against dragons."

Finn clenches his jaw, but before he can say anything Luz touches his shoulder. "Lucas gave us five minutes with him. Alone."

He opens his mouth to argue, then throws a scathing look to Tytus. "Just watch yourselves."

When he leaves, some of his angry energy lingers. Only Tytus seems unbothered, instead turning curious eyes on us.

"What's going on?" Luz asks, stepping closer. "I know you're not trying to hurt us. You helped me, not so long ago."

One shoulder lifts in a shrug. "Perhaps it was all part of my master plan."

"Bullshit." Luz gets even closer. "I don't believe that."

"Neither do I. Why would you have bothered warning me about my magic, helping me with everything?" I frown. "You even joined our fights. It may be you were looking for something, but that doesn't take away from the fact you helped."

Tytus turns his gaze away, sighing. "This is beyond your understanding."

Luz crosses her arms over her chest. "Try us."

He's silent for a long time, and I whisper, "They only gave us five minutes. Two of those are up."

Luz softens her tone. "Let us help, Ty." I fully expect him to correct the nickname she gives him, but to my surprise, he doesn't.

"This is beyond your help, Red. And yours, little wolf."

I kneel in front of him, trying to catch his eye. "Not going to happen. You helped me with my magic. Without you, I wouldn't have been able to face my brother once – let alone twice, and win."

Tytus snorts, his expression twisting in a sneer. "I didn't help you, I used you. Needed you to get me closer to your brother. Not that it helped..." He looks away.

"Nice try," I say, "but you're not fooling us. So are you saying you don't want this?"

I reach into my pocket and pull out my father's pendant. It's similar to my mark, a pagan star with a snake around it. Except the body of the snake is actually a little vial, with a cap on the head. The weight of the liquid inside it sinks into my palm.

Tytus' eyes widen, as if unable to believe what is being presented mere inches from his face. "Where did you get that?"

I grin at Luz, happy we got his attention. "Where you said it'd be – my father's neck."

Tytus frowns. "You wouldn't have taken it from him, you're too good for that."

"You're right, but my father's dead now, so he won't miss it."

Tytus' gaze is glued to the pendant, assessing, thinking. He wants this thing, needs it, but I don't know why. And unless he opens up to us and lets us help him, Lucas will have his way.

"What's in this, Tytus? Why do you need the pendant?"

He still refuses to talk, and turns his head away from us. But I won't give up, not when I feel us this close. "Say what you will, but you helped me. And I need you to do it again. Thiago controls the ravens, and somehow I managed to as well. But I don't understand how he uses *magia* when he's in wolf form... How can I defeat him, when it comes down to it?"

Without looking at me, Tytus says, "The chance to defeat your brother was long ago. The only thing you can do now is defend."

"I refuse to believe that. There has to be a way! What about the witch he keeps imprisoned?"

Tytus looks up sharply then, his expression hungry. "Where does he keep her?"

"I...don't know. It used to be in a cave near Bow's Arrow, but I'm sure he moved her since then. Now that our father's dead, he'll probably bring her to the house and keep a closer on eye on her." I think back to the first time Tytus joined us in a fight, how he'd been circling the ground, as if searching for someone. I'd thought at the time it was my mate, but now something tells me I was wrong. "Is that what you wanted? The witch? When you helped me save Tristan..."

His stormy eyes hold mine for a beat, and he nods. Then his gaze flickers to the pendant still in my hand. I raise it to his eyes once more. "I'll give you this, Tytus, and I'll release you. All I ask in return is you tell me how to defeat my brother."

A beat passes. Then another. And another.

Finally, he says, "Your brother might have been gifted the magic, but he has sullied it, taken to using it for selfish gains. Every act he has done, has turned him worse than he was in the beginning. There is no saving him, you have to understand that. That is why he wants you, wants to mate with you. To own you – body and soul."

"Why?"

"So he can kill you after, and gorge on your blood. Then he'll be the alpha he wants to be, with the lobisomens fully subservient to him."

I frown. "His pack already listens to him."

"They may listen, but they cannot *hear* him, little wolf. The ravens are in his head, leaving no room for the lobisomens. Thiago is slowly going insane from the lack of contact with his fellow wolves. Your death, the true leader of the pack, would make him their uncontested alpha, and break the last bonds of loyalty to you."

I stagger to my feet, looking down at him. "Thank you." He nods, then looks away again.

"Ty, please," Luz begs. "Talk to us. Tell us how to help you, too."

He takes a deep breath, then releases it. "Can't. You should remove yourselves from this town as soon as you can."

"Kind of hard, considering we both have men we love here," I snap. "Let's try something else. What does Lucas have on you?"

His eyes flash at that. "Nothing."

"Didn't look that way to me. You practically kneeled before him when he mentioned a *she*."

A growl escapes his lips, and he actually bares his teeth. "A dragon never kneels."

"Oh yeah?" I know I'm taunting the beast, but at least he's talking. And we're down to no more minutes. "Isn't it funny then that you're here, bound by ropes I know you can cut, imprisoned in a building I know you can explode?"

Luz picks up on my words and tries again. "Let us help, Ty. We're the only ones who believe in your innocence."

Then I remember something. "Is it the bakery? Is that what Lucas has on you?"

Tytus tries to avoid a reaction, but his eyes flicker to mine. Then I think back to last time, when I'd been there with Luz and Finn. He'd been the handsome stranger with the stormy gaze outside the bakery. Except there had been no one inside it, except for...

"Elle."

Luz gapes at me, but I know I'm onto something. Footsteps echo in the hallway – we've run out of time.

Bending over Tytus, I reach into the front pocket of his jeans, sliding the pendant in there. "Keep it. It's Elle you're protecting. Lucas followed you and he knows you have an interest in her. You don't want to put her in jeopardy."

He scowls at my sure tone, but there's a hint of panic in those stormy eyes. "Stop meddling. Go help your wolves. The Reapers will attack soon."

"No," Luz shakes her head. "There's more than one menace out there. If we warn Elle, keep her safe, will you stop fooling around and join forces with us?"

The door opens before Tytus can answer. Lucas stomps in, followed by Dom, Tristan and Finn. And he doesn't look happy. "Five minutes are up. It's our turn."

My stomach clenches and I catch Tristan's eye. He's innocent, I know he is, but Lucas won't listen to reason. I probably wouldn't either if I was head of a pack and needed to protect everyone. But this isn't right.

By the door now, I glance back to Tytus. And just before Lucas steps and blocks my view of him, he catches my eye and nods.

Luz sees it too, and we try to exit the room without giving anything away.

Tristan

Tytus looks up at Lucas, a defiant glint in his eyes, and I know we won't get anywhere. Lucas must realize it, too, but he takes off his jacket instead and throws it in a corner.

"What was your deal with the Reapers?" Lucas asks. Only silence answers him. "It's a simple enough question. Think hard before you don't answer it."

Tytus' jaw clenches, and he releases a heavy breath. "Their territory hunts don't impede on my territory."

"And what would that territory be?"

"You should know."

Lucas stays silent, and something tells me he *does* know. Only he's not sharing with us.

"Why did you join the fight to save Tristan?" This comes from Dom.

Tytus spares me a glance. "His mate was very convincing."

The smug grin is aimed at getting me riled up. But I don't bite. Lucas does – and then punches him.

Bound, Tytus doesn't strike back. He spits out blood, then meets Lucas' glare with one of his own. His expression darkens further and I know a line's been crossed.

An hour later, Lucas and I are the first to walk out. We didn't get anything from Tytus after that hit.

"You shouldn't have gotten physical," I say.

Lucas shrugs. "Maybe. But he wasn't going to talk anyway."

"Don't you think we should take Ileana's warning seriously? About being attacked tonight?"

It's then I notice how quiet the reception area is. I check everywhere, cursing under my breath. "Where did they go?"

"Who?"

Lucas stares at me like I'm crazy, but I gesture around. "The girls!"

Luz and Dani are nowhere to be seen. Finn and Dom walk in after us then, and I gulp. How the hell am I going to tell him my crazy girlfriend took his away, probably on a suicidal quest for justice? If I know them at all, they're out there trying to clear Tytus' name.

Turns out, I don't have to tell Dom anything. The vârcolac takes one look around, nostrils flaring, then his darkened blue gaze settles on me. "Where's Luz?"

"They must have taken off," Lucas says. "Tristan was just about to go look for them."

"Fine, I'll join him."

"No, Finn will. I need you here."

I walk past the scowling Dom, Finn trailing me. "I'll get her back, meu amigo."

He nods in a way that leaves no room for error, and we disappear.

Finn takes one look down the street, and starts heading to the bakery store. We walk in, the bell ringing above our heads. Guilty faces turn to us – Luz, Dani, and another young girl that looks familiar.

"What the hell are you two doing?" The growl escaping my throat is no human sound, and the other girl moves back.

Dani rolls her eyes, which only pisses me off further. "Trying to fix something. What's gotten up your butt?"

I want to tell her to come to me, but I shake my head and instead walk to her. A glance to Luz shows her being fidgety. "Dom's looking for you."

She bites her lip, looking guilty as sin. Then I focus on Dani, wrapping my arm around her waist and pulling her to me. I lower my head to her ear. "Are you done making me sweat?"

She tilts her head back, eyes twinkling. "Maybe. Maybe not." Then her expression grows serious. "How's Tytus?"

I shake my head. "Lucas crossed a line, and he's not talking."

"So he's still imprisoned?"

No sooner do I nod, that I catch her side glance to Luz. "You're not planning anything, are you?"

They both look up at me with innocent expressions. "Of course not."

We turn to leave, and only then do I notice Finn staring at the girl behind the counter like he's never seen a woman before. "Amigo," I tease, "you okay?"

He snaps out of his daze, and a flush covers his cheeks. He's actually blushing. I glance behind, and Luz reads the question on my face. "Her name is Elle."

"Elle." Finn whispers. And it's only loud enough for our wolf ears, but she perks up like she's heard him.

Before I can say anything, Finn storms out.

∞ ∞ ∞

∞ Isca ∞

"Better to shun the <u>bait</u> than struggle in the snare."

-William Blake-

Daniela

"What do you think got into Finn?" Tristan's nuzzling my neck, and I'm tempted to give in and get back in bed. But the night's events are keeping me awake.

After dropping Luz with Dom, we took off to give them some time alone. Lucas was nowhere to be found, and Finn had stormed out after the bakery. So we came back to Tristan's place and after ordering a pizza, ended up lounging in bed.

I still haven't cried over my father's death. Probably another sign of how broken I am, but I can't make myself shed tears for someone who stood by and let his son ruin everything his wife had ever worked for.

Tristan's whispers in my ear thankfully remove such thoughts from my head. "Not sure how I feel with you thinking about another wolf while in bed with me, meu anjo."

I chuckle at my mate's words. His arm is wrapped around my waist, and he's spooning me. I turn enough to capture his lips with mine. "You've got nothing to worry about."

Tristan growls in appreciation into the kiss, then his hand starts wandering down my front. With his heat at my back, I'd only kept on my tank top and underwear, which I now realize is the perfect invitation.

"You still haven't told me what you were looking for at the bakery," he whispers, and my half-lidded eyes fly open.

"Are you...serious...right now?" The words come out breathless, because it's really hard to ignore his touch on my skin, and the tingles it provokes.

Tristan's lips leave butterfly kisses on my neck, and shoulders, then nibble on my ear. In contradiction, his fingers duck in my underwear with precision, finding a particularly soft spot.

"*Very* serious."

I spread my legs, giving him better access, even as a soft moan escapes me. "Tristan..."

Before long, I'm panting as his skillful fingers drive me crazy. Then he stops, and a frustrated noise escapes me. "Tristan!"

He chuckles against my back, pressing closer to me. His hard-on digs into me, and I know this can't be easy for him. But he's holding back, and it's pissing me off.

"An answer for an orgasm seems a pretty sweet deal, no?"

I try to move out of his grip, but he tightens it on me. His chuckles vibrate, and I'm fighting a grin. "You're mean when you want to be."

"Mmm," he murmurs, then pushes me on my back. Hovering above me, his chocolate eyes bearing into mine, his hardness holding me hostage, I relish the safety, the warmth – my mate's irresistible touch. "So, what's your answer?"

While I think on it, he teases me, spreading my legs and holding himself at my junction. I bite on my lip, meeting his burning gaze.

This stubborn male of mine. I roll my eyes, and give in. "It's Elle, the girl in the bakery. There's some connection between her and Tytus, that's what Lucas has over him." Then I shift my hips, and grin. "Now, where's my reward?"

Tristan shakes his head, then removes his boxers in record time and covers me with his body. His mouth moves against mine, drawing more moans from my lips. Then Tristan nips on my neck, while burying deep inside me, and I know I'm gone – falling to a place I won't recover from.

∞ ♦ ∞

I don't know what wakes me up. At first I think it's the rain outside, but the more I blink at the darkness, the more I don't believe it.

Then my phone rings. A single buzz, on my nightstand.

I slide out from Tristan's embrace, and glance at the glowing screen. My blood freezes. "Shit."

The text is coming from Luz's phone and it's a picture. I already know what I'm going to find before I open it.

My eyes take in the gag over her mouth, the tousled hair. Somehow they managed to capture her from under Dom's nose. Which alone tells me who we're dealing with.

Then a second text vibrates. ***Come alone.***

"Fuck You, Thiago." My mutter lingers in the darkness, then I get up. It's about time I bring this to its ultimate conclusion.

I'm no fool. It's a trap, and he must have figured out I'd listen. After all, it was his raven I'd seen when I fought Cade, trying to save Luz. And he must have figured out I'd hate for Luz to be suffering.

The smart play would be to wake Tristan up and call Dom.

Only there's no time, and I'm not about to risk her life. Or my mate's. I've seen what my crazy brother did to him once, and there's no way in hell I'll let him do it again.

There's also the matter of Lucas. Tristan and Dom would have to run their plan by him, and the alpha might not agree. Going against his orders would mean being in a precarious situation and risk being kicked out of town. Or, in my case, I've only been afforded protection. And if all things go well and I defeat Thiago, I'll still have a pack to go back to.

Either way, it's a no brainer. So I get dressed in record time and grab Tristan's truck keys. There's an address in a third text and I step on the gas with a vengeance.

The area it leads me to is an abandoned row of trailers off the side of the town. I don't even need to follow my nose. The pack of ravens sitting atop one particular one is enough indication of where I can find my brother.

I park in front of it, noticing the four burly guards. By the time I reach them, the door opens and out comes Thiago.

"So that's all it took to make you come running? Capturing a puny human?" He laughs. "Had I known, I would've saved us a lot of trouble."

"How the hell did you get to her?"

Thiago snickers, leaning against the door like he's got all the time in the world. "Easily. Now, as for my previous terms. Come home with me and once the deal is sealed, she will be released."

I clench my hands. "Fuck you. I'm not going anywhere and neither is Luz."

"We'll see about that."

I make the mistake of not paying attention to my surroundings. All I see is the flash of eagerness in my brother's eyes, then something hard hits me and everything goes black.

Tristan

The knock on my door is loud – almost fisting. I struggle out of bed, and open the door to find a crazed-eyed Dom, panting.

"Tell me Luz is here."

"Wh–"

Before I can finish my thought, he's bursting inside my place and looking everywhere. I'm left scratching the back of my head. "Why would she be here?"

"Because her and Dani are thick as thieves." He stops mid-pacing, sniffing the air. "Where's your girl?"

"She's just..." My gaze goes to the bedroom, finding it empty. I glance back at the door – her boots are gone. And then I notice the cold scent. Our eyes meet across the room.

"Merda!"

∞ ♦ ∞

We make it to the shop in record time. Lucas is already there, joined by Finn. They glance up from a map they're studying.

"What's going on?" Finn asks, noticing our distressed moods.

I shake my head. "Dani and Luz are gone."

Lucas straightens from the map, frowning. "What do you mean, *gone*?"

"They're not home, Lucas, what the hell do you think he means?" Dom snaps. "They were taken!"

"Forget this." I don't waste my time with more explanations, instead storming past the alpha, straight to his office – and the prisoner still held there.

I burst through the door, my eyes meeting Tytus'. He takes one look at me and Dom who follows behind, and smirks. "Lost something?"

I'm lunging for him before I can think otherwise, my fist connecting with his jaw. Again. Then again. Shouts echo around me, but it's Dom who finally manages to pry me off Tytus.

Panting, I yank myself out of his grip. "I got this. I'm good." Then my eyes narrow on the dragon. "What happened yesterday?"

"I'm sure I have no idea what you mean."

I take a deep breath, forcing my wolf to chill. If I lose it and go at with the dragon, it won't help anyone. "Dani and

Luz both thought you're innocent, that you're not in cohorts with the Reapers. Is this true?"

For all answer, Tytus shrugs. And it's enough to make me see red.

Dom steps forward then. "You saved my mate once, and for that I'm very grateful. But she's gone now, too. And she may be in danger."

Tytus' expression changes then, thoughtful. His eyes flicker over my shoulder, and I turn to Lucas. He's leaning against the wall, not doing anything. And my rage suddenly reroutes. "You going to talk, alpha, or what?"

Lucas' eyes glint dangerously. "Say that again. *Calmer.*"

I stomp to him, and before either of my buddies can intervene I shove him against the wall hard enough to rattle it. "I said, *talk*. You know something, and I'm not going to sit by and let this shit get out of hand."

"Perhaps you should ask him why, exactly, he afforded a witch protection. And what he gained out of it." Tytus' words only throw fuel to my fire, and my grip on Lucas tightens.

"Is that true?"

"You're delusional," Lucas bares his teeth, eyes glittering with danger. "And you," he says to Tytus, "shut it."

The zmeu smirks, I see it out of the corner of my eye. Dom takes a step towards me, as if to move me off Lucas, and I growl. "Don't move. I'm trying to get answers here."

"Either you let me go, or we need to deal with this in another way." Lucas' hiss is dangerously low.

I still don't budge. Instead, I slam him against the wall again. "*Talk*, dammit!"

"Love has made you lose your mind, amico." Lucas shoves me backwards and tries to move past me, but Dom's there, blocking his way.

"Time to talk, Lucas."

Our alpha glances at Finn, but he's also quiet. Finally, he shrugs. "Yes, I knew about the zmeu. We've been playing a game of cat and mouse, each keeping an eye on the other. It wasn't until he started training Daniela that I realized the danger we were in. So I followed the dragon. He has an interest in Elle, the girl at the bakery store. She's his weakness. Same as Luz and Dani are yours. So what if I used it against him?"

"You had no right."

I turn to Finn, surprised to see my usual calm buddy enraged. His brow is furrowed, hands clenched at his sides, and his nostrils are flaring. Tytus is watching him with interest. At first, I think his rage is directed at me, for breaking pack rules and raising my hand to the alpha. After all, our Irish friend is all about the rules. It takes me a longer moment to realize Finn's rage is aimed at Lucas.

"What is going on with all of you?" Lucas looks at us one by one, scowling. "I protected our pack. And you'll recall it's you two," he points to me and Dom, "who brought these females into our lives. So what if I gave Daniela protection in order to lure the zmeu out of hiding? It's about time we find out what his purpose here is." His glare settles on Tytus, then falls on each of us in turn. "You're a bunch of hypocrites, expecting me to save your girls, but not at the price of being a little ruthless? Mio Dio, give me a break!"

"Don't invoke God's name in vain." Finn takes one step closer, and something about his energy draws my attention. He's... seriously mad. "Since when does protecting our pack mean toying with innocents?"

Lucas gets up in his face. "I didn't *toy* with anyone. I watched her, tried to find out who she was. I never interacted directly with the dragon's precious...whatever she is to him."

For once, I feel the snap coming before anyone else and step between them. The second after, Finn tries to lunge at Lucas. My body's the brick wall he can't get through, and I make sure to keep it that way.

"Enough," Dom says, his voice low. "All this useless fighting isn't helping when Luz and Dani are in danger. So, does anyone have any idea what might have happened, and how to help them?"

Silence lengthens between us. I feel the blood rushing to my temples, and the murderous rage builds with it. But something about Lucas' words when talking about Tytus' weakness...

"Merda! I know what happened." I meet Dom's eyes. "Did you catch any weird scents in your house?"

"None."

"Thiago must've gone in, taken Luz last night. And if he did, I bet you anything he blackmailed Dani to go after."

"Shit." Dom runs a hand through his hair, then paces in the small office. His eyes dart to Lucas. "What do we do?"

Silence lengthens between us.

"I think," Finn says, "that one thing is clear." We turn to him, but his eyes are on Tytus. "He has nothing to do with Thiago or the attacks on us. Even less with the Reapers' coup."

"Fair point," Tytus drawls, "coming from someone who hates my kind."

We ignore the zmeu, and instead I meet Finn's gaze. "Your point?"

"He's saying it's time to free me," Tytus grins. "And I agree." In front of our eyes, he snaps the restraints binding him in two. Then he stands, dusting himself off.

"Why didn't you do that before?" I ask. "You obviously could have."

He snorts. "Before, your alpha was ready to murder me and intended to hurt something very dear to me. Now, he sees the point in using me, without hurting." His eyes travel on each one of us, stopping on Lucas. "I can help. Or you can let your girls die. It's up to you, wolf."

I'd sell my soul to the devil if it means getting Dani back safe and sound. And I'm definitely ready to battle my alpha for it. It turns out, I don't have to.

Lucas glances at all of us, and clenches his jaw. He nods to Tytus. "Talk."

Daniela

The noise takes a while to get to me. Then it makes me open my eyes – to darkness. Judging by the rolling noise under me, I'm in the trunk of a car. And I'm not alone.

I cue in to someone's heavy breathing, and take a whiff. My mouth is gagged, but I definitely feel someone squirming next to me. A few movements later, my cheek hits something rough. I start rubbing against it, until the gag moves down my mouth enough so I can speak.

"Luz?"

The person next to me stills, then a whimper escapes her. I take is an affirmative. "Hang on, I'll get us out of here. Try to rub your cheek against the backseat, it'll help to get the gag off."

She moves around a bit, and a few seconds later she exhales loudly. "Finally. Are you okay?"

"Am *I* okay?" I frown at the darkness. "You realize it's my brother who kidnapped you, right?"

"Only by my own stupidity," she whispers, and I sense the anger at herself in the words. "Dom told me not to go anywhere without him. I saw a glow in the backyard and thought it might've been Ileana. But it wasn't."

"It's not your fault," I try to reassure her. "Thiago's good. Too freaking good. He must've been following me for a while with the ravens."

"But why pick me?"

"Because he knows I'd never let him hurt an innocent." I sigh. "Enough about this. We need to get out of here. If I know my brother – and I do – he's taking us back to my town. And as soon as we get there, he plans to mate me."

"Ew."

Luz's whisper draws a chuckle out of me. "Yep, my thinking exactly. So what do you say to getting out of here?"

"Let's do it. What's the plan?"

"Look for something sharp. He won't have paid attention to details..." As I go on telling Luz what to look for, I do what I haven't done in forever – I pray. And can only hope by some miracle, the guys will come help out.

Thiago's not a foe I can fight on my own. I need Tristan, and the pack, to help me.

Tristan

"Are you sure about this?" We're in Dom's pickup, with Lucas and Finn following behind in another car. And we're all heading to where the dragon tells us to.

Tytus rolls his eyes. "Yes. Thiago is headed to Bow's Arrow."

"Why? Can't he get what he needs here?"

"Sure," he snorts. "He can mate your girl here. But he doesn't have the witch to bless the union – which will ensure he gets Daniela's powers, as well."

Something rises in my throat at the vile image, but I manage to push it down. "If he hurts one hair on her head..."

"He won't," Dom tries to reassure.

"Not until he gets near that witch," Tytus adds.

"Why?" I ask, though my voice feels hoarse.

"Because her powers will ensure he gets his due."

"So how do we find them?"

Tytus moves at the back, then pulls a pendant out of his pocket. I squint at it, then my eyes widen. "Dani's father had that around his neck!"

"Indeed. And it will lead us to the witch."

Dom throws us a look. "How?"

"Because of the blood sealed inside it." At our blank gazes, he rolls his eyes and pockets the pendant. "Just trust me."

I slouch in my seat and mutter, "Kind of hard to do, when you only release information bit by bit."

Tytus is silent for a bit, then shrugs. "It's the way of the world, wolf. I know some things you don't. And I get to choose when you find out about them."

Dom throws me a look I know is intended to make sure I don't punch the shit out of Tytus – again. Then he says, "Why is the witch the key to this ritual?"

"It's she who gave them the powers, even though they're not hers to give. That is why I need to get my hands on her."

I glance at Dom. "Lucas knows about this?"

He shakes his head, then his eyes meet Tytus' in the rearview mirror. "That's your price? Why didn't you ask our alpha?"

Tytus leans back in his seat, smirking. "I'm asking *you*."

Dom grips the steering wheel, taking one deep breath. I know he'll do whatever he needs to get Luz back, as will I. *But will Lucas understand?*

"No, he won't," Dom whispers. Then he glances at me. "You sure about this?" I nod. He meets Tytus' expecting glare. "It's a deal. But only after you've helped us secure Luz and Dani. And that means sticking it through to the end."

Tytus hand comes between us, and Dom shakes on it. But when they touch, something else hits me.

Two hands shaking, a child between them. A truck coming closer, its driver dead, brains splattered all over the windshield. Me yelling to get out of the way. The child, bleeding in my arms...

My hands grip the side of the car. There's more building at the back of my head. I know what it is – it's another episode. And I can't fucking have one now. They've been on the edge of my consciousness, kept at bay because of my wolf taking over and Dani's presence. Now neither is fully present, and the stressful situation causes my mind to sidetrack.

"Tristan?"

I grit my teeth, closing my eyes. That doesn't work – all I see is blood. My breathing grows shallow, and my nails grow, sinking into the sides of the car.

"Buddy, snap out of it!"

Then Dom slams on the brakes and I hit the front of the car. Blood trickles down the side of my face, and I look up. Dom throws me a concerned look, but then I realize I'm not the reason we stopped.

There's a line of wolves blocking the way – Reapers.

"Figures," Tytus mutters.

∞ ∞ ∞

∞ Surpresa ∞

"The backbone of <u>surprise</u> is fusing speed with secrecy."

-Carl von Clausewitz-

Daniela

It takes us the better part of twenty minutes to look around, without finding anything. I'm about to give up, when Luz whispers, "Dani, what about your magic?"

I shake my head. "Tytus didn't teach me everything, I wouldn't know where to start."

She pauses for a second, then says, "What about claws? You've done that before, morph only your hand. Do you think Thiago will sense it?"

I chew on my bottom lip for close to a minute, then shake my head. "It might work. But just in case he does, we'll have to be ready."

"Okay. Free my feet first if you can. I'll use them to kick and buy us time."

A chuckle escapes me. "Good point." Then I focus on my hand, letting the change come over it. One claw digs into my back, but I grit my teeth against the pain.

"Ready. Don't move now, I'm going to shuffle near your feet." Inch by painful inch, I move closer, until I feel her boots. Then I raise my hand to be level with the rope tying her, and cut through.

It takes a few tries, then Luz wiggles her feet. "Awesome! Now, my hands."

"I'm going to need you to move to me, though." Luz does as I ask her, and again I make quick do of her bindings. "Okay, that leaves me."

"I have an idea," Luz says. Then she moves around, and I hear a zipper. Out of her inside pocket, she pulls a nail file. "I wouldn't have been able to reach it bound, but it should be enough if I pick at the ropes to make them easier to break."

"Worth a try."

I hand her my feet and she goes to work. It takes close to ten minutes, and I start worrying we might not succeed. But then I feel the rope give way. I tug at it with my feet, and it snaps.

Luz grins in the darkness. "Now, hands."

She's just about done when the car comes to a harrowing stop. We smack into the sides, and my head hits the metal.

"What the hell?"

Ignoring Luz's mutter, I look around for the latch that opens the trunk. Thiago must've done something, because no matter how much I feel my way around, it's nowhere to be found.

"Luz..." The doors to the car open and slam closed, and panic seizes me. "Listen to me. I'm going to use magic to blast this open. Then you run – run as fast as you can. If you can bring help, do so. If not, get the hell out of here."

Her hand finds mine. "I'm not leaving you to face this psycho alone."

"He'll kill you." I feel tears on my cheeks, and footsteps resound outside. "We don't have time for this. Just run, okay?"

Without waiting for her answer, I move as far back into a corner as I can. Luz does the same, curling up and covering her face. Then I hold my hands up to the trunk.

With my index finger, I draw a rune in the air. It's something I've only ever seen Thiago do once, months ago. I'm not even sure it's correct until it glows in the dark.

One, two... "Three."

A blast of burgundy light escapes me, hitting the trunk and blowing it open. The next moment, I jump out, Luz right behind me. I turn to face Thiago, only to find him grappling with beasts.

They're large like wolves, with dark fur and yellow eyes, tinged with red. And the scent – ugh!

I raise a hand when one comes closer to us, but Luz grabs it. "No! Wait. I don't... I think they're here for me."

And in front of my stunned gaze, the massive, scary creature sits down and tilts its head to the side. Its eyes are focused on Luz, and they're not filled with hunger but...reverence.

Tristan

"What do you mean, figures?"

Instead of answering me, Tytus opens the door and steps out of Dom's truck. Lucas is also out, followed by Finn. I'm about to join them, but Dom reaches for my arm.

"You okay?"

I nod tightly. "Yeah."

"Cause you weren't, for a second there."

A sigh escapes me, and I rub at my face. "It's these damn nightmares, man. Sometimes they seep in the daily. But I'm dealing with it."

He nods, then looks away. A muscle ticks in his jaw. "I'm here if you ever need something."

"I know." Then my eyes get drawn to the outside, where Cade has stepped forward. "We better get out there."

Dom steps out first and I join him, walking straight to Lucas.

"Don't trust them."

Tytus' words are only for Lucas' ears, but since I'm behind them, it's easy to eavesdrop. And harder to keep my mouth shut. "And why not?"

Tytus throws me a look, then straightens up and takes a step to the side. "Your funeral."

I've never seen Lucas this pensive. His dark gaze levels on the Reapers, now led by Cade. Under our less-than-impressed faces, Cade morphs to human. Naked in front of us, he smirks.

"Thought you'd need a little help."

"What for?"

"To get your girls back, of course."

Lucas narrows his eyes. "And how do you know they're missing?"

Cade shrugs. "We kept an eye on our territory. When those wolves came back, my scouts reported what they saw."

Tytus snorts. "Reported, but didn't help, hmm?"

Cade's expression darkens. Those onyx eyes look dangerous, and I know this change for the Reapers is for the worst. Especially where we and the humans are concerned.

"Are you allied with the zmeu, now?"

Lucas glances at Tytus. "We do what we have to for our pack."

"As did I," Cade smirks. "I'm glad you understand that." His excuse for the coup makes me want to hurl, but I hold back.

"Let's get one thing straight," Lucas says. "The Reapers' business has never been mine to worry about. But if it impedes on mine or endangers my pack, it will be. Capisci?"

Cade holds his gaze for a moment longer. "I don't speak Italian, but I get you."

He holds his hand out to shake. The gesture makes me fear another episode, but nothing happens. My sigh of relief does not go unnoticed by Dom, who throws me a worried look.

I got you, my wolf whispers back.

Lucas stares at Cade's hand. He doesn't have to make a show of authority, it's in his voice when he speaks. "And why would Reapers help us, of all things?"

Cade shrugs. "Wolf solidarity. Plus, the she-wolf was almost part of our pack."

A low growl escapes me at the reminder. "I don't recall you being there before, when we were trying to kick Thiago out of town. Why now?"

Lucas throws me a look to shut me up, but Cade only smirks. "Maybe it took us this long to realize we'd rather live in peace than fight a war."

"That's odd," Dom says, sarcasm dripping with every word. I know this truce makes him uneasy, what with the Reapers' stance on humans, and Luz being caught in the middle. "I thought the whole reason you killed Jared was because he was soft. What gives?"

Cade's eyes flash, betraying his hate for a second. Then he catches himself and shrugs. "Hey, if you don't want our help, no harm done." He turns to leave. "We'll be on our way."

"No." Lucas takes a step forward, extending his hand. "You're welcome to join us, and we accept your truce."

Cade turns and shakes his hand, grinning. Behind the outward peaceful exterior, I sense something that makes my skin crawl. I glance at Finn, who meets my gaze on the other side of Tytus. He shakes his head, but it seems more regretful than anything I've seen from him.

Shit.

Then Lucas nods to us. "We're close enough to Bow's Arrow. Let's morph now, and we can go the rest of the way on foot."

He shifts first, followed by Dom and Finn. Then they take off, following the Reapers. I linger behind, uneasy. Cade's scent is all wrong, and after what he did to his own alpha, what's to guarantee that he'll stick by his word? Apparently, Lucas is willing to trust it. Which makes me wonder what else he's not telling us.

"You are right not to trust them," Tytus says. "Watch your backs. The Reapers in this for the same thing I am."

Tytus steps back from me then, and it takes me a moment to realize why. He throws his head back, clenching his fists by his side. The same burgundy light of his magic envelops him, coating his entire body. He trembles, gritting his jaw as a snarl rips from his throat.

Then the mist hides him from my eyes, but he grows larger, and larger. He's only a huge shadow, increasing in size, in the midst of a cloud of bloody ash. Within moments, all sounds stop, and an eerie silence descends.

With a roar, the zmeu escapes the mist, and with two beats of his powerful wings he's up in the sky. Jaw gaping, I stare at him until he's out of sight, wondering how I got to be the one witnessing a dragon shift.

After a few moments of stunned silence, I morph into my wolf form, and give in to the run. If Tytus is right about Cade's pack and their motivation to help us, that begs another question. *What the hell would Reapers need with a witch?*

Daniela

"Umm, Luz?"

My voice has the unfortunate side effect of drawing Thiago's glare our way. He's on the opposite side of the car, surrounded by creatures. And once he notices we're out of the car, and unbound, he starts walking towards us.

One of his hands is raised in a way that makes me think he's about to use magic. I lift mine in response, ready to block whatever he's planning to throw at us – never mind the fact I have no clue how to do that.

"They're with me," Luz whispers.

"How?" My gaze is drawn again to the gory creature.

"That's Dom's pack of vrykolakas."

I recall then something Tristan told me about their last fight and how these creatures are bound to Dom and Luz. "How did they find you?"

"Dom told them to protect me, whenever I'm in danger. I guess..." She looks at them, noticing there's about twenty in total. "That's not all of them. They must have been looking for somewhere to hunt."

Her attention falls on the nearby creature, and she motions for it to move closer. Step by step, as if afraid to scare Luz, it nears us. Then it plops down near her feet like a good puppy. Luz kneels in front of it, meeting its eyes.

I'm not at all comfortable with those massive canines near her pretty face, but it's not like she'll listen to me. Then her eyes widen, and she tilts her head to the side.

"Is that thing...*talking* to you?" I hiss back.

Luz doesn't answer. A ray of burgundy light hits near her, scorching the ground too close. She yelps and steps back, and the creature moves, blocking her body – protecting her.

My human friend glances up at me with wonder in her eyes. "They felt me in danger, and came to help. Dani, this is our salvation!"

"I don't suppose you know how to, um, order them about?"

She bites her lip, then meets the creature's gaze again. "Attack?"

It stares back for a second, as if assessing the truth of the command. After a beat, the creature turns to the rest of them, and a hair-rising howl escapes it. A weird silence falls on the vrykolakas – then they all jump in action.

Half of them split in two teams, going after Thiago and his wolves. And the other half forms a semi-circle in front of Luz and, by association, me.

"It's like we have our own security guards," I whisper.

Luz grins my way, and reaches out to the pet one of the creatures. It leans into her, practically making her fall. The damn thing reaches her waist!

A blast not too far off draws my attention. Thiago's closer to us, and there are far fewer obstacles in his way. Contouring the car, he keeps advancing. His expression is cold, fire burning within. I finally take a moment to inspect our surroundings, and notice the woods. My back tightens.

"What is it?" Luz whispers.

"We need to get out of here. Soon."

The next blast from Thiago is aimed straight for Luz. One of the creatures jump up, and it hits him. Fur scorching, he falls a few feet away, whining.

"No!" Luz takes a step forward, but the vrykolakas by her side grabs her shirt in his canines and shakes his head.

"They want you to stay in the semi-circle," I interpret.

Luz's teary eyes focus on the hurt creature. "But..."

I shake my head, stepping around the semi-circle. Two of the creatures lift their eyes on me, suspicious. I raise my hands up. "Easy, I'm with you guys."

Then another blast comes our way. This time, I'm on automatic. I write the rune, and catch the fire in my hands. Just like Tytus taught me, I roll it over and re-launch. My aim's a bit off, but it's enough to make Thiago stop and reconsider.

Luz's voice comes from the side. "Dani..."

"What is it?" I can't afford to break eye contact with Thiago.

"Why did you say we have to leave?" Her voice wavers and whatever it is, it can't be good.

"Because this isn't safe. We're too close to danger."

"Yes, you really are."

I can't explain it – not in the two seconds we have before Thiago attacks. But I know my brother didn't bring me here to mate. He brought me here to sacrifice.

And the voice, at my back? She just confirmed as much. Because when I eventually turn to face her, I know I'll be seeing the witch who gave us these freaking powers.

Tristan

I catch Dani's scent and force onwards. My body shifts, growing larger. I intend to take down as many of Thiago's wolves as possible. I just hope they're not all privy to the bastard's magic.

By my side, another wolf appears. I recognize Cade's darker shade and throw him a look. *What do you want?*

He snorts and lengthens his stride. *You can't handle it, that your precious girl wanted to join the Reapers huh?*

Fuck off.

I want to outrun him, but he's faster still. *Kinda rude to outrun a partner.*

Shut up. Lucas may trust you but it doesn't mean I have to.

Cade snorts again. *And you shouldn't.*

Before I see it coming, he slams into my side, and I go spiraling down a ravine. We were at the back of the packs, and no one's seen it. So I stand and shake myself off, then get back on the path. By the time I join Lucas, Cade is in the midst of his wolves acting like nothing happened.

Everything okay? Lucas asks.

You know it isn't.

He's silent a beat, then he pants, *Yeah, but let's get your girl first. Then we can deal with them.*

Lucas and I exit first into the clearing, and we come to a dead stop. Dom joins us next, and Finn. Our stunned gazes take in the scene below.

A car is stopped in the middle of the otherwise empty road. Forests line it on one side, a cliff on the other. Its occupants are out and surrounded by twenty or so black creatures – their scent tells me they're vrykolakas.

Did you call them?

Dom shakes his head at my question. *No. I...*

Then how did they get here? Lucas' growl is plenty indication he's not happy. I'm not surprised, considering the deal he had with Dom. Then again, we're off our territory and the wolves aren't really evil...anymore.

Dom's silent, trying to assess the situation before he answers. His gaze lands on Luz, and the creature at her feet. Then he takes in the semi-circle around her. *Holy shit. They came for her, like I ordered them to!*

Lucas shakes his head. *Go get them in line. Make sure they don't attack any Reapers.*

Dom takes off, and I take a step forward to follow him. Finn glances at the Reapers behind us, and Cade moves forward. *Are those creatures with you?*

Lucas nods. *Yes, don't hurt them.* He pauses, as if weighing his words. *The dragon will be with us, too. You've nothing to fear.*

I see that flash again in Cade's eyes, but it's gone the second after. Then shouts from below draw my gaze. Dani's facing some girl, and Thiago's getting way too close for comfort. *Lucas, let me go. She needs me.*

He meets my desperate gaze, but holds back on the approval. I know it's payback for earlier, for how I stepped out of line.

Please. The word is ash passing through our mental bond, but it seems to do the trick. Lucas nods my way, and I take off like lightening.

Daniela

I manage to shift my weight, at least enough to turn and be able to keep an eye on both Thiago and the witch.

She's exactly how I remember her, only more bedraggled-looking. Her white hair streaked with green is split at the ends, and a mess in dire need of combing. Her face is young, barely a few years older than me, but the dark circles under her eyes speak much of what she's been enduring. The faded jeans and sweater can't hide the bruises around her ankles and wrists, and I know where they come from. It's the ropes my brother puts on her when he's done getting what he wants.

Her pale eyes settle on me, filled with sadness. "Lower your hands and surrender," she says and her voice is empty. Worse than empty, it's dead.

"What did Thiago do to you?" I whisper.

She frowns at me. "Nothing I didn't want."

"That's not true and you know it, Fiona."

She gulps, and blinks rapidly as if biting back tears. Then Thiago's voice comes behind me. "What the hell are you doing, capture them!"

Fiona lifts her trembling hand and starts drawing a rune. One of the vrykolakas moves at my back, presumably to protect me.

Then Luz takes a step forward. "Wait."

Fiona looks at her, and her frown deepens. "You're...human."

Luz nods. "I am. My mate is a wolf. I've been where you are, before I met him. Fiona, you can fight back."

"You can," I add. "You just have to want to."

Tristan's right. Luz really sees the best in everyone, because I never bothered to look past it. Yet now I am. And I'm done letting my brother hurt more people.

"He branded me," I whisper, taking another step in her direction. I throw a look to Luz and hope it's enough to keep her where she is. The last thing I want is to put her in danger again. I shouldn't have worried though. The vrykolakas by her side is doing a good job watching over her while the others time their attacks on Thiago, keeping his attention away from us.

My attention focuses back on Fiona. "He hurt you enough. Let me help you, free you. You never should have been stuck here."

"I...."

Thiago's angry shouts can be heard behind us, and Fiona looks ready to crumble.

"Don't listen to him. He killed my father, drove my sister to kill herself. He ruined this pack and branded all the females like cattle." My heart clenches at the thought of the pain I've left behind. One Fiona never had the luxury to escape. "I can help you, get you away from here. I'm here to kill Thiago and end this, once and for all."

Her eyes fill with tears again and her gaze flickers behind me. I don't look. "You have to run," she whispers. "He'll kill you."

Then she glances over my shoulder again, and this time I can't help but foolishly do the same. Fiona steps behind me in that second, wrapping an arm around my neck and tightening it. "I'm sorry. I'm *so* sorry," she says in my ear. "But I need to do as he says."

Then she lifts her hand, drawing another rune. "Stop!" She shouts to the creatures. "Or she dies."

The vrykolakas around Thiago pause their attack, then turn their gazes to Luz. She's gaping in open-mouthed horror my way.

And in front of my wide eyes, the rune Fiona drew vibrates, and morphs into a flaming dagger. The only thing worse than its size and dangerously-looking sharpness is the fact it's pointed right at my heart.

∞ ∞ ∞

∞ Luta ∞

"Strength and growth come only through continuous effort and <u>struggle</u>."

-Napoleon Hill-

Tristan

As I'm running towards Dani, I feel the rest of my pack and the Reapers disperse. More of Thiago's lobisomens are coming out of the woods, and they jump in the fray with the vrykolakas. It's a freaking free for all.

I only have eyes for one – Dani. And she's currently in a bad spot, with some girl holding her hostage. The closer I get, her scent wafts to me – a witch. And she has a dagger pointed at my mate.

Increasing my speed, I zig zag between creatures, desperate to get to her. Nothing can happen to Dani. I won't allow it.

I couldn't live with it. My wolf agrees, pushing us forward, demanding we stand between her and any danger.

I'm here, meu anjo.

Dani turns her head to the side, seeing me coming. Relief spreads in her expression, and her faith in me is enough to give me wings. Stupid, I know, but real.

Luz is a distance away, and Thiago looks like he's about to make his move. But I'm no fool, I've seen that look before in Lucrezia's eyes. And I wish to hell Dom was around to warn his girl off, but it's too late.

Luz crouches next to the vrykolakas at her side and whispers something. I don't know how the putrid scent doesn't bother her. It makes me want to gag, and even as I'm heading towards them I feel the memories I've tried so hard to keep at bay press on me. I can't have another episode, not while trying to rescue them.

Let me help.

My wolf wants to take over, and despite having had a good run before, I'm afraid to try. Seeing all these creatures here makes me even more aware of what could happen. How it could go wrong.

It wouldn't.

I don't believe that. Not enough, anyway.

Then I'm distracted when Luz moves. She's holding her hands up, talking to the witch. I'm closer now and slow my gait, listening in.

"Harming Dani won't do anything, Fiona."

The witch spares her a glance. "I'm not going to harm her! Just keep her, for him."

She jerks her chin towards Thiago. His cold eyes are on Dani and I know he's relishing the near-win.

Luz moves again, only this time, she's not alone. The vrykolakas by her side jumps Thiago with a vengeance. And another one I hadn't seen approaching hops on the witch. With a loud scream, she lets go of Dani, who rolls out of harm's way.

A blast of burgundy to the right draws my gaze. The vrykolakas that was keeping her brother is dead. And Thiago is vibrating with anger, heading towards my girl.

I get to Dani just as Thiago jumps on her, then morphs. Only, he's not fully wolf. His arms are hairy and end in claws, and his body grew, but the rest of him is still human.

His snarls, however, are all beast. And when I see him on top of Dani, a haze of red descends on me. I jump him, digging my canines in his back. He howls and throws me off, then tries to go back to Dani.

She notices me in wolf form, and shifts under him. Thiago tries to clamp his hands around her throat, but then she's a wolf, and he's grappling with fur. I run into him, smacking my body against his from the side with enough force to throw him away.

The second he's off balance, Luz's vrykolakas step between him and us, effectively creating a wall. Step by snarling step, they close the circle around him, forcing him to backtrack – away from us.

Dani gets back on her feet and, and joins me, panting. She nuzzles me, and I feel her tongue snaking out to lick my wounds. *Where's everyone else?*

Lucas and Finn are coming. Taking advantage of the brief reprieve, I return the favor. My saliva closes two of her worst wounds. *Dom's in the middle of his pack.*

Dani looks around. *So it's true? They're really his?*

Yeah. How did they find you?

Not me, she shakes her head. *Luz.*

We duck under Thiago's men and join Lucrezia. Knowing since her initiation she should hear me, I decide to test the link myself. *You need to get yourself out of here.*

She meets my gaze. "I would if I could. But I'll either run into Reapers eager for my blood, or Thiago's lobisomens. Like it or not, the vrykolakas are keeping me safe."

I'm about to say something else, when a shadow moves behind her, but it's nothing I expected. My wolf whines at the back of my mind, trying to warn me off.

I'm deaf to it.

What I'm looking at shouldn't be possible, shouldn't be real. But everything else around me narrows on the image a few feet away. It's a soldier, with half his face missing and blood coating his uniform. I blink, but he's still there.

And I know him. I fought alongside him, I even watched him die, torn apart by the same creatures that are now surrounding us.

It's my CO. The same one who led multiple expeditions in the wilderness, helping us fight creatures of the dark.

And if there's one thing I know, is he shouldn't be here.

"Tristan?" Luz glances behind herself, then back at me. I'm already gone, side-stepping her and heading towards him, ignoring the shouts behind me.

Daniela

Fucking Thiago and his damn illusions. I can't talk to Luz in this form, since I haven't been sworn into the pack like Tristan is. So I shift back to human to explain. "Thiago spelled him. I don't know what it is that Tristan's seeing, but it's no good for us."

Luz bites her lip. "Can you stop it?"

"Yeah, but only if I can kick Thiago's ass."

I glance around, looking for my brother. He's by the edge of the forest, watching as his – *my* – lobisomens are torn apart by vrykolakas or Reapers. Lucas and Finn are making their way to us, and I try to point them in Tristan's direction.

My old pack steps between us and draws their attention. Now no one's keeping an eye out for him, and the sound of the battle is getting to us. *Shit.*

"Thiago's escaping," Luz points out. "We need to go after him, Dani."

"I know that."

My gaze is drawn back to Tristan, and the uneasiness in my gut intensifies. I need to help him. But I have to stop Thiago. Who's my first priority, my mate or my pack? *Fuck.*

Luz notices my distraction with Tristan, lost now in a sea of wolves. "I can go after Thiago with a couple vrykolakas," she says.

"Absolutely not!"

Her green eyes flash. "I can help, Dani. For better or worse, I'm sworn into this pack, and I have these guys guarding me. Tristan needs you right now. How else are you going to get through to him?"

By killing Thiago. The thought enters my mind, and won't leave. Tytus had alluded, not so long ago, to me having to make tougher decisions. *Guess it's about to come by much faster than I expected.*

"No, I'm not letting you go alone." I glance around again. "We'll need backup. Can you call out to Dom, tell him what's going on with Tristan?"

She nods and finds her man through the haze of the wolves. It's easy with the white stripe on his back, and the vrykolakas surrounding him like guards to a king. Then Dom's attention focuses on us, and Tristan in the distance.

Luz cringes, and I have a feeling Dom's telling her exactly what I did – to get away. Before he can move our way, a wolf jumps on his back.

Only, it's not one of Thiago's. I gasp, recognizing the colors of the wolf, and his build – it's a Reaper. My gaze collides with Luz's. "What the hell?"

Everywhere we can see, the Reapers are now jumping on either our pack or the vyrkolakas, like they've suddenly changed sides. Cade, off to the side of the battle, is keeping an eye on his people and nodding. *The bastard's up to something.*

His gaze drifts elsewhere, and I follow it to see Thiago drawing runes in the air. He's going to do something stupid, by the feel of it. And I need to stop him. Now, more than ever.

Still, the hesitation grows. After everything Thiago's done, it's my duty – my burden – to put an end to it. Yet no matter how much I feel the weight of that decision, Tristan's predicament holds me back. I can't move forward, not if he's in such a shape he can't continue fighting. Or worse, gets hurt. No amount of defeating Thiago will be worth the price, especially if Tristan ends up having to pay it.

With a frustrated noise, I point my index at Luz. "Go by the edge of the forest and wait for me. No matter what you hear, Luz, I mean it. Dom will kill me if something happens to you."

She nods, and it's the freedom I need. I morph back into wolf, and run towards Tristan. From a distance, I see him ripping apart anyone that dares come near him – be it friend or foe. Whatever illusion Thiago's put him under, it's powerful. I only hope there's a way to undo it. Fighting my brother will be impossible, unless Tristan's waiting for me on the other side.

As I make my way to him, I know Tristan won't hurt me. That's one certitude I could put my life on. So when I land in front of him, blocking his way to whatever illusion, I don't expect the empty eyes and snarl. I take a step back, shocked, and he crouches low as if ready to pounce.

Tristan...

Tristan

Everything's a haze. I'm no longer with my wolves, but in the desert, then the mountains.

Sand crawls up my throat, choking me. My eyes burn. Grappling with the sand, I move through debris and fallen bodies to the one I need to see.

My CO is gasping, blood escaping his mouth. He's shifted back to human, and there's a large laceration in his chest. No, more than one. It looks like he fought with a tiger and lost. Half his face is missing. Tears fill my eyes, blurring my already impaired vision.

I reach out to him, and he gasps. Blood spittle flies in the air, and I managed to pull him to my lap. "Sir, hang on. I'll get help."

His gaze meets mine, and he opens his mouth to speak. Whatever he meant to say is lost as one last breath escapes him. Now those eyes filled with fight and wisdom stare unseeing.

Growls tear all around me, and I know the creatures have found the rest of our camp. With a trembling hand, I reach for the hunting knife in my belt, coated with silver. "I'll avenge you, I swear it."

Then I'm in the fight, and nothing can get to me. It's survival. It's...

Then a wolf hops in front of me, disturbing the image. The vision cracks, as if a mirror just broke, and I'm facing a sandy-haired wolf. There's a snowy meadow behind her, and more wolves. Her sweet scent gets through me, enough that I blink. And for a moment, I see Dani.

You have to snap out of it.

Snap out of...

Her face flickers in and out like a bad movie connection. The soldier's back, as is the sand. And the blasted heat, burning my skin.

It's Thiago, meu amor. He's doing this to you. It's not real.

It is *real.*

She shakes her head. *Listen to my voice. Come back to me.*

I can't...

Let me help. It's not Dani's voice, but my wolf's, at the back of my mind. He tries to take over, push the rest of me at the back, but I fight it with a vengeance.

A vrykolakas gets too close, and in the heat of my confusion, I can't distinguish between the past and present. I claw at his back, then dig my canines into his shoulder.

Tristan, stop!

The voice is familiar, and she's been able to help me before. On some level, I know I need to trust it, listen to it. Then she howls, in pain, and through my haze I see another wolf jump her from behind. Dani tries to fight back, but a second one joins in the fight.

Our mate is in trouble, my wolf says. *I cannot force you, but you need to trust me. Now.*

Distrust is in my gut. I look between the soldier, and the sand. Dani, and the snow. Which is real, which is fake? Which is my mistake, which is my redemption?

TRUST ME!

My wolf's roar jostles me out of thoughts I don't have time for. And in that moment, I make a conscious decision to move to the back of my mind. My wolf takes over, relishing the control. The vision shatters, and we lunge at the Reapers attacking Dani.

My wolf body shifts, growing larger. My claws elongate, and I dig them in the lobisomens' backs, picking them off Dani like they weigh nothing. She crumbles to the ground, but I'm not about to let her be easy prey.

Hold on to me, querida. Then I dig my head under her, and manage to lift her to her paws. Leaning heavily on me, I manage to bring her to the edge of the fight. Chaos surrounds us, but Dani burrows into my side, seeking heat and comfort.

What's going on? My eyes are taking in the multiple fights taking place, feeling like I'm finally getting the full picture.

Reapers turned on us. They're not just fighting Thiago's men, they're fighting us and Dom's wolves.

Shit. This is what Tytus warned against.

Tytus?

As if his name calls him out of hiding, the dragon appears in the sky.

Bastard took his time, but yeah, he warned us about the Reapers. Lucas chose to not listen.

Dani's amber eyes are sad when they meet mine. *He'll regret that choice, but Dom, more so. His vrykolakas are bearing the brunt of the losses.* She hesitates for a beat, then says, *I'm sorry for running out in the middle of the night. I thought I'd spare you this, another fight, and Lucas' ire should you go against it... But I realize now how stupid it was.*

Stepping closer to her, I bury my muzzle in her neck. *Never do this again, Dani. We face it together – all of it.*

We both look up as Tytus circles above our heads. With everyone so tightly intertwined, he can't shoot fire without harming us too.

Dani moves away, her gaze darting around. *I have to go.*

Where?

Luz is in the woods, we're going after Thiago.

I take a step forward, bending my head to hers. *Let me come with you. Together, right?*

Dani looks around, taking in the carnage surrounding us. *I want to say yes, Tristan, but not today. You need to help Lucas and Dom and I couldn't ask you to choose. I'll handle my brother.*

She nuzzles me, and I make her promise. *Swear you'll come back.*

I swear it.

With a single leap, she disappears in the forest.

Daniela

Please let her be there, please let her be there...

Thankfully, Luz listened. She's waiting by the edge of the forest with ten vrykolakas. I morph back to human and smile in relief. "Good thing you brought back-up."

She rolls her eyes. "Let's just say I remembered a certain promise I made to your man about not playing hero." Her worried gaze moves over my shoulder. "Is he okay?"

I nod, "As okay as he can be. He's helping Dom and the others." We both look to the darkness of the forest. It's a no moon kind of night, still. "You sure you're ready for this? There's still time to change your mind."

Luz throws me a look like I'm crazy. "Lead the way."

I shake my head, then take the first step forward. Our feet crunch in the snow, and after moments of trekking I realize Luz is shivering. She's still only wearing the sweatpants and the sweater Thiago kidnapped her in.

"You sure you'll be okay?"

With blue lips and chattering teeth, she still manages to smile. "Yeah. Girl power and all."

A chuckle escapes me, then we grow quiet. A few more minutes, the vrykolakas following us in eerie silence, and the woods give way to an abandoned cabin. Luz trails behind me as I go to the side, opening a latch that goes to the wine cellar – and the tunnels below.

"What is this place?" she whispers.

"Our family retreat." Memories of a happy childhood and running around with Izzy are tarnished now by my brother's actions. "Thiago'll be in here with his witch."

I take a deep breath. "Last chance to stay behind."

Luz shakes her head. "As if." Then she looks at the vrykolakas. "Two of you should stand guard. If anything happens, go and find Dom. The others, you're with us."

They split as ordered, and soon we're going down the stairs, following a flicker deep within the earth. I've been here before – the night we got our powers.

Moments later, we emerge into the wine cellar, and I lead us through another tight hallway. We finally exit into a subterranean cave.

In the middle is Thiago, gesturing wildly at Fiona. She's looking worse for wear, with a bruise developing on her cheek. Her white hair is a mess, streaked with mud instead of green. A cloak is thrown carelessly over her back. I can see her shivers from here, not that Thiago cares.

I squeeze Luz's hand, placing myself to shield her from Thiago. The vrykolakas join me, creating a semi-circle again. Thiago doesn't even glance around. He's too focused on the witch he has in tow to notice us.

"Is the place dark enough?" he asks.

"Yes, it will do." Despite her words, Fiona doesn't seem ready to proceed.

"What the hell are you up to now, brother?"

Thiago doesn't even turn our way. Instead, he whispers something to the witch and throws her to the floor. Her eyes lock with mine across the distance, and I catch one word she mouths. *Run.*

Considering what happened last time I gave in to my softer instincts, I want to hold my ground. But then I sense Thiago's entire being vibrating, and the cave shakes.

Something shines in the air, blocked by his head. No, more than *one* something. It's runes, and each one –

Bolts of red lightning exit them, each hitting a vrykolakas. Their aim is ruthless, and perfect. Each creature falls on the floor, a burning hole in their chest. The charred smell fills the closed up space as we stare in horror.

Luz cries out – a delayed reaction. It's enough to spark me into movement.

I don't think. Pulling Luz after me, I take off running. Thiago roars behind us, then I hear the crunch of bones as he morphs.

"Go!" I push Luz through the opening, then turn, morphing my hand in claws, strong enough to smack him. If it's a fight to the death my dear brother wants, it's what he'll get.

He reaches me and this time, I know there's no escaping it. Using the only runes I know, I blast magic into him, throwing him backwards. With Luz out of the way, there's one more innocent I need to free before I can focus on him.

I run to Fiona, using my claws to release her from her bindings. "Get out of here, while you can."

She looks at me as if not believing her eyes. "But I..."

"I know," I glance over my shoulder, where Thiago's getting up and shaking his head. "You've been too much his slave to know what you're doing. Get out of here. Have a good life."

Fiona's eyes fill with tears. "You don't owe me this."

"Then maybe you'll repay the debt one day." A growl from behind has her scurrying away, and I nod. "Go!"

With one last look, Fiona takes off as if her life depends on it – which, it does. Then I turn and face my brother. We're finally alone.

"You shouldn't have done that," he growls. "That witch is bound to me."

"Not anymore, she's not. You're done hurting the innocent."

We circle each other, and I morph into wolf form. *Let's make this fair, brother. You've wanted alpha for a while, right? So fight me for it. Once and for all.*

He lunges, teeth bared straight for my jugular. I paw him out of the way, then whirl around and jump on his back. My claws dig into him, tearing into the skin. By the time he shakes me off, rivulets of blood are running up and down his sides.

He claws at the ground, and I think he's doing so out of pain. I've forgotten he's had more time to master the *magia*. Then he throws the rune in my face, and all I feel is fire.

I run to the basin of water, burying my face in it. Its coolness helps, but then something rips into my back. An agonized howl tears from my throat.

Tristan

I'm jaws-deep in a Reaper when a howl echoes over the grounds. Finishing him off, I move towards Dom and his vrykolakas, trying to see what's going on.

Above us, Tytus stops circling and dives into a further part of the forest. Another rallying cry echoes, and this time the Reapers drop the fight with us, retreating in front of our stunned gazes.

Dom glances at his creatures, and nods to one. A group of five detaches from the rest, following in the wolves' trail. Tytus is nowhere to be seen, but I hope whatever's drawn his attention is worth it.

Filled with blood and gore, I close the remaining distance between me and Dom, both morphing to human at the same time. "Where's Luz?"

"With Dani."

He narrows his eyes. "I told her to get out of here."

"And they never listen," I roll my eyes. "But a few of your wolves are with them, so they should be safe."

Dom throws me a grateful look.

"What?" I ask.

"Thanks, for calling them wolves. I know your experiences with them haven't been...pleasant."

I shrug. "Maybe, but what happened wasn't with this pack. Plus, with you at their head, they're turning out alright."

We turn to Lucas, also morphed back human. Only Finn remains in wolf form, keeping an eye on the vrykolakas and the four members of Thiago's group they're surrounding.

Then out of the woods, Luz emerges. Her hair is disheveled and she's got only two vrykolakas following her. "Tristan, you have to get in there!"

I'm already moving towards her, though it feels the ground is shaking under me. "Where's Dani?"

"Fighting Thiago. She pushed me away."

Dom comes and picks her up in his arms, but I'm already moving. Until Lucas steps in front of me. "This is a fight for alpha. You know it as well as I do. You cannot intervene, you have to wait it out."

"Like hell I will!"

I rip my arm out of Lucas' grip and rush forward, morphing mid-run. I'm surprised to feel someone by my side, and when I turn, it's Tytus, in human form. Yet he has no issue keeping up with me.

What do you want, dragon?

Against all odds, he hears me. Yet another mysterious perk of a zmeu, apparently. "I thought it would be obvious," he grins. "You cannot do this on your own."

In that moment, I don't care what his intentions are. All I care about is Dani.

∞ ∞ ∞

∞ Possibilidades ∞

"When you've exhausted all <u>possibilities</u>, remember this: you haven't."

-Thomas Edison-

Tristan

I follow Dani's scent into the bowels of the wine cellar and beyond. By the time me and Tytus emerge, she's bloody and on the ground. Gashes have her wolf's skin cut open, and her breathing is laborious.

Thiago's standing off to the side of the cave, drawing runes in the air and with his back to us. I want nothing more than to rip him apart. But I also know Lucas is right. What we've stumbled into here is definitely a fight for alpha. And no matter how much I want to, the rational part of my brain tells me I need to let Dani fight it alone.

My wolf is less prone to listening to these old pack laws when he sees Dani in so much pain. He struggles against my control, wanting to rip Thiago apart – and write his obituary in blood.

I shift back to human in an effort to hold myself back. Even so, my fingers itch to hold her, and I take a step forward. Tytus throws me a look, then rolls his eyes and next thing I know, I'm dressed in jeans.

"Thanks," I mutter, but my gaze won't leave Dani.

"Don't mention it." His gaze narrows on Thiago, and I have a feeling he's reading the runes. Then he growls. "Ah, hell no!"

I'm still trying to figure out how to help Dani without making her forfeit this fight. With Thiago using magic, and her in a wolf form that can't reciprocate, the odds aren't even.

Tytus seals it for me. He takes two steps forward, one index raised in the air. He draws a rune tinier than Thiago's. It ripples in the air, and with both hands the zmeu maneuvers it and throws it on Thiago.

The bastard freezes, his hand raised, then his entire body starts shaking, shuddering, until he drops to his knees. His head's thrown back and he howls in pain, then bends over and his claws dig into the ground. His pitiful sounds and pants are like music to my ears.

Then he gets back up to his feet, and I frown. "What did you to him, and why didn't it last?"

"Your alpha was right," Tytus smirks, retreating to my side. "I didn't directly intervene, only evened the score. They can finish the alpha fight now. Only, with no magic."

Hope blossoms in my chest and I kneel on the ground, tapping it to get Dani's attention. "Meu anjo, did you hear? No magic. He's all yours now."

She still doesn't move, a whine only escaping her.

"Please, Dani," I whisper, praying she has enough strength to bring this to the end it deserves. No matter how much I want to fight this for her, I can't. It's not my battle, nor my score to settle. This vengeance is all Dani's to take, and I have no right to stand in the way of that.

"Meu amor, you can do this." My words carry across, echoing. After a beat, Dani blinks, her amber eyes settling on me. I read the pain in there, and it breaks my heart. "It's your time to shine, Daniela Da Silva. Be the Luna you were always meant to be, the one I see in the depths of your soul."

Her eyes close, but rather than stay immobile, Dani moves. First one paw comes up, and she struggles. Then the other, and she manages to get herself to a half-standing position. With one last grunt, her back legs lift up and she's finally standing.

She reaches behind and lets her tongue lick away the two worse wounds, watching as they heal. Then she shifts her body, and though she's moving slow, I have faith she can do this.

Daniela

Thiago faces me, and this time I don't sense the magic rolling off him. Tristan was right, he's only a wolf. And though he's bigger, and stronger, he was never meant to be leader of my pack. Izzy was, then I.

Remembering everything he took from us, all that he caused, is enough to fuel the rage in my veins. My adrenaline kicks in, and the pain in my muscles and lacerations evaporates.

Time to end this, meu irmão. It's the first and last time I'll be calling him brother.

Thiago snarls and runs towards me. I paw the ground, holding steady and avoiding unnecessary movement. When he's close enough, I move and pick up speed, then jump over him. Only my claws elongate, and they tear through his back through my journey in the air.

When I land on the side, Thiago's panting, and his blood taints the ground underneath us. Still, he turns to face me, his canines extended. His bulk grows impossibly larger, more the size of a polar bear. In comparison, I must look no bigger than a regular wolf.

Size isn't always better.

That part, I learned from our mother. So I push my legs and run in circles around him, forcing the last bit of power through my tired body. Thiago's paws land in my way, and I have to zig zag to avoid being turned into a pancake.

Still, he's moving slower, and he can't see what I'm planning. The moment his paw lifts again, I run towards his belly, this time rolling over my back. Using the slickness of his blood on the ground to slide under him, I claw at his stomach.

Blood pours over me and by the time I end under his tail, it's as if I've showered in his organs. Disgusting, but needed. Thiago's snarling and howling, but none of that affects me. He moves away, this time not able to control his shift. The human him shows up, naked, and stumbles to the ground.

He's holding one hand to his stomach, turning away and trying to staunch the blood and intestines tumbling out. I watch him, waiting, assessing. Not so long ago, he thought he could own the females in my pack. For them and everyone who's suffered under him, I cross the ultimate line.

I lunge and fall on his back, forcing him to the ground. My jaws dig into his throat from the side, and the last of his blood coats the ground.

Frozen, I stand on four paws on my brother's back, feeling the life pour out of him. When the last heartbeat stops, the adrenaline in my body runs with it and I stumble off him.

The shift comes over me, and then I'm on human legs. I limp away from my brother's body, leaning heavily on Tristan.

He turns me over, lifting my shirt, and I feel his tongue tracing my wounds, and the healing saliva soon starts working. Some of my weakness ebbs away, and I can think again. I recall a stormy gaze in the darkness of the cave, and magic flowing.

"Where's Tytus?"

Tristan looks around, but our dragon friend is nowhere to be found. My mate shrugs and tightens his grip on me. "He'll come back. He always does."

By the time we join everyone else, Thiago's men are dead and vrykolakas are rallied around Dom and Luz. They look like a king and queen in their midst, with the way those creatures stare at them adoringly.

Dom seems in deep conversation with an elder vrykolakas, so we head over to Lucas and Finn. They're dressed, which makes me think the fight ended long ago for them.

"Thiago's gone," I whisper to Lucas. A glance around confirms none of my lobisomens survived the fight. Between the Reapers and the vrykolakas, they had no chance.

Lucas' gaze softens on me as he takes in my injuries. "You should get some rest, while you heal."

Before I get a chance to reply, Finn glances behind us. "Incoming."

We turn to see Tytus. And by the look of it, he's not happy, practically stalking towards us, hands clenched by his side. "Where's the witch?"

I recall her bedraggled form running away, and shrug. "Fiona's free. Gone far away from here, by now. At least I hope so."

Tytus scowls, and Tristan freezes by my side. Lucas' eyes narrow on Tytus. "Why do you act as if you were robbed of something?"

"Because I have been. We had a deal."

"Not that I recall," Lucas says coolly.

"It wasn't you I was speaking with," Tytus growls.

Then Lucas turns and notices Dom's expression. Contrite and defiant would probably describe him in that moment.

"Before you blow a fuse," Tristan intervenes, "Dom did what he had to. It was a deal we both struck for the sake of engaging Tytus in this fight."

"It was a deal that should have been run by me," Lucas growls.

"You're right," I whisper, moving away from Tristan's hold. "It was a deal made in my name, so I should be the one to pay for it."

Tristan's presence is steady at my back, but he doesn't try to hold me back. I throw him a grateful look over my shoulder, and he nods. That small gesture is enough.

Facing Lucas again, I say, "There is no pack here, Lucas. My Luna lineage is as good as useless, but the *magia* I have could be of worth to you. With the developments with the Reapers, you'll need as many hands on deck as possible. They've retreated from here, but they'll be back, you can be sure of that."

His expression remains unreadable, which makes my task harder. But not impossible. "You offered me protection, Lucas. Dom and Tristan did what they had to, ensuring that protection continued. And now I'm willing to offer you my loyalty, and pledge allegiance to you. If you'll have me."

Lucas holds my gaze, then glances over my shoulder at Tristan. He knows what I'm saying – in exchange for my allegiance and never contesting his authority, he has to let this matter go. Tristan and Dom are to leave this forest unscathed, without consequences applied for their rebellion. It's a big price to ask of a man who's not used to giving in.

Whatever he sees in my mate's expression wraps up Lucas' decision, as he moves towards me then. "I accept, Daniela Da Silva. Welcome to my pack."

He pulls out a knife from his back pocket, and cuts into his palm. I wait patiently until he offers it to me, then press my lips to it, licking the wound. The blood tastes like metal to my human tongue, but my wolf whines. I've surrendered the last of my power, but at least it was done willingly, and for the better.

Satisfaction shines in Lucas' eyes, and then Tristan is there, kissing my neck and hugging me from behind.

Tytus is not as eager to let it go. "Except there is still the matter of my payment."

Finn, ever the peace-maker, sighs. "Would you let it go, already, mate? What's done is done, no point in lingering."

Lucas doesn't answer. Instead, his eyes scour the surroundings. "The Reapers are gone," he points out.

I don't see where he's going with it. "And?"

"Perhaps there is a reason why they disappeared, at the same time as your witch."

Tytus' eyes narrow, but he doesn't dismiss the idea. "I warned you they were here to seek something."

"And you were right," Lucas acknowledges. "It must have been the witch. To what purpose, I do not know. But perhaps you could find what you seek in their lair."

Tytus growls, then jumps. Mid-air, he turns to a dragon and takes off. Leaving us in the clearing, with all the dead bodies.

"Now what?"

Lucas sighs. "We need to clean this up. Dom, lead your vrykolakas away from here. We'll rendezvous back at the shop."

Tristan

By the time we get back to my place, Dani's wounds are mostly healed. She still has bruises, but they're turning rainbow colors on their way to healing.

She drops on the couch, her head in her hands. I lean against the wall, trying to see where her head's at. Having just killed her brother, it can't be easy. The itch of the battle left me feeling empty, and I don't know if I can trust myself going closer to her. I'll want to protect her, and it may come across as smothering. When I needed her, she gave me space... But this is different.

As I'm standing there, debating, Dani lifts her head slightly. Without looking at me, she whispers, "Tristan."

That's all I need to hear. I move off the wall and next to her side, kneeling in front of her. She refuses to look me in the eye, grappling with her emotions.

"Talk to me, meu anjo."

She's playing with her hands, wringing them at first, then picking at the skin around her nails. I reach out and grab both in mine, tugging enough to draw her attention. Those soulful amber eyes meet mine, and my heart seizes. "I'm here, whenever you need me."

Dani nods as if not really hearing me. Halfway in her motion, her eyes start tearing up, and the first sob comes. Then another. And another. I open my arms and she crashes into me, curling her body around mine and letting go into my chest.

I'm alone now, really alone. Her thought echoes in my mind, and I squeeze her tighter. "You'll never be alone, querida. Not while you have me, and the pack."

Dani pulls back from my arms, and despite being a mess, I couldn't find her more beautiful than in that moment. I move one of my hands off her back to push her hair off her face, then kiss her forehead, followed by her nose. "I've got you. *Sempre.* Always, querida."

Fresh tears fall down her cheeks, and I let her bury her head in my chest again. If what she wants is to hide right now, to cry it out, then I'll allow that. Once she's ready, I'll talk her out of the guilt she feels. But for now... I can hold her.

Hours must have gone by. I'm only guessing at the time because I feel my legs cramping, and my lower back hurts like a motherfucker. But I'm not planning to move, not if it wakes the beauty in my arms.

After a heartfelt cry, Dani fell asleep. And amid fitful dreams, she ended up finally relaxing in my arms. I'm not about to disturb that because of my physical discomfort.

"Are you sore?"

Her voice, rough with sleep, surprises me. I lift my chin off her head, and try to peer down. "You're awake?"

Dani nods in my chest, then pulls back. Her eyes are red-rimmed, nose red from crying, but she seems calmer.

"Woke up a few minutes ago. You've been holding me this entire time?"

My hand cups her cheek, and I steal a kiss off her lips, then rest my forehead against hers. "I'd hold you forever if you'd let me."

She smiles then, and I see a bit of my girl. Then she disentangles herself from me, and moves back up on the couch. I cringe as I stretch my legs, then stand and try to stretch my back. After a few deep-felt cracks of bone, I can move without feeling eighty years old.

I look at Dani, holding out my hand. "I'm about to step in the shower, wash off the grime of the battle. Want to join me?"

She looks at my outstretched hand, then at me, and smiles. "Maybe later."

After a hesitation, I move to the bathroom, shedding clothes that I fully intend to burn to the floor.

The water's hot, and steam rises, filling the small space. I let it cascade down my back, feeling it hit my muscles. So many fucking questions gone unanswered. How the hell is the pack going to move on, how do we survive with the Reapers in town now?

And better yet, how can I help Dani get over this?

The answer soon makes itself known. I'm holding the wall with both hands when the door to the shower opens and

Dani steps in, naked. My gaze roams over her body, my mouth going dry. I don't want to read into anything, which is why I force myself to focus on her amber eyes instead.

The look buried within tells me enough. Releasing the wall, I turn to face her and hold out a hand. She steps towards me, letting me pull her closer. My hand travels to her waist, then her hip. Dani tilts her head back, offering me her mouth, and our lips meet. Fireworks explode, and I'm willing to give her anything she wants, like she's done time and time again for me.

Daniela

I know he's hesitant, I feel it in the gentle way he's touching me. But I don't need this right now. I need *him*, inside me, and I need to be *feeling*. So I let my head tilt to the side, offering him my neck.

Tristan's mouth moves to it, nibbling at it, sucking on the skin. I gasp, and have to hold onto the wall for balance. Then he's moving lower, kneeling in front of me, his mouth never leaving my skin.

When he moves my thighs, burrowing deep for a taste, my legs buckle. It's only his strong grip on my hips that keeps me standing upright.

"Tristan..."

He looks up at me, not stopping his movements. "Yeah, querida?"

"Inside me. Please." My voice wavers on the plea, and he stops. Then he takes his sweet time standing, again trailing kisses all over my body.

"Not yet." Ignoring my wishes, he reaches behind me and grabs the soap, starting the painful task of washing us both.

With his slick hands moving all over me, I soon lose sense of all time and space. Nothing else exists except Tristan's newfound torture, and my submission to it.

"Please..." I try again, after my second powerful climax. "Tristan..."

He listens then, trailing his lips from my ear to my mouth. Then the kiss deepens, and my skin tingles. Tristan's hands move under my ass, and he hoists me up, pressing me against the wall. Then he's there, right where I need him, and he buries himself inside me with a groan.

I echo the sound, my breathing quickening under the steam. Between the water running over us and Tristan moving inside me, I don't know where I end and he begins. Then he shatters me when he cups my cheek.

"Open your eyes, querida. You need to hear this."

It's hard to do when all I want is to focus on the sensations he awakes in my body. But I listen, and my eyelids flutter open. Tristan's chocolate eyes look into me, piercing me, and he whispers against my lips, "Let the guilt go, meu anjo. You did what you had to, and none of that makes you a bad person. I love you. I always will."

Then he kisses me with newfound intensity, and lets go, burying himself deeper inside me. I lose myself in Tristan, in his expertise, and let the water do exactly what he asked.

I let the guilt go.

In bed that same evening, Tristan spoons me from behind and makes sure to leave no inch of space between us. I relish his heat at my back, and this newfound peace between us.

"Will you have nightmares tonight, do you think?"

I know his episodes are something that will be around forever, and I'm perfectly prepared to deal with that. But I also know he's strong, stronger now than ever, and that he and his wolf have a new coping mechanism.

Tristan admits as much into my neck, peppering it with kisses. "Not tonight, querida. My wolf will watch over me. And with you in my arms, sleep will be heaven itself."

I grin at the night, and close my eyes. Had anyone told me years ago that I'd be forfeiting my Luna status for an inferior one in a different pack, I would have laughed in their face.

Yet all happens as it has to. And while destiny and fate may be senseless words to some, to me, they've proven they exist when they brought me to the only guy who could ever understand me, ever hope to get me.

So I burrow deeper under the blankets, reassured by Tristan's breathing at my back, and let sleep claim me.

The next day, we join the shop. A tension's taken over Lucas and Dom, but we can only hope it won't come to blows. Tristan's at ease, and I try to relax. No more ravens, no more psycho brothers. No family. These people are all I got. And it's true what they say – blood doesn't make a family, not always. The people you choose do.

Which is why it's hilarious when I'm joking with Luz, and Elle walks in. Her doe eyes take us in, and she smiles feebly. "Do you have room for one more appointment?"

In the garage, something clatters. I glance over, and see Finn's eyes riveted on her. Luz elbows me, and I turn to Elle with a grin. "Hell yes, we do!"

∞ ∞ ∞

EPILOGUE

Tytus flew above the town, drawing onto elements to keep himself hidden. When he landed in a meadow, his massive form shrunk to accommodate his surroundings. Then a beautiful woman stepped out of the forest.

"Interesting night you pick to roam, zmeu."

He tilted his head to the side. She was older, wiser than he remembered, but that flowery fragrance was impossible to forget. "Ileana?"

A faint smile played on her lips. "So you remember my name."

"I thought the wolves were joking."

"Not quite, no. And while you may have caught most of what's been happening in this town, you missed one important part." She pointed to the path she had left. "Come and see."

Perplexed by her cryptic words, Tytus nonetheless followed in her footsteps. Moments later, they reached bushes that

341

blocked another clearing. When Ileana gestured for him to peek through, Tytus lifted an eyebrow. In the end, he gave in.

Cade and his Reapers occupied the entire clearing. Most were in wolf form, but some, like Cade himself, were using their human form. They were all staring at a captive figure in their midst, covered by a cloak.

Tytus' nostrils flared, and he lifted the pendant Daniela had given him. "The witch."

"Yes, they have her." Ileana's voice was sad, but not surprised.

He pulled back from the image, and retreated a few feet away. His narrowed eyes settled on her. "To what end?"

"Immortality, I would presume? Or perhaps more." She turned her gaze to him. "And while this *will* spiral out of control, you have other things to worry about now."

Tytus leaned against a tree, giving the immortal his full attention. "Such as?"

"Your descendent, Elle." Tytus opened his mouth to dispute the claim, but Ilena lifted a hand. "Remember who I am, zmeu, and do not lie to me. If someone does not teach her how to master the fire burning in her veins, she might harm herself."

His eyes glinted at the truth she voiced so freely. "And your suggestion?"

"Do not intervene with the wolf. He may succeed where you have failed." Ileana laughed, then disappeared in a cloud of smoke. Tytus was left brooding.

Preview of Book III

Third to Tumble — A Moonlight Rogues Novel

Elle

"I'm sorry, what?" Not for the first time, I wish controlling blushes was a thing. Grandma always makes fun of me, but there's nothing more embarrassing.

Especially when I'm being stared at like the most delicious morsel.

The onyx-eyed man in front of me grins, and it's shiny enough to blind me. There's something about his hard jaw, the ebony skin and the muscles on display that has me feeling all kinds of wrong things.

Wrong, but so, so good.

I realize he's been speaking this entire time, and I haven't heard a thing. "Sorry," I mutter, avoiding his distracting gaze. "You'll have to repeat that – again."

"Would you like to grab a drink with me later?"

I drop the cash machine on the counter, and gape at him. Yep, jaw open, eyes wide, the whole bit. What in hell about me could he like? I've got flour on my apron, my hair's a mess, and I sure as hell don't wear any makeup.

Yet this guy, who walked in here barely ten minutes ago and has been taking his sweet time choosing sweets, won't let me out from under his gaze.

Before I can answer, the door behind him opens. And the guy who walks in steals my breath away – literally. Until he opens his mouth and speaks.

"Get the bloody hell away from her, Cade."

Finn

Breaking rules is not my thing. Anyone who knows me will attest to that. Being a lawyer, the eldest in a family, and the only one with a brain not ruled by hormones in this pack – well, it weighs on a person.

Which is why this isn't me.

Barging into a bakery? Not me.

Clenching my fists so I don't smash Cade's pretty face into a bloody pulp? Not me either.

Wanting to claim the girl behind the counter so bad it leaves me breathless? Yup, that's *definitely* all me.

Sign up for an ARC now![1]

---

1. https://www.alexawhitewolf.com/third-to-tumble

Sign up for my readers' group at
www.alexawhitewolf.com/contact and receive a
copy of *Unconditional Love* for **FREE**, as well as
first dibs on cover reveals, discounts, giveaways,
prizes **and more!**

Cheers,

Alexa

Did you love *Second to Surrender*? Then you should read *Avalon Dreams* by Alexa Whitewolf!

"It was impossible they had met before - of that she was certain. Yet his hold on her was undisputable, an irrational pull to the utmost recesses of her soul." Vivienne du Lac has everything she could wish for - a normal, peaceful life, a good job, cushy nest egg, and a semi-social nightlife. The only problem? She's clueless to being the reincarnation of the Lady of the Lake, mythical sorceress from King Arthur's time, and Merlin's apprentice.Sébastien Dubois is the guy you wouldn't take home to mom and dad. He's the one you jump off on a motorcycle with, to ride into the sunset. The sexual chemistry between them is sizzling from the start -

but there's more to the tall, dark and handsome stranger. When a magical past tumbles into her orderly reality, he is Vivienne's only hope at survival. Caught between darkness and light, a battle she has no intention to fight - let alone the knowledge to win - Vivienne quickly finds out not even closest allies can be trusted. Can she look within and access powers from long past, become the enchantress Merlin meant her to be... Or will she lose it all over love, for Sébastien's salvation? This is a battle between good and evil you don't want to miss.

Read more at https://www.alexawhitewolf.com.

Also by Alexa Whitewolf

Moonlight Rogues
Moonlight Rogues: Origins
First to Fall
Second to Surrender
Third to Tumble

The Avalon Chronicles
Avalon Dreams
Avalon Wishes
Avalon Nightmares
The Avalon Chronicles - Complete Series

The Sage's Legacy
The Dragon Medallion
The Dragon Manuscript
Relics of the Underworld
The Sage's Legacy - Complete Series

Standalone Novels
Unconditional love
Blood Ties, Love Binds
Blazing in a Storm of Ashes (Coming Soon)

**Watch for more at
www.alexawhitewolf.com.**

About the Author

Alexa Whitewolf is a dog-loving, caffeine-addicted, all-around traveling enthusiast. Author of three series of fantasy, paranormal and young adult, she spends her nights dreaming up new stories and her days fighting reality. She lives in Ottawa, Canada, with her husband and two mischievous furballs- Zeus and Achilles. Check out her website at www.alexawhitewolf.com !

Read more at https://www.alexawhitewolf.com.